PRAISE FOR
THE WOUNDED HEART

"This relatable story, which launches Senft's Amish Quilt series, shows that while waiting to see God's plan can be difficult, remembering to put Jesus first, others next, and yourself last ('JOY') is necessary."

—*RT Book Reviews*

"With this quaint, gentle read, Senft's promising series is off to a good start and will make a nice alternative for Jerry S. Eicher readers who want to try a new author."

—*Library Journal*

BOOKS BY ADINA SENFT

The Amish Quilt Novels

The Wounded Heart
The Hidden Life

Available from FaithWords wherever books are sold.

The
HIDDEN
LIFE

AN AMISH QUILT NOVEL

ADINA SENFT

New York Boston Nashville

Copyright © 2012 by Shelley Bates

FaithWords
Hachette Book Group
237 Park Avenue
New York, NY 10017

www.faithwords.com

Printed in the United States of America
RRD-C

First Edition: June 2012
10 9 8 7 6 5 4 3 2 1

FaithWords is a division of Hachette Book Group, Inc.
The FaithWords name and logo are trademarks of Hachette Book Group, Inc.

The Hachette Speakers Bureau provides a wide range of authors for speaking events. To find out more, go to www.hachettespeakersbureau.com or call (866) 376-6591.

The publisher is not responsible for websites (or their content) that are not owned by the publisher.

Library of Congress Cataloging-in-Publication Data

Senft, Adina.
  The hidden life / Adina Senft. — 1st ed.
    p. cm.
  ISBN 978-0-89296-855-8
  1. Female friendship—Fiction. 2. Amish—Fiction. I. Title.
PS3602.A875H53 2012
813'.6—dc23
                                    2011052229

For Nyree, Skully, Jenny, and Jackie

ACKNOWLEDGMENTS

Thanks go to my agent, Jennifer Jackson, for her help and encouragement—and for taking me to cool New York restaurants I can subsequently put in books. My thanks, as well, go to Melody, Police Services Representative with the Springfield Police Department, for walking me through the process by which someone could find a missing person—it's harder when they're Amish. And as always, love and thanks to my husband, Jeff. You make a great tour manager, sweetie.

The
HIDDEN
LIFE

Behold, thou desirest truth in the inward parts:
and in the hidden [part] thou shalt
make me to know wisdom.

—Psalm 51:6 (KJV)

CHAPTER 1

In the absence of a husband or children, the written word was pretty much the only way a woman could prove she existed. Of course, God knew the existence of every sparrow, and had numbered the hairs on her head, but to Emma Stolzfus, this knowledge no longer held the comfort it used to. Not when her thirtieth birthday had come and gone and she was left staring at the wasteland of spinsterhood on the other side.

Had she said anything like this aloud, her mother would have suggested in her humble but inflexible way that she plant something in the wasteland and ask the Lord to make it yield some fruit. Well, Emma was doing that very thing. She loosened the strings of her black "away" bonnet and pulled open the glass door to the Whinburg post office. She laid a large manila envelope on the counter.

"Sending off another article?" Janelle Baum had told Emma once that reading the addresses on people's mail was as good as reading their diaries. People sent care packages to their boys in the Middle East. They returned clothes that didn't fit. They sent each other presents. And Janelle found out about all of it, mostly because for the foreign packages you had to say what was in there, and for the domestic ones, she'd act interested and ask nosy questions until you told her.

Emma nodded. "*Family Life*, this time." Which was written right there on the front, so there was no point in trying to hide it.

"Too bad you Old Order folks can't have the Internet," Janelle said. "It'd be a lot faster, sending things back and forth."

"I wouldn't want to put you out of a job." Emma smiled, paid the postage, and left, feeling as though she'd put one over on Janelle at last. If *Family Life* depended on electronic submissions, there wouldn't be much of a magazine, since its audience and its publisher were plain. She got along just fine without the Internet or a computer. Her pen and her old turquoise Smith-Corona worked no matter what the weather did to the power poles running down the side of the highway, and if that wasn't an advantage, she didn't know what was.

She untied Ajax's reins from the rail in front of the post office and patted his nose. "Patient boy. You weren't expecting to go all the way to Strasburg earlier, were you? Now we can go to Amelia's and I'll put you in her nice warm barn to visit with Daisy for a couple of hours."

Ajax snorted and allowed her to back him around before she climbed into the buggy, pulled the heavy wool blanket over her legs to keep the chilly air out, and shook the reins over his back.

What nosy Janelle didn't know was that she had two envelopes to mail, but she'd gone all the way over to Strasburg to send the other one. Its address would have told a tale she wasn't ready for anyone to read, and the postal employees in the bigger town didn't know her. Why should they care that an Amish spinster was sending an envelope to New York City? Or that it was addressed to a contest coordinator care of one of the biggest publishers in the country?

Emma gulped and tried to calm the sickening swoop in her stomach at the thought of her envelope, probably already on a truck and heading down the highway.

She took a deep breath and let the cold air blow away her nerves. Winter might have eased its grip on Lancaster County just a little, but it hadn't given up yet. Here they were at the beginning of March and you'd think it was still January. Emma eased onto Whinburg's main street and kept Ajax under tight rein until they were out on the county highway, which was straight and offered the cars coming up behind her plenty of warning that there was a gray buggy in the road, even if its color matched both asphalt and sky.

The men were probably gathered even now in Moses Yoder's barn, leaning on bales of hay and anxiously watching the sky for signs of change in the weather. If the planting were delayed, it would throw the whole year out. From her point of view, there was an even worse consequence.

Wedding season would go on even longer than it already had.

No, she wouldn't think about wedding season. That was worse than thinking about her envelope. About the sweet young brides and awkward grooms, about the oceans of food, about the gatherings of everyone in the *Gmee* and neighboring communities—during every one of which at least one person would ask her when her turn was going to come.

She'd stopped making up witty answers years ago. Now she was reduced to a sickly smile and a swift return to whatever task occupied her. It was safer to become one of the many pairs of helping hands at a wedding. That way, you always had a reason to disappear and no one questioned you about it.

And now, here was her best friend Amelia Beiler putting

her black dresses away, dressing in purple ones, and looking at courtship a second time. If she didn't love her so much, Emma would be tempted to give in to despair, which was a sin. Everyone knew, even if they didn't say so, that there were more women than men in the church. Much as her heart was gladdened that Amelia's smile now held genuine happiness instead of the wistful sadness of the last year or so, in the dark of the night she allowed herself to think, *It just isn't fair for you to have two and me to have none.*

Which was ridiculous and selfish and—for that brief second—a betrayal of the friendship they'd treasured for more than two decades. In the practical light of morning, Emma knew herself to be a healthier person than that. But practicality tended to keep its mouth shut in the middle of the night.

She pulled on the reins and Ajax slowed to take the turn into Amelia's lane. The cure for dissatisfaction was to remember that the *gut Gott* held her life in His hands to use for His own purpose. And if that purpose was that she should care for Mamm in her old age, then she, Emma, must rejoice that she had good, rewarding work to do.

What would happen to her after Mamm passed on to be with God, she didn't know. Would she be permitted to live in the *Daadi Haus* on her own? Her sister Karen's John had aging parents also, and it wasn't too far-fetched to imagine he might want to bring them here. Her practical side told her that Karen would welcome someone in the upstairs bedroom to give her some help with the children and the household, since there was a fifth baby on the way. But somehow, living under Karen's thumb in the big, noisy farmhouse when she'd learned to appreciate the quiet of the little *Daadi Haus* wasn't very appealing.

And most important of all, where would she write?

I should never have mailed that envelope. What was I thinking? I have an eighth-grade education and I've never been farther from home than Lebanon County. What do I know about the world that smart folks from the city didn't learn when they were babies? They'll laugh at my pages. Of course they will.

She would put it out of her mind. She'd done what she'd done and now she knew how foolish it had been. So when the letter from the laughing people came telling her some bright young city person had won the contest, she'd accept it as being only right, and that would be that.

No one would know but herself.

But at least you'll have tried. And then maybe you'll have learned a little humility and you'll be satisfied with writing articles about canning bean pickles and putting indoor plumbing in the schoolhouse.

When she'd unhitched Ajax and made him comfortable in the stall next to Daisy, she crossed the neat little yard and looked up to see Amelia on the back porch, wiping her hands on her kitchen apron.

"Come inside, quick!" Her friend gave her a hug and practically dragged her through the door. "It's raw out here."

"March came in like a lion and will probably go out the same way." Emma pulled off her bonnet and coat, and unwrapped the knitted scarf that she'd wound around her neck, crossed over her chest, and tied in the back. She knitted them long just for that reason. "No Carrie yet?"

While the Stolzfus place lay just on the other side of Moses Yoder's alfalfa field, Carrie was way over on the other side of the highway and had farther to come.

"She's walking, I think, since Melvin had the buggy when he came to the shop this morning. I've been watching at the window."

"Oh, I wish I'd known," Emma said in distress. "I'd have gone around that way to give her a ride. When is Melvin going to sell that poor mess of a farm and move closer to town?"

Amelia opened the oven door and pulled out two pans of cupcakes. As she lifted each papered cupcake out of its well with a knife and lined them up with the others cooling on racks on the counter, she spoke over her shoulder. "Every time I'm tempted to ask, I bite my tongue. It's not my place to poke my nose into his business, much as I want to. I do know he's leased his fields to Young Joe Yoder's Amos, since his land marches with Melvin's."

"I should hope so. If he doesn't plan to plant them, he may as well lease them to someone who will." And just in time, too. Amos Yoder was probably one of the men in Moses's barn eyeing the sky. A Yoder to the core, he was a faithful steward of the land and would make a much better job of those fields than poor inept Melvin ever had.

A movement outside the sitting-room window caught Emma's eye. "There's Carrie. I'll get the door. Are those carrot cupcakes?"

Amelia grinned. "Carrie's favorite."

"Mine, too. With lots of cream-cheese icing."

Laughing now at a hint that couldn't be any broader, Amelia dug the knife deep into the bowl of frosting and dropped a heavy dollop onto a cupcake in the coolest row. "You have to promise to save some for Matthew and Elam. My little men will be hungry when they get home from school."

Amelia's boys were six and eight, and both Emma and Carrie enjoyed honorary aunt status. That didn't mean they could eat all the cupcakes, though.

"I'll only eat one, I promise." Emma swung the door open

and gave Carrie a hug. "I'm so sorry. If I'd known you were walking, I would have come and got you."

Carrie pulled off her wraps and hung them on the coat tree next to Emma's. "I wouldn't say no to a ride home. Goodness, it's cold out there. If a crocus tried to lift its head, it would be frozen right off."

"They'd be smart to stay underground." Trust Carrie to think about the crocuses. But that was the way she was—mothering her chickens and giving them names, seeing personalities in flowers, talking to the birds digging worms in the garden. To her, everything was her family. Which made sense, when you considered the pain she carried inside—married ten years and no children. As she'd told Emma once in one of her rare gloomy spells, there were worse things than being single.

But now her smile was as warm as the stove, where they both gravitated to toast the backs of their dresses and watch Amelia ice the cupcakes. "You two are like a pair of starlings in a cherry tree," Amelia observed. "I'm going as fast as I can."

"I'll wash your baking dishes as soon as I get one of those," Emma said. "I'm like to fall down from hunger and they smell wonderful." Amelia handed them one each and Emma bit into hers, her eyes sliding closed in bliss. She'd start watching her desserts tomorrow. If her waistband was getting the tiniest bit tight, she only needed to get out the brushes and mop and attack the kitchen floors and that would take care of it. A person just couldn't pass up carrot cupcakes with cream-cheese frosting, could she?

With the sustenance of the cupcake and the promise of good hot coffee and a raisin pie besides, Emma detached herself from the woodstove and made short work of the baking dishes. Carrie dried and put everything in its place while Amelia shook out the Crosses and Losses quilt top that Amelia had taken to calling "Sunrise Over Green Fields," and draped it over the bed in the guest room. Emma had never given a quilt a name in her life, but then, Amelia looked at these things differently. To her, if you could make something beautiful at the same time as you were creating it to be practical, then you should do it for the glory of God. But in Emma's mind, a quilt was a quilt. It was meant to use up fabric scraps and keep you warm in the winter, and the simple fulfillment of its purpose would glorify God. It didn't need to have a name as well.

But to each her own. Amelia made beauty with physical things, and Emma made it with words. As long as a person didn't fall victim to pride while she was doing her making, that was the main thing.

She was sure God must be proud of his handiwork in creating Amelia and Carrie. Because each of them in her own way was beautiful. Amelia's dark hair, so thick and shiny, lay neatly coiled in its bob under her heart-shaped prayer covering. When they'd been teenagers, Emma had envied her that hair and wished her own mop were as well behaved. And Carrie? Behind that smooth blond hair and china-plate blue eyes, she was one of those people who appreciated small things and took a simple joy in them. She'd even told Emma once that she thanked the spiders in the corners of her attic. "Think how many more moths and mosquitoes there would be if the daddy longlegs weren't there, Emma."

Think how many more moths and mosquitoes there would be if she didn't have a good, old-fashioned fly swatter hanging by the door. But Emma would never say such a thing to her. Carrie had enough things looking to dim her smile. Emma would not add to them by even the smallest degree.

"Will you survive until we have this measured up?" Amelia teased her. "Or should we have *Kaffi* now instead of after our work is done?"

"Such rebels we'd be, playing first and working after." Emma bumped her shoulder. "That cupcake will tide me over. So, what have we decided for our borders?"

Amelia and Carrie exchanged a glance, and then Carrie said, "What do you think, Emma?"

Why were they asking her? "I think that you two should decide. You're better at making things pretty than I am." Another glance. What were they up to? Did they think they were taking on too much and leaving her out? Because that was not so. "Anyway, we talked about this a little, before all Amelia's excitement."

The arrival of Eli Fischer back in town when he'd heard outlandish rumors about Amelia's health had broadcast to everyone in the settlement that he was head over heels for her, even if Amelia was the last person to find out. No one was surprised when he had quietly moved into a room at his cousin Martin King's, since Martin's boy Aaron had recently vacated it to go who knew where looking for work.

"We did," Carrie agreed now. "So then, a narrow strip of green around the piecing, then a narrow strip of color, and a wide border to quilt those twining feathers on, *ja?*"

Emma nodded, and after a moment, Amelia did, too. "And why don't we use the black and some burgundy as backing and binding? We can piece it in some nice way and use it up. The boys already have all the pants and shirts they need for the spring."

"Eli might need some, too," Emma said slyly, and tried not to smile when a blush crept up Amelia's cheeks.

"He already has Sunday pants and vests," she said steadily

while her face flamed. "What he's really going to need are denims if he and my brothers ever stop talking about building a shop and actually do it."

"So he's still going ahead with the mechanical conversion idea, then?" That would be wonderful *gut*. Right now, folks who wanted their washers and stoves converted from electricity to gas or hydraulic power had to go all the way to Strasburg to find someone to do the job. According to Karen's John, having someone right there in Whinburg was a blessing akin to having vegetables in your own garden instead of going to town to buy them.

Carrie turned from contemplating the quilt top. "But he can do that in Martin King's barn. Building a real shop on your land for his business is a little premature, isn't it?"

Again, Amelia blushed. "It would be premature. And it would say something I'm not quite ready to say yet. No, such a shop would be for me to make pallets in. I still need to make a living, you know. It isn't fair to ask Daed to support me until—I mean, if—"

"But Amelia," Carrie broke in, "it wouldn't be fair to sell Melvin a share in your pallet shop and then start up another one so close."

"No," Amelia agreed, and patted Carrie's sleeve in reassurance. They all knew what it had meant to Carrie that her husband now had steady work as part of Amelia's business. "All the commercial customers will stay with Melvin and Brian Steiner. But if a farmer out here or a smaller business in the district should happen to need some, then I can do it. Brian and Melvin will likely be too busy for the small, one-off orders, so we'll be able to help out."

"We?" Emma raised an eyebrow.

"I." Amelia went to her sewing box and came back with a

measuring tape. "Sometimes we. Eli can make a pallet as well as anyone."

Why didn't Amelia just come out and say what all of them already knew? There was nothing wrong with *we*. Emma would be happy to say *we* if she ever got the chance. And why insist on Eli keeping his fledgling business in the King barn when by this time next year, it would be in Amelia's shop anyway?

But then, Amelia had always cared much more about how things looked than Emma had. Maybe that was why Amelia had had two men to love—because she had a better spirit of conformity. Nothing about Emma seemed to conform to what men wanted. She was too tall, too angular, and too apt to say what she really thought, without the leaven of submission, grace, or tact.

"—feeling these days, Emma?"

Emma came to herself with a start. "Sorry, what? I was woolgathering."

"I'd say so." Carrie's eyes twinkled. "I said, how is Lena feeling these days? She looked awfully frail in church on Sunday."

Emma nodded. Her *Mamm*, so hearty and hardworking in the past, was frail, there was no getting around it. The oxygen tank had to go everywhere with her now, and aside from church, she didn't stir much from the *Daadi Haus*. "Mary Lapp said that she should have a chair with a back for church, instead of sitting on a bench. That's why she was up front."

"She's not doing so well?" Amelia asked. "Do you think one of Mamm's vitamin mixtures will help her?"

Here was a switch. "I thought you didn't believe in your *Mamm*'s vitamin mixtures. The only thing I've seen you take are her packets of *Kamilletee*."

"What I think isn't the point," Amelia said, her cheeks reddening again. "If Lena thinks they're helpful, then it has nothing to do with me."

Maybe she'd better stop teasing. Emma had heard enough of Amelia's frustrated rages about her mother to know the subject was as sensitive as a bruise with her. But the fact was, the whole *Gmee* held Ruth Lehman in respect as a *Dokterfraa* for her herbal mixtures, teas, and tinctures. During cold season, the Lehman lane could be as busy as the main street in Whinburg—minus the cars—as people came to get remedies. And what Ruth couldn't cure, Dr. Shadle the *Englisch* chiropractor could.

Amish folk preferred to doctor their own; why, look at what had happened to Amelia. Because of that fancy doctor she'd gone to at first, her loving spirit had been nearly demolished by despair. Her experience had firmed the conviction in everyone's mind that fancy doctors should stick to the business of mending broken bones and suchlike, and stop trying to take the place of God.

"I'm sure Mamm would appreciate a course of vitamin drinks," Emma said after a moment. She didn't have much in the way of money to pay for it, but Ruth often took bartered items in exchange. "I'll ask Karen if she has any honey left, and maybe you could split half a gallon with Ruth."

"That would be wonderful *gut*. I'm nearly out." Amelia was on some strange diet to cleanse her system, and natural honey was on the list of things she ate. "The boys are used to me baking with honey now, so I go through it faster than ever. I have to watch the liquids in things, though. You should have seen the first batch of cookies I made. I had one great big square cookie, all spread out on the sheet."

"I bet Eli likes anything you make." Emma couldn't resist.

"He was not here at the time." Amelia looked down her nose at her and Carrie, just in case she planned to get lippy, too, and Emma had to smile. Where would the three of them be without each other? Their friendship had weathered school, and *Rumspringe*, and marriage, then babies and households and the business of being grown up. Through sunshine and shadow, like the old quilt pattern with its bands of light and dark, they had learned that no matter what God sent them, they could share the load with each other and find it lighter.

Then why, she reflected a little uncomfortably, had she not told them about the package she'd sent off from the Strasburg post office this morning?

CHAPTER 2

Thursday evening was as good as any to go over and see about the honey. Emma wrapped a black knitted shawl around her shoulders and looked in on her mother, who went to bed with the sparrows. The lamp was on, and she was reading her Bible in bed instead of in a straight-backed chair downstairs—a great concession to the state of her health.

"Mamm, I'm just running over to the house to see if Karen has any honey left. Do you need anything?"

Lena shook her head. "You've provided everything I need, and I have everything I want right here." Her smile included Emma, who stepped out into the cold evening with a glow in her heart.

When Pap died, Emma had confessed some awful things to Amelia and Carrie—how she had resented being the one to care for him as his dementia progressed, while all the time he thought she was Karen, his favorite child. How distressed she was sometimes that life held nothing wider than this lane between the *Daadi Haus* and the old family farmhouse. But under all that she had one thing that she could count on, and that was the bedrock of her mother's love.

Lena never played favorites, but Emma knew she kept one special smile just for her. She might not have much, but God had blessed her richly there, and she'd best not forget it.

Karen was still doing the supper dishes with her eldest girl, Maryann, who was eight. "Everything all right?" she asked over her shoulder, up to her elbows in suds.

"Hi, Auntie Emma."

"Yes, everything's fine. Hi, Maryann. How was school today?"

"We're learning fractions. I hate them."

"Ah, but you can't make a pie without fractions, and I know you don't hate pie."

"What?" Maryann gave her that look that said, *There goes* Aendi *Emma, making things up again.* She was a very practical child, just like Karen.

"If you didn't know fractions, when Bishop Daniel comes for coffee and says, 'I'll take a quarter slice,' how would you know how much to give him?"

"Bishop Daniel would never be so greedy," Karen put in.

"But if he was sharing with Mary, he might," Emma persisted. "How much of the pie would a quarter slice be?"

Maryann put down her dishtowel and diagrammed a quarter of a pie in the air.

"Exactly. See? That's a perfectly sound use of fractions—not to mention you can find out how greedy people are or aren't."

Maryann tipped her head from side to side as if to say maybe, maybe not. "But if someone said, 'Give me one and five-sixteenths of a pie and divide it by three eighths for my *Kinner*,' that's when it gets hard."

"It would be hard," Emma agreed. "Sounds like you have too many people and not enough pie, in that case, and Bishop Daniel needs to share his quarter slice with more than just Mary."

"Honestly, Emma, you talk such nonsense." Karen

drained the sink and dried her hands on Maryann's towel. "Where do you get these ideas?"

"They come in the mail."

Karen couldn't have detected a joke if it landed on her nose. "Then I suggest you put a stop to it."

Emma let it go. "I came over to see if you had any honey left. I want to trade it for some of Ruth Lehman's vitamin drink for Mamm, and Ruth loves your honey."

Karen was not a proud woman—only unbearably convinced that she was right about most things—but when it came to her honey, her face took on the glow of accomplishment. She led the way to the cellar steps. "How much do you need?" She picked her way down the stairs carefully, one hand gripping the banister, the other rounded over her stomach. She was about six months along, and looking eight.

"If you have half a gallon, I can give a quart to Amelia."

"I think I can do that." Her shelves, which had been loaded to the point of bursting in December, were now showing space. But they were still beautifully organized by type and by color—yellow beans before peaches, beet pickles before cherries and strawberry jam. Looking at Karen's pantry was like looking at a stained-glass window, meant to draw the soul up to God.

At least, that was what Emma imagined such things were for. She'd never actually seen a stained-glass window except in books.

Karen kept the honey on the floor out of the light, in plastic buckets with sturdy lids. With the ease of long practice, she scooped out partially crystallized honey with a paddle and into quart canning jars. With quick twists of her wrists, she lidded them and handed them to Emma. "Is that all you need? Sure you don't want an extra one for Mamm?"

Just smelling the cool sweetness was enough to make her crave the stuff drizzled on hot toast. "*Ja*, all right. She enjoys it for breakfast, so it doesn't take long to go through it."

Karen filled another jar. "Melt a little at a time in a saucepan as you go, otherwise it'll crystallize again."

She said that every time, as if Emma couldn't keep a fact in her head. No, that wasn't fair. She probably said it to everyone who came for her honey, automatically, like the *Englisch* said *Have a nice day* at the checkout counter. Carrying three jars, Emma climbed the stairs and emerged into the warm kitchen in which she'd spent most of her life.

In the living room, she could hear ten-year-old Nathaniel reading the nightly chapter out of the Bible to his younger siblings, prompted every now and again by Karen's John. John's name was also Stolzfus, being a distant cousin from the family of one of Pap's father's brothers, so neither Karen nor the farm had had a change of name when they got married. Trust Karen to be efficient, even in the matter of the man she married.

Emma would be happy to take Eireschpiggel for a surname, if only God would send her someone to marry.

Never mind. Don't think of it. The good Gott *has given you all you need, and whining for more is selfish and proud.*

Karen put the kettle on the stove and leaned on the counter. "So, what's new across the lane?"

I'll have another article published, and I entered a worldly writing contest. If I win it, maybe someone out there in the wide world will hear me and think I have something worthwhile to say.

"Nothing. Mamm was a little tired today."

Karen nibbled on her lower lip. "She seems tired a lot."

"I'm keeping a close eye on her. She has an appointment next week." When her sister looked alarmed, she added, "It's just a routine check, to make sure everything is fine. I'm sure it's just this time of year. I wish spring would come."

"You're not the only one. Every time the sun comes out, I think, is this it? Can the men finally plant?" Casually, she added, "John is thinking of renting Melvin Miller's north field. Between him and Amos Yoder, they should get some use out of those acres. More than Melvin ever did, that's for sure."

Emma resisted the urge to defend her best friend's husband because she certainly couldn't deny that Karen was right. Hadn't she thought the very same things Tuesday afternoon? "That will mean more work for him."

Karen nodded, and as the water boiled, she got out the teapot, shaking in a packet of what Emma recognized as Ruth Lehman's *Kamilletee*. Ruth always folded the packets in interesting shapes, like diamonds and boxes. "Oh, that reminds me of what I meant to tell you. It's going to be busy around here, and maybe noisy. John is hiring Grant Weaver to build an extension upstairs, and when he's done with that, he'll replace both porches on the *Daadi Haus*."

Emma was torn between the need to have those porches refloored before someone—namely Lena—put her foot through a hole and fell, and the fact that John had hired Grant Weaver to do it.

"Surely you don't need that expense?" she asked, trying not to look as if she had any opinion, which wasn't easy. The minute Karen thought something mattered to you, she'd be all over you to find out why. "We've lived with the porches for years now. We know just where to step."

"*Ja*, well, other people don't," Karen said crisply. "And I don't want anyone saying John doesn't take as good care of this place as Pap ever did."

"Your John works hard." Clever Emma, redirecting the conversation.

"He does, but he also knows when to ask for help, and Grant needs the work, what with having three kids under seven and that wife of his gone nearly two years now." Clever Karen, bringing it right back. "He'll start over here on Monday. I have no idea how long it will take, but you should warn Mamm anyway that there will be men around the place and if the noise bothers her, she should hunt out the earplugs."

"Does Grant have someone to look after the children?"

"Old Joe's great-granddaughters take turns. Muriel's girls, I think. Grant's not the kind to ask for help, but that family would never let anyone else take care of them."

Pretty, lively Lavina Yoder had been one of Old Joe's many great-granddaughters. So pretty and so lively that she had attracted the attention of every boy their age for a hundred miles around ten, fifteen years ago. The fact that she'd chosen stoic, silent Grant Weaver to marry had astonished everyone—and the fact that she'd done something bad enough to be put under *die Meinding* and left six months later had surprised no one. The Yoder clan still grieved her, even if they no longer spoke of her.

No one knew what Grant thought. And no one had the courage to ask.

"Grant and his helpers won't be the only new faces around here. John's going to ask Joshua Steiner if he wants to hire on and farm the new section."

Goodness. There were men falling out of the sky today, after a drought of at least a decade. "Joshua wants to farm here? I thought he was working up in Indiana at an RV factory." Where there were lots of girls who might not know about the trouble he'd gotten into as a teenager—or about Bishop Daniel's suggestion that he take a trip to visit his extended family and live somewhere else until he settled down.

"John says he's coming home. Time to find a wife, he says."

All at once Emma saw where this was going, and she turned to get up before Karen could see her face. "I'm surprised he hasn't found one in Indiana." She reached for her shawl and stood. "I'd better be getting back to—"

"This could be your chance. Grant is still married, no matter where on earth Lavina might be, so he's out, but you and Joshua used to be thick as thieves back when."

"I don't think so."

"Why not? I'm sure he's settled down by now." She laughed, gazing past Emma's shoulder into memory. "Remember that time you and he floated those inner tubes down the river and got halfway to Strasburg before Mamm realized you were gone?"

"I was ten years old, Karen."

"And what about the time you two made ice cream with the gallons of cream his mother had set aside to be sold at the market? You weren't ten then. More like fourteen."

That had been the last time she'd done anything with Joshua Steiner, who had been ridiculed to the point of cruelty by his buddy bunch after that caper. The fat boy and the four-eyed girl had been permanently separated, and it was after that that his more questionable escapades began. No doubt they had all been rooted in Joshua's trying to prove to his friends that he was a real boy's boy and not someone who would share adventures with a homely girl.

Those childhood adventures had been fun. Even though mostly she had been buddies with Carrie and Amelia, there were things that Joshua would do that neither of the girls would. Each had recognized the outsider in the other.

"If he's coming home, he must have settled down some," Emma said. "I wonder that he hasn't married."

"You were good friends once. You could be again, is all I'm saying."

Emma gathered up her jars and paused at the door. "Don't even think it, Karen. I'm not interested in anyone that way, and you'll just embarrass me if you say anything."

"Poor Grant," Karen mused. "Such a hard row to hoe, believing God had led him to the woman He wanted him to have, and then finding out she was a..." She glanced at Emma. "Well. We all know what she is. I wonder if Grant knows *where* she is. Or if they communicate at all."

"The sad thing is, he won't be able to find happiness with anyone else until death do them part." Not for the world would Emma say what she was really thinking: *If only he'd chosen me. I would never have left him and our children. Never.*

Since Grant was on the Not Eligible for Emma list, Karen was forced to dismiss him. "As for Joshua, he might have changed. He has to have, or Bishop Daniel wouldn't allow him to come back."

Emma would far rather talk about Joshua than Grant. "It doesn't matter if he's changed or not. I have. I know too much about that boy to ever believe he'll make a good husband."

"People can surprise you."

But they didn't. Not very often.

Emma let herself into the *Daadi Haus* and out of habit, glanced into her mother's room. Lena had turned out the light, and in the silence, Emma heard the labored but still re-assuring sound of her breathing.

As quietly as she could, she put the jars of honey in the pantry, saving one out to take over to Ruth tomorrow. After that, there was nothing to do but sit next to the stove in the lamplight—no dishes, no mending, nothing. Well, she could write longhand, but the only things she wanted to say were best left in her mind and not on paper where anyone could read them.

It wasn't dark yet. She could walk over the hill to Amelia's and have a cup of coffee and a piece of pie and a good talk.

And what do you want to share with her most? The very thing that would cause the most talk, that's what. Shame on you, harboring this ridiculous softness all these years for a married man. One who didn't choose you when he could have, and one who hardly knows you're alive now.

Except that when he was working on her porch, he'd know, especially if she offered him a sandwich at noon or a nice slice of cake at coffee time.

Fool. You're a sorry fool and pining after another woman's husband is a sin. And what have you got to base it on, anyway? He took you to a singing once. Once. Never again. Not after Lavina Yoder's family moved back into the district and he got a look at her—him and every other boy you knew.

Emma sighed. It would feel good to talk it out with Carrie and Amelia. She should open herself up like a book and let them read the shameful lines she'd written there herself. Let them scour them away with sense and good counsel, and she'd leave feeling as though anyone could read her and not judge her again.

Yes, she should.

But *should* was a fantasy. *Should* wasn't real. It was an obligation, and she'd never handled obligation very well.

They are your best friends. Helping you through this sin would not be an obligation. It would be a gift, one they'd give you gladly.

Maybe. Maybe she would talk it over with them on Tuesday at the next quilting frolic. Then by the time she saw Grant in the yard, giving instructions to his crew, walking back and forth wearing his carpenter's belt, holding the tools of his trade in strong, capable hands that always knew what needed fixing, she could smile and speak like a rational person, like a neighbor or a grateful customer.

Not like the woman he hadn't chosen—and whom no one else had chosen, either.

A sound on the steps made her lift her head and look at the calendar next to the kitchen archway. Thursday! How could she have forgotten?

She crossed the room swiftly and closed her mother's bedroom door, then went to the front of the house. Alvin Esch stood shivering on the porch, a canvas messenger bag that might have seen service on an ambulance in the Second World War clutched to his side. "Am I late?" he whispered as she held the door open to let him in.

"Not at all. I just forgot what day it was. Lucky we don't have company."

"I'd have just kept going," he said. "As it is, my folks think I'm courting Sarah Grohl, so I'd probably have turned left instead of right and gone over there."

"You should be careful." She opened the tallest cupboard in the kitchen—the one out of reach of everyone but her—and handed him the packet that had come yesterday from the correspondence school where he was getting his GED. "Sarah's liable to think you really mean it."

A hot flush of color under his fair skin and white-blond hair gave him away. "Would that be so bad?"

"Only if you really do. If you're just using her for a handy excuse, that's a different story."

He ducked his head and Emma smiled. Lucky Sarah, to have a boy who cared so much.

She got up and began to measure coffee into the old pot as he ripped open the packet and read his grades from last week. "How'd you do?"

When he lifted his head, he was grinning. "A minus."

"Good for you. You worked hard on that paper." She didn't know a thing about Shakespeare except that reading him was a lot like reading the Bible and there was a lot of very colorful swearing. But Alvin, apparently, knew a bit more than that. He'd been working hard to get his high-school diploma so he could go on to college in Lancaster. He didn't rest on his laurels, though, just tucked the papers into his bag and spread out this week's work on the table.

She watched his busy pencil on some math problems for a while, then got up, poured the coffee, and cut a couple of slices of snitz pie. She liked hers with a splash of rich cream poured over it, and once he'd gotten over the fact that it wasn't ice cream, he'd come to like it that way, too.

One thing about teenage boys—they loved to eat and she very rarely found a fussy one.

"Do you ever think about what you're going to do if your parents find out?" she asked when he put his pencil down and pulled the pie in front of him. Her shameful secret was safe inside, but his was not. His involved the U.S. Mail and buggy rides to the other side of the district, which made it exponentially more dangerous.

He shrugged, his mouth full of pie. With a swallow, he replied, "I'm not stopping even if they do find out. My instructor just sent the sheet with our choices of final essay for

English and history. I have ten weeks to go and my junior year will be done."

"What if your dad takes all your papers away?"

"I'll write and get new ones. Besides, all my essays are stored on the computer down at the library. I just write out the drafts by hand when I'm here."

He looked up at her and she realized he'd had his hair cut in the *Englisch* style, like Aaron King, who used to come on Thursday nights, too, to write, when he still lived in Whinburg. He'd had some kind of falling-out with his father and had gone to visit his aunt and uncle in upstate New York.

"What would *you* do if they found out?" he asked.

"How would they find out unless someone followed you over here?" Or Carrie or Amelia told them.

"But if they did."

Emma had often wondered that herself. It was one thing to encourage talent in the younger folks. It was quite another, as Amelia and Carrie had taken pains to point out not long ago, to aid and abet a young man in deceiving his parents. Will and Kathryn Esch had no idea he spent this time in her kitchen, and her own mother had no idea the packets came to their post box, because Emma collected the mail every day. Karen was glad to let her, because cooking breakfast for her family and getting the children off to school in the morning was so chaotic that the mail was the last thing on her mind.

It was the first thing on Emma's. Not just because of Alvin's packets, but because once in a while a check might come from a magazine for her, or a circle letter from her old buddy bunch, or a flyer from some women's clothing emporium that would give her ideas for characters in her book. The mail was full of inspiration no matter how you looked at it, and if Karen got hold of it, she'd never see half of it.

So what would she do if they were discovered? "I'd ask forgiveness of your folks, I guess," she mused aloud.

"What if they put us in the *Bann*?"

"If we asked to be forgiven, they wouldn't do that, Alvin. It's only if we refused to, if we weren't sorry for doing what we're doing and kept on doing it, that they might consider something more serious."

"Are you sorry?"

"*Nei.*"

A snort of laughter made him scramble for a napkin to mop pie crumbs off his chin. "But you'd say you were if we got caught?"

She gave him a level look. "Alvin, we're not stealing honey-dews out of Mary Lapp's garden. In your parents' minds, this is a serious thing. You should treat it seriously."

He sobered, and pushed his empty pie plate away. "I know it is. I also know I couldn't say I was sorry and be willing to give up my courses. Because you know the second part would have to go along with the first."

That was the thing about repentance. It didn't just mean being sorry. It meant turning away from what you were sorry for, and not going back to it, ever. Her thoughts turned to Lavina Weaver. Would she one day realize all she'd left behind? Would she repent and return to Whinburg?

"I'm glad to see you've thought about it," she said. "I just hope you're prepared if that day comes. Can you finish out your senior year living under *die Meinding*?"

He met her gaze, and when he didn't answer, she got up and cleared the dishes. When she looked over her shoulder from the sink, he was hard at work again.

Which, she supposed, was answer enough.

Trent O'Neill
1440D 37th Street
Springfield, MO

Dear Trent,

We have never spoken, but I am Lavina's husband. I am writing to you because this is the only address I have for her. Since she left Whinburg, she has written at least once a month to get news of the children and for money. I have not heard from her since Christmas and I am getting a little worried. If she is no longer willing to write, I understand, but maybe you could let me know she is all right.

I am enclosing ten dollars for her. It isn't much, but it's all I have.

Thank you.

Grant Weaver

Grant Weaver
P.O. Box 254
Whinburg, PA

Hey man, I can't remember the last time I wrote a letter on real paper. I think I was eight. Anyway, here goes with the bad news.

Here's your ten bucks back, plus Lavina's stuff in the box. The truth is, I don't know where she is. She went out to get whipped cream or something at Christmas and I haven't seen her since. Chick was flighty, but man, that takes the cake. I figure if she's going to contact anyone about her stuff, it'll be you.

We had some good times, but I'm moving on. You want the truth, man—so should you. She might have asked about the kids and stuff, but there was no way she was going back. Just thought you should know.

T. O'Neill

Whinburg Township Police Department

Missing Person Report

CONFIDENTIAL

Case Name/Number 2012-3-1470	

Date: March 29, 2012	Time: 14:57	Location: Whinburg, PA

Interviewer's Name: BECKMAN, T. #17516	Title: PO	Agency: WTPD

Information given by Grant WEAVER	DOB 27 APR 81

Address: P.O. Box 254, Whinburg, PA

Home Phone n/a	Business Phone n/a

Cell Phone, Other Numbers: 717-555-1212 Phone booth Hwy 1240

Occupation: Carpenter	Employer: Self

Relationship to missing person: Spouse

Missing Person

Full Name: Lavina Yoder WEAVER	Nickname(s) n/a

Subject's primary language: Pennsylvania Dutch, English

Home address: Last known 1440D 37th Street, Springfield, MO

Business or local address n/a

Home Phone n/a	Business Phone n/a

Cell Phone, Other Numbers n/a

E-mail address n/a

Description

Age 29	Race WHT	Gender F	Hgt 5'4"	Wgt 120	DOB 02 FEB 83

Build Slender

Hair Color BLND	Length Waist		Style Amish		
Eye color GRN	Glasses	N	Regular	Sun	Contacts

Facial features, shape: Pretty

Complexion: Fair

Distinguishing marks, scars n/a

General appearance: Amish

Details of Loss

Location missing from: Home address, Springfield, MO

Point Last Seen (PLS) : Going to store for whipping cream

Day/Date Last Seen: Christmas	Time Last Seen: Unknown

Last seen by whom: Trent O'Neill

Vehicle description, if driving n/a

Destination(s), stated intentions: See above

Events of last 24 hours leading up to time of loss: Christmas baking

Reported missing by: Spouse	Why? Has not heard from her since Xmas. Usually writes once a month re kids and money.

Where can this person be reached in the next 12 hours? Home address

Subject's Experience

Resident of Springfield, MO	How long? 2 yrs 2 mo
Previous residence: Whinburg, PA	How long? 13 yrs

Birthplace: Whinburg, PA

Has this person been the object of a search in the past? No

Identification

Drivers License: n/a	State	No.	Date Issued

Other Identification: Dental records

Detailed Subject History

Single		Married	X	Divorced		Widowed	

Spouse's Name: Grant WEAVER	Phone n/a

Education level: 8th Grade

Religion or belief system: Amish	Active?	N

Hobbies, special interests: Cooking, sewing

Experience in outdoors, backcountry: Gardening

Favorite places to visit: Florida
Athletic ability, mobility: Healthy
Active/outgoing or quiet/withdrawn? Outgoing
Attitude toward authority: Questions, disobedient (quote)
Recent, current or anticipated financial, legal or other problems: Left spouse for O'Neill
Who does subject confide in and/or whom does he/she frequently talk to on the phone? Unknown
Who last talked with subject at length? Trent O'Neill
When and what was topic? Unknown
Recent letters or writings? Letter to spouse at Christmas 2011
Does subject have access to a computer? No

Planning Information

Local Responsible Agency: Springfield PD

NCIC Y	Date 29 MAR 11	Time 13:40	Agency WTPD
Amber N	Date	Time	Agency
Obtain:	Identification N	Photos N	Scent Article N

Actions to date: (Date and time of this report)

Took report from spouse. He will obtain dental records and ask if photo exists from O'NEILL. Report to be sent to Springfield PD for follow-up. Subject is Amish, therefore no DL, no credit card, no criminal record, no identifying marks such as wedding ring.

Person to be notified when subject located: Grant WEAVER

Signature of interviewing officer: Signature of reporting party:

     T. BECKMAN   G. WEAVER

CHAPTER 3

March 30, 2012

Dear Ms. Stolzfus,

Congratulations! We're delighted to inform you that your entry in the Commonwealth Prize fiction contest has been judged by two panels of readers and has progressed to the final round. Competition was steep, as we had 742 entries. The finalists comprise the top one percent of the total.

Please send the complete manuscript to me by April 7. Finalist manuscripts will be judged by an editor from a publishing house and an agent from a well-known literary agency. We wish you the best of luck in the final round.

Sincerely,
Tiffany Hickman
Contest Coordinator

Emma staggered over to the phone shanty from the mailbox and slumped against the wall, clutching the letter with its New York return address.

Finalist! She was a finalist!

She'd never been a finalist for anything in her life, except in sixth grade at the school spelling bee, when she'd come within one word of beating an eighth grader for the prize. But this! Out of 742 stories, hers was one of the top seven.

Thank You, dear Lord. Thank You for giving me this gift. If I never achieve anything else in this life, this moment is enough.

Because of course she would never win. Someone would find out that she was an Amish woman living miles from anywhere, and would realize how impossible it would be. And even without that, there were six other people with more talent than she who would be fighting it out for the prize. She was outnumbered, and that was that.

Emma folded up the letter and stuffed it deep into the pocket of her work dress, under her apron. Relieved to find her legs were operating again, she walked up the lane, methodically separating Karen and John's mail from hers and Lena's as she went.

How had it gone? Had her pages been passed from one hand to another, or had someone made copies and mailed them all around the country? It didn't matter. Someone—several someones, maybe—had read her words and thought them good enough to pass on to the next round. And the next. Who knew how many people had heard her—had maybe been changed just a little by what she'd written?

And not *changed* as in they now knew how to keep cucumber pickles crispy. But *changed* as in perhaps they had an inkling about the goodness and greatness of God.

Such a gift!

She'd heard the expression *burning a hole in his pocket* all her life, but had never applied it to herself. Now she knew what it meant. Throughout the morning she felt the folded paper in her pocket every time she reached or turned. When she was alone, she took it out to read again and again, until she could recite it verbatim. By the time she saw Amelia coming over the fields and got her sewing things together, she could hardly wait until they got to Carrie's house to share the news.

As soon as her coat was off, she pulled the letter from her pocket and held it out to them. "Read! Read my good news."

Carrie grabbed it and Amelia read over her shoulder. Then both of them looked up at her, their faces slack in identical expressions of astonishment.

"Isn't it amazing? Isn't God good?" Emma clapped her hands in delight.

Amelia turned back to the letter, as if it might say something different this time, pulling it from Carrie's fingers altogether. Then she slumped into a kitchen chair. "You entered a contest?" she finally managed. "A writing contest? This isn't from a magazine?"

Emma shook her head so that the strings of her organdy prayer covering danced against her chin. "I read about it in one of those writer's magazines that they have in the bookshop. I copied down the address and what they wanted, and typed out the manuscript as neatly as I could. They only wanted the first three chapters but you had to have a whole book. And now look! It's in the top seven, and they want the rest; so I mailed it this morning. Can you believe it?"

Carrie leaned against the counter, completely oblivious to the fact that the kettle was boiling madly on the stove. "But I thought—when you were so happy, I— Oh, dear."

She was supposed to be jumping up and down, sharing Emma's delight. "What? Oh, dear, what?"

Carrie plastered on a smile and took the kettle off the flame. "It's wonderful *gut*, Emma, of course. It's just that we had no idea. And I thought... Well, obviously, that will get me in trouble every time, won't it? Thinking?"

"What did you think?"

A shamefaced glance passed between the two of them. "We both thought you'd had a letter from someone, that's all," Carrie finally said.

"I did. A wonderful letter. The best letter ever."

"I meant, from a special someone."

Emma let out a long breath, then held out her hand for the letter. She folded it up and slipped it into her pocket again, where it should have stayed to begin with, obviously. "And who do you suppose might be writing me letters like that?" she asked in an even tone.

"Don't be mad," Carrie pleaded.

It was impossible to be mad at Carrie. She was as transparent as a running creek, and just as refreshing, even when she was being a wet blanket. "I'm not mad. But it was silly for either of you to think such a thing. If anyone would know I was corresponding, it would be you two."

Amelia had begun cutting the widest of the borders they'd planned. For a moment, Emma watched her hands. Amelia noticed the direction of her gaze, and waggled the fingers holding down the dark green fabric. "They're working pretty well. Not a hundred percent yet, but more and more as the days pass."

She was going to change the subject, and leave Carrie's foolishness where it lay. "You're using them, at least," Emma said. "I remember when all you could do was use that hand like a paperweight."

Amelia nodded. "I have a lot to be thankful for."

"Speaking of things to be thankful for, did you hear that I'm to have some work done on the *Daadi Haus*? John has hired Grant Weaver to replace both porches."

Carrie smiled at the prospect of any good thing happening in Emma's life, even the most prosaic. She had obviously decided to let the subject drop, too. "That will be *gut*. But Lena? Will the noise bother her?"

"The sound of work getting done has never bothered her. In any case, it won't be until later in the spring. John is putting an addition on for the new baby, upstairs over the kitchen."

"Grant Weaver is a good carpenter," Amelia said. "He helped Daed and my brothers build the new barn a couple of years ago. Before..."

Before Amelia's Enoch died. And before Grant's Lavina left. All of them thought it. "Does anyone hear from Lavina?" Carrie asked.

Amelia shook her head. "If any of the Yoders do, they don't say so. She's still under *die Meinding* for...for that business with that *Englisch* boy."

Emma looked up from the narrow strip of fabric, blue as the summer sky, that they'd measured and cut the previous week for the first border. "What business?"

"They tried to keep it quiet at the time, but some of us knew. She was having a—she was looking outside her marriage vows for attention. And since she couldn't get it from any of our men, she looked outside for it."

Oh, my. Emma's heart swelled with sympathy and sorrow for poor Grant—sympathy she could never, ever express to him. He wouldn't thank her for knowing about his shame.

"Is that where she went?" Carrie asked. "To be with this *Englischer*?"

Amelia shrugged and resumed cutting. "I don't know. I wouldn't have known about it at all except that I saw them once on my way home from the shop, standing in the door of the post office so close together you couldn't get a butter knife between them."

The post office, with its glass doors that concealed nothing. Foolish Lavina. Foolish in so many ways, and now having lost her family, she might lose her eternal hope, too. Had it been worth the price? Because she was not the only one to suffer. She had made Grant to suffer as well. She might have left him and gone off to begin again, but he was the one who would be alone for the rest of his life. A few brief years of marriage set against a lifetime of loneliness.

At least Emma had hope that her situation might change. Grant had no such hope.

"Poor man." The words came out before she realized she'd spoken them.

Amelia looked up from the scissors. "At least he has his work. And his children. She could have taken them, you know."

"She wouldn't have been so cruel." Carrie's tone was firm. "Besides, if you're going to step out on your husband, you wouldn't take the *Kinner* along, would you?"

The butterfly loved to flit from flower to flower, preening its wings and soaking up the sunshine. With baggage, it couldn't fly.

"I guess he should have chosen me when he had the chance," Emma said, hoping the words came out with airy nonchalance. A joke. Ha ha.

Carrie's pale eyebrows rose. "He had a chance with you? When?"

She should have kept her mouth shut. They would make

more of it than it really was. "Not really. He gave me a ride home from the singing once, that's all. Years ago."

"Why, Emma." Amelia's voice was soft with revelation. "You never said a thing to us."

Emma could feel the blood seeping into her cheeks, and ducked her head to concentrate on her seam. "It was only the once, so there was nothing much to say."

"There must have been something, or you wouldn't be blushing."

Drat. The girl had eyes like a cat. "Maybe there was once, on my side. Not now, of course."

Her cheeks felt like they were on fire. Why did her body have to pick now to betray her?

"Oh, Emma." Carrie's eyes were so full of sympathy that Emma was tempted to leap up from the treadle and run outside, scattering Carrie's chickens and not stopping until she was safe two fields away.

"It was nothing, so stop trying to make it something," she mumbled. "He's married and it's wicked to even talk about it."

Now it was Carrie's turn to jump to another subject. She began to tell them about Amos Yoder's plans for their rented fields, and the fire faded from Emma's face as she sewed.

But the pain remained in her heart, and not even the thought of the letter would make it go away.

Karen's John, no doubt prodded by his wife's advancing pregnancy and shortening temper, wasted no time in making the arrangements, even though the weather was as fractious as a teething baby, with sunshine one minute and a cold downpour the next. Emma heard the sound of a wagon coming up the drive and stepped out on the spongy porch to see who it was.

Grant Weaver guided his horse past the turn to the lane, but just as she moved to step inside before he saw her, he turned his head to look over at the *Daadi Haus*.

He's just giving his next job the once-over. Of course he was. But that didn't stop the lightness in Emma's heart as he raised a hand in greeting and drove on past.

You're a fool. He's married and if he ever dreamed the sight of him gave you such pleasure, he'd make sure never to venture over to this side of the settlement again. Never mind his shame— at least that wasn't his fault. Your shame would be all yours.

People had entertained themselves enormously over the rumor that she and teenaged Aaron King were courting. But if word got out that she was pining for a married man, their pity would be savage—and so would their opinions on the matter.

Oh, no. She would have to walk very circumspectly once Grant began work on this house, and never let him see anything but the sober, studious woman who cared for her mother. The girl who had once thought the world held no greater gift than a ride home in his buggy under the stars must be buried so deeply she could never come out.

So Emma told herself as she got on with scrubbing the kitchen floor, which never seemed to stay clean for more than a few hours at this time of year. She and Mamm didn't track it up so much, but the *Kinner* running in and out to visit their *Mammi* brought half of Nature in with them.

She'd just finished and had begun on the bathroom floor when a knock sounded at the back door. "*Aendi* Emma?"

Emma got up off her knees and waved both hands at six-year-old Victor, as if to shoo him back toward the door. "Careful, I just washed it."

He teetered, the toes of his muddy boots on the edge of

the linoleum, and grasped the door jamb. "Mamm says can you come over to the house for lunch. Mammi too, if she's feeling up to it."

"I am feeling up to it," came Lena's voice from the front room. "What a treat."

What brought this on? was more like it, but Lena would never say so. The fact was that it was typical of Karen to send one of the children as a messenger instead of coming for a visit herself. She always sounded flustered and busy when they hinted at seeing her more often than a couple of times a week, and usually made some comment about how Emma's help would be very much appreciated in the big house instead, since as a single woman she had much more leisure time.

Maybe Emma didn't have four children with another on the way and a big household with its canning and cleaning and sewing to do. But it wasn't because she didn't *want* those things.

Besides, she couldn't leave Lena for hours every day. What if she took a turn and there was no one there to help? Wasn't that why the family had singlemindedly decided Emma's place was here, caring for Mamm and Pap until he had been taken away from them? It was she who had gone in to the hospital in Lancaster and taken the training on caregiving and how to administer medicine and operate the oxygen tank. It was she who gave Lena needles in the middle of the night when she had to, much as she hated it and cried herself to sleep afterward.

It was she who acted on her love for Mamm every single day, and if all she asked in return was a little quiet in which to write, then she would not feel guilty.

"*Denki*, Victor," she told her nephew, and padded over the expanse of the drying floor to give him a hug. "We'll be there at noon sharp. Can I bring anything?" He looked unsure, as if Mamm had given him no instructions on that score. "What if I make that coleslaw you like?"

"That one with the cranberries and peanuts?"

She'd been thinking of the one with the pickles in it, but all right. Luckily she still had dried cranberries left from Christmas. "It's my favorite, too. Even if nobody else likes it, that means more for you and me."

Delighted, he nodded. "I'll go tell Mamm." He took off at a run.

Lena put a cautious foot on the shining floor and made her slow way over to the kitchen table. "I'll shell the peanuts for you while you shred the cabbage."

"You're supposed to be resting." Emma got the ingredients out of the fridge and hunted up the jar of cranberries.

"I have all afternoon to rest, and besides, I like peanuts."

Lena would no more miss an opportunity to help than she would tear off her oxygen and run across the fields. Before long, Emma was walking slowly down the lane, the bowl of coleslaw tucked under one arm and Lena's tank dangling from the other hand.

When they climbed the front steps one at a time, the door swung open. "Mamm," Karen said, managing to kiss Lena's cheek and take Emma's bowl in one smooth motion. "Come right in. We're just sitting down."

Emma tossed her shawl over the back of a chair in the sitting room, but Lena kept hers wrapped around her shoulders as Karen guided her into the kitchen and seated her in the chair closest to the woodstove. Out of habit, Emma moved to help Karen get the food on the table, and had no sooner picked up a bowl of mashed potatoes when she realized there were two extra people. Grant was one of them. And the other was . . .

"Hullo, Emma." A man got up and it was a good thing she was already leaning over to put the potatoes down, because she dropped the bowl with a clank.

"Joshua?" Her mouth would hardly form the sounds. It was too busy hanging open like a trapdoor in the hayloft.

"The very same. It's been a long time, hasn't it?"

They had only recently been talking about him, but still, she barely recognized him. The fat boy of her childhood escapades and the stocky youth of his troubled teens were both gone, and in their place was a tall, handsome man whose hazel eyes snapped with humor—as if he knew a grand joke about the world and wasn't letting you in on it. He still had curly hair—lots of it, too. Nothing as prosaic as a bald spot for Joshua. And no beard, because he wasn't married.

"When did you get back?" she finally managed, reaching over the table to shake his hand.

"Just this week." He resumed his seat and she got her feet moving over to the stove, where Karen was dishing up chops in mushroom gravy. She handed Emma the platter and Emma put it at the head of the table in front of John's place.

"Hullo, Grant," she said to the man sitting opposite Joshua. Did he think she had been rude, paying all her attention to Joshua and none to Karen's other guest? "*Wie geht's?*"

"*Gut,*" he responded. "Your sister was kind enough to invite me for lunch when she already had company."

Karen made a deprecating noise. "People come and go all day long around here. What's one or two more, especially when we haven't seen either of you in a long time?" She put Emma's coleslaw in front of him. "As I was saying, John has hired Joshua to farm the new section we bought. John! *Kinner!*" she called over her shoulder. "*Alliebber kumm!*"

John came in on a tide of children and they washed up at

the kitchen sink. When everyone was settled at the table, silence fell as they said grace over the steaming food. Emma raised her head and helped little Andrea, who was four, to some potatoes and chops. When she dished up her own plate, she found Joshua's twinkling gaze on her.

"So you didn't recognize me, hey?"

"You've changed a bit in ten or twelve years."

"You haven't. You look exactly the same."

That was a pity. And here she was thinking she'd become a ravishing beauty. "I hope the changes with you have been on the inside as well as the outside," she said smoothly. "Have you seen Daniel and Mary Lapp?"

He flinched theatrically, as if she'd wounded him. "As it happens, they were the first folks I visited after my own family."

She'd bet that was true. If Bishop Daniel had sent him away, only Bishop Daniel could welcome him back. "And were they glad to see you?"

"I think so. I'm not the rapscallion I was when I left, you know. I can see what you're thinking." Emma very much hoped not. "I was honest with the bishop, and he with me. We agreed that the past should stay in the past and the present was in God's hands." He paused, a silence filled with the clinking of cutlery on stoneware and the sound of little Victor gulping down his milk. "I hope everyone else will agree, too."

"No reason why they shouldn't," John said, his deep voice a rumble in his chest. "If God and the bishop say the past is forgotten, then it is."

"Did you do something bad?" Victor piped up, wiping his mouth with his sleeve.

Joshua smiled at him while Karen vainly attempted to wipe her son's face. "I was a bit of a prankster when I was younger," he said. "Things got out of hand and I got into a fast gang—faster than was good for me or them. Bishop Daniel suggested to my pop that I spend the summer with some cousins up in Shipshey. One summer turned into a winter, then a permanent job, and before I knew it, I'd been there ten years." He shook his head and turned his attention to spooning a small mountain of Emma's coleslaw onto his plate.

"And you never found a girl up there to marry?" Karen asked, handing him the pickles.

"Never found one who would have me. They're smart cookies up there in Shipshey. I figure I might have better luck back home."

"Don't get your hopes up," Emma said. "The girls here are pretty smart, too—and they have mighty long memories."

Grant chuckled into his yeast roll and Joshua looked offended. "Come on, now, Emma. Go easy on a fellow or he won't give you a ride to the singing on Sunday night."

"I can drive myself, thank you." She hadn't gone to the singing in several weeks. It was just too awkward, feeling like somebody's mother at a table full of giggly sixteen-year-olds sneaking glances at boys she used to babysit.

"Don't listen to her—she'd love to go with you," Karen told him. "What time will you be by?"

Emma gawked at her, unable to believe what she'd just heard. She'd suspected why Joshua Steiner had been invited to lunch, but hadn't expected Karen to involve herself further. Clearly Karen had given up on Emma's abilities in the courtship department and had decided she needed a little more help.

And when Karen got the bit in her teeth, there was no stopping her.

CHAPTER 4

Could there ever have been a lunch more uncomfortable than this one?

In all her years, Emma couldn't remember feeling like this—even when she'd been sixteen and full of raging emotions and hormones that had no outlet except in the pages of her little dime-store notebooks. So here she sat, one chair away from the man her wicked heart still yearned for, while the one she didn't want let her sister manipulate him. The question was, why did Joshua allow it? He couldn't be interested in her as a woman. Was he just entertaining himself? And what did it say about a man that he would allow her to be mortified like this and do nothing to ease it?

Maybe he didn't know she was mortified. She should be grateful, in that case. Pride was a sin, but a woman still had to hold her head up. There were some things that the people around you didn't need to know.

After dessert, John let out a belch that made Karen beam with satisfaction. He didn't need to say, "Another *gut* meal, *Fraa.*" The second helping he'd taken was proof enough that it was, and the clean plates of her guests backed it up.

"Karen, *denki* for the lunch," Lena said when John pushed his chair away from the table. "I must be getting back now."

Emma got up at once, only too happy to hurry the meal to its end. "I'll take you."

Karen and Maryann began to stack the dessert bowls, which held the crumbs of a preserved-plum cobbler. On any other day, Emma would have stayed to help. Today she was going to get out that door as fast as Mamm could walk, and Karen could send as many pointed glances at the stack of dishes as she wanted.

"I'll walk you over." Joshua pushed his chair back as well.

And add fuel to Karen's fire? Not likely. "No, thank you, Joshua," Emma said with firmness. "We know our way, and have done for several years now."

"But you need help with the oxygen tank."

"I brought it and a bowl of coleslaw without help. *Denkes* for the offer, though. It was nice to see you."

"Such an independent woman." His humor restored, he set his winter hat on firmly and hooked his coat off the tree by the door. With a word of thanks to Karen and John, he started out to his buggy.

Emma wasn't so sure he'd meant to be humorous. *Independent* was hardly a compliment.

"I'll walk over with you, if I may," Grant said from behind them. He'd hardly said a word during lunch. The few sentences he'd exchanged with John about estimating how much wood they'd need hardly counted. "If I'm going to put in an order for lumber, I might get a better price if I look the porches over and include all of it at once."

Emma did her best to keep her breathing even. "Certainly."

What a sense of humor God had. He had switched things about so thoroughly that now Emma was more uncomfortable than ever. At least she knew how to handle Joshua—and could give as good as she got. Grant just left her tongue-tied and miserable, afraid that anything she said would expose too much.

Then again, how much could she expose in a hundred yards?

Emma, you think too much about yourself. Think about him and all his troubles and you'll be less likely to dwell on your own.

"How are the children, Grant?" Lena asked, clutching his arm and stepping carefully over the ruts and puddles in the lane. John graveled it every year, but somehow it all managed to travel away, so that by spring, a fresh wagonload had to be raked down its length again.

"They're well," he said. "Sarah wanted to go to school so bad last fall with all her cousins that I let her go, even though I didn't think she was ready. She's not so forward as Katie is. But she's proved me wrong."

For a moment, Emma imagined herself in the little girl's place. Who wouldn't want to go to school with other children you knew and learn about the world, instead of staying with a babysitter in a house empty of your mother's love? Emma would have begged to go, too.

"And the baby? Some of the mothers were saying that a bad cough was going around this spring."

"He hasn't got it yet, but I'm sure it's just a matter of time."

"You called him Zachary, didn't you?" How did Lena know this? Emma wondered. Did she keep track somehow of every child in the settlement?

"*Ja*. I wanted to name him David after my father, but Lav—" He stopped and cleared his throat. "Mostly we call him 'babes.'"

"How old is he now?"

"He's a little over two," Grant replied.

The poor little thing. His mother had left so soon after he was born, he'd barely had time to get attached to her.

Emma stepped into the moment of awkwardness with a smile. "I hope you start calling him Zachary when he goes to school. Otherwise he'll have a terrible time."

Grant's lips flickered in what Emma hoped was an answering smile. "We'll do that. Here you are, Lena." He helped her up the front steps, Emma following close behind with the oxygen tank.

"*Denki*, Grant," Emma said. "It was kind of you."

"I was coming over anyway." He settled his hat more firmly. "I'll just take a few measurements, if that's all right?"

"Of course. Do whatever you need to." *And I'll have the pleasure of watching you do it. Our windows are wide so we can see the beauty of God's creation.*

But Lena had other ideas. "Emma, I'd like to take a rest. Could you read to me for a little while?"

A knot of dismay and truculence formed instantly below Emma's breastbone, but she fought it down. What could she say? *No, I'd rather watch this married man working outside, Mamm.*

The sound of boots treading back and forth on the porch was familiar, and at the same time utterly new. She should be thanking God for her mother's gentle way of removing her from temptation, instead of indulging in invisible rebellions. As Lena took off her shoes and stretched out on top of the quilt, Emma opened her Bible at the bookmark in Ecclesiastes.

Better is the sight of the eyes than the wandering of the desire: this is also vanity and vexation of spirit.

Emma sighed and began to read. Yes, between the two of them, Lena and the good Lord had quite the sense of humor.

* * *

Emma closed Moses Yoder's pasture gate behind her and walked through the wet grass. Thank goodness she'd put on her gums—rubber overshoes that the *Youngie* tended to avoid because they were ugly and favored by old ladies. But Emma figured she was old and eccentric enough to choose practicality over fashion without any noise from anyone. The seasonal creek at the very back of Amelia's place was in full spate, and the sun had finally gotten down to business and caused the forget-me-nots to make a blue cloud of tiny blossoms over the grasses. By next month they'd be a sticky cloud of burrs, but until then, she'd enjoy their fleeting beauty.

Hm, that would make a good article. Not "The Signs of Spring," which any farmer could write, but maybe "The Practical Side of Beauty." Because, to a forget-me-not, those burrs would ensure the continuation of the species.

Amelia's five acres were too small to farm, but the perfect size for a home, a barn for the horse and buggy, a chicken yard, and a huge garden. It was evident that, in between converting motors, a certain someone had borrowed equipment and plowed up a couple of big plots out of what had been wild grass. Amelia was definitely planning on planting enough to feed a hungry man all year.

Smiling, Emma mounted the steps and let herself into the house, where, to her enormous surprise, she found Ruth Lehman in the sitting room where they usually worked, regaling Carrie and Amelia with some big piece of news.

"Oh, Emma," Carrie said, turning from the table to look up at her. "Did you hear? Isn't it strange?"

"Hear what?" Amelia turned as well, and Emma's stomach plunged. "What is it? It's not the children? Or Eli?"

"No, no." Amelia crossed the room and gave her a hug—a harder hug than usual, as if she were glad Emma was standing there in the flesh, unharmed. "It's Grant Weaver."

Emma sucked in a lungful of air and felt herself go lightheaded. "Grant? Oh, no, no. I just saw him at lunch yesterday. It can't be. He's working up at our place. He—"

"No, not Grant himself," Ruth said. "Goodness, child, you look like you're about to faint. Sit down."

Emma pulled Amelia down on a chair beside her at the table. "What then? What happened?"

Ruth resumed her place as the bearer of the news. "It seems Lavina has gone missing. Grant told his grandfather that he went to the police station and filed a missing persons report. And Will Weaver, being a great friend of Isaac's, told him when Isaac was helping him put the corn in. So of course Isaac told me when he came in for lunch. Did you ever hear the like?"

Emma had lost the thread back at *gone missing.* "But she's been gone for years. What would make him do such a thing now?"

"Apparently they've been in touch all this time," Ruth said. "A regular correspondence. I don't know whether that man is a saint or a fool for keeping it up, but anyway, he hasn't heard from her since Christmas. Turns out the man she was living with hasn't, either. She just didn't come home one day."

The lightheaded feeling was swimming through Emma again.

They've been in touch all this time. Two years of regular correspondence. He never gave up on her, even when she left him, left the children, left her church and community for an Englisch *man. Oh, Grant . . .*

"Well, where is she, then?" Carrie asked of no one in particular. "How do you just not come home?"

Ruth shrugged and got up. "I suppose if you walk away from one life, you can walk away from another."

"It doesn't sound as if Grant believes that," Amelia said. "A missing persons report sounds serious to me. Oh, I hope no harm has come to her."

It sounded serious to Emma, too. Their people had as little to do with the police as possible. Oh, they obeyed all the laws and carried their identification cards and made sure they knew the laws of the road when it came to driving a buggy, but aside from that, some folks could go their whole lives without speaking to a policeman.

What must it have taken for Grant to walk into that station and tell them his wife, who had left him two years ago, had gone missing? And what about the man she'd left with? Was he not concerned? Were the two working together to find Lavina?

Questions buzzed in Emma's head like wasps looking for something to land on and sting.

Because they did sting. Oh yes, they did.

Corresponding all this time. He had never stopped loving her. Not once, despite what she'd done. And now he was prepared to involve the police to find her.

Emma Stolzfus, you are the biggest fool God ever made. Now will you stop mooning over this man?

When the door closed behind Ruth, Amelia shook out the quilt top, and Emma opened her bag and took out the strips for the long side that she planned to sew today. There was comfort in the orderliness of piecing a quilt—the way each piece went together with its neighbor, each fitting against the next. There were plenty of rough edges—no getting around that—but they were concealed on the inside, so all you could see from the outside was the beautiful pattern.

Lavina Weaver had been like a piece of silk tossed down in a patchwork of kitchen cottons. She had always been different—prettier, livelier. If one of the girls had news, they told it to her first. If a boy told a joke, he would look at Lavina to see if she laughed. And if she had something to say, the whole room fell silent with interest while she said it.

Emma fingered the border of dark green. She herself was like this—solid, dependable, good for working in the background so that others showed to their best advantage. No one would ever accuse her of trying to attract attention. No one would believe that her dearest wish was to be heard the way Lavina had been heard.

That was why she wrote, wasn't it? To make people listen.

But no one could hear Lavina now.

Except maybe her husband.

During the weeks that followed, the addition took shape on the big house as different helpers arrived every day to augment Grant's core crew. The sheathing went up, then insulation went in, and when the roofing crew arrived, Emma knew it wouldn't be long before Karen would be able to move in the crib and all her baby things.

On the Monday following the spring Council Meeting, the men arrived with paint cans in their buggies, and Emma saw Grant turn and walk down the lane to the *Daadi Haus* instead of climbing up onto the scaffolding at Karen's. Hastily, she slipped around the side of the house and got busy pegging out the wash on the line, which ran from the back porch out to a pole on the far side of the lawn.

"*Guder Mariye*, Emma." He stepped carefully through the

beds of budding day lilies, giving her time to school her face into that of a friend instead of a woman whose treacherous, foolish heart had just thrilled to the sound of her name on his lips. "You might need to move this end of your clothesline when you bring your clothes in tonight."

"*Guder Mariye.*" Good. A calm, friendly tone. "Are you boys ready to start over here?"

"Does tomorrow morning suit you?"

"*Ja.* Would you like breakfast first?" Karen had been feeding the crew and there was no way Emma would do less. She could not offer much in the way of comfort, whether he knew the whole community knew his business or not, but she could feed him, at least.

"*Nei.* I don't like to put you to any trouble."

"It's no trouble. Mamm and I have to eat anyway, and we're early risers."

He nodded, slapping his straw hat against his knee. A little puff of fine sawdust drifted to the ground. "I'll have a few of my crew with me. Three of us okay?"

As long as he was among them, she would feed as many as he could bring. "Sure. Say, seven o'clock?"

He nodded, turned as if to leave, then paused. He looked up at her, swinging his hat against his leg. "I suppose you heard about Lavina."

Goodness. She had not expected him to speak so bluntly about something so personal. "I did," she said awkwardly. "I—I hope she is all right and that you will hear from her soon."

"I hope so, too. I spoke to a police officer in Whinburg, but he only said they were still looking into it. He said to tell him if I heard from her." He paused. "You're quite a writer, Emma."

A blush rose into her face. On the tip of her tongue teetered her news about finaling in the contest, like a red-winged blackbird balancing on a reed singing its heart out. But she bit it back. Instead, she savored the gift of his compliment. Already she knew she would be taking it out again and again, a treasured heirloom in a chest of silence, to turn it over and marvel at its beauty in private.

"I know you write for *Family Life*," he said. "And those letters I see in the *Whinburg Weekly* signed E.S.... I wonder whose those could be?"

"I wonder," she replied. What was he getting at? The beating of her heart slowed to a workaday rate. Did he plan to go to the bishop about this troublesome woman who too conveniently forgot the principles of *Gelassenheit* with her attention-seeking ways?

Was that a smile hidden in his beard? "I won't say a word. When God gives a talent, it would be a sin to bury it in the ground."

"You're the only one who thinks so, then," came out of her mouth before she could stop it. Heat rose in her cheeks again.

"I keep my thoughts to myself as a general rule. God has given you this talent. Be sure you use it for His glory and there will be no harm in it. There might even be some good."

Emma's heart turned over in despair. Here was someone who understood—no, more than that: who was everything she admired in a man—hardworking, kind, even perceptive. And she could never, ever tell him or so much as hint that she felt this way.

"I wonder if I could ask you to do something?"

"Of course." What could she possibly do for a man who was so capable?

"I wonder if you could write a little article about Lavina for *Family Life*. It goes to Amish folks all over the country. I was thinking maybe if somebody read it and saw her, they could ask her to write home. Or they could write, themselves."

All she could do was nod. Her powers of speech had deserted her completely.

He slapped his hat on his knee with the sound of finality. "*Gut. Denkes*, Emma. I appreciate it. We will see you in the morning, *ja?*"

When he was out of sight and hearing, she turned her face into a cold, damp towel hanging on the line and wept.

CHAPTER 5

May 7, 2012

Dear Ms. Stolzfus,

We have received our judges' feedback on the finalist entries in the Commonwealth Prize fiction contest. While the competition was very strong and your entry received close consideration, we regret to say that it was not chosen as the winner of the publishing contract.

However, your entry showed such merit that it was the judges' consensus that you should pursue publication through the normal channels. We on the contest committee wish you the best of luck in your literary endeavors.

Sincerely,
Tiffany Hickman
Contest Coordinator

Emma folded up the letter with its New York postmark and stuffed it in her pocket. She had never expected to win; had never even allowed the possibility to take root in her mind.

To believe she was better than six of the best writers in the contest smacked of arrogance, and her soul flinched from that.

But oh, how wonderful it must be for the person who had received a different letter this morning!

Well. *Genunk.*

She had exercised the gift that God had given her, and it had produced a few moments of fleeting joy, as worldly gifts tended to do. She had done what she had done, and now it was time to move on and be realistic. When they sent it back, she would not burn the manuscript, because the story was part of her and to harm it would be like cutting off her hair and burning it. So it would stay hidden in the closet and maybe once in a while she would take it out and read it, the way one read old letters from a close friend simply because they were good for the soul.

Meanwhile, God had given her other gifts—and one of them was the cause of the squeaking sounds she could hear through the trees. Emma delivered Karen's mail to the big house and paused at her end of the lane to watch Grant and one of the teenage boys he employed as they labored over her porch. Each rocked the claw end of his hammer against the wood, yanking up the nails one by one. The porch already looked like a skeleton, and soon even the supports that had held up the roof as well as her purple clematis would be gone. Behind the house, the boy's brother did the same, the shriek of wood yielding up nails a sound sweet to her ears.

The men had made short work of her eggs, ham steaks, and biscuits this morning. It wasn't often she got to appreciate a hungry man at her table, so to have three of them all at once was a novelty she would almost rather have sat back to watch. And she learned one more thing about Grant Weaver: He was a coffee drinker. Not just at breakfast, but all through the morning. She had already made three pots and it was only eleven o'clock.

She hugged this knowledge—the kind of knowledge a wife might have—to herself as she went in through the kitchen and got busy making another pot. They'd be in for lunch at noon.

You are pathetic. You're like a sparrow, darting under the table for a tiny crumb and calling it a gift from God. Probably half the women in the district know he's a coffee drinker.

If a person ranked God's gifts by size, she was walking a dangerous, arrogant line.

Stop thinking about him. That's *the dangerous line you should be worried about.*

But Emma couldn't.

God had shown her abundantly how silly and pointless her feelings were. Grant was married. Even though she'd been gone two years, he still loved his wife. Emma knew that. But try as she might, she couldn't make them go away.

What would Amelia and Carrie say if she didn't turn up for their quilting frolic this afternoon, and stayed to savor the experience of having him around the place instead? By this time next week, she would have new porches and Grant would move on to his next project. If what the other women had been talking about after Council Meeting were true, he would be building a home for Daniel Lapp's daughter Mandy and her new husband, who had been married the previous fall. She was the last of five daughters to be married, but the first who had chosen a man who loved farming, so Daniel had ceded a hundred acres to the young couple. Now they needed a home to live in.

The Lapp property extended from the county highway in the north down to the far side of Edgeware Road from the Stolzfus place. Emma would be able to see the new house going up in the distance if she stood at the mailbox. Maybe she would see the builders arriving if she happened to be down there picking up the mail.

Ja, and maybe they would all get a clue about what you were doing there, and the talk would go around the district that Emma Stolzfus was setting her Kapp *for a carpenter.*

Never mind. Better she spent her time on profitable things, and Tuesdays were sewing days, not mooning over men days. The Crosses and Losses quilt was going together so slowly that the average Amish woman could have made two in the time it was taking. But no one was judging them on their speed.

"Just because it's a winter project, doesn't mean we have to complete it in the winter," Carrie said when Emma told them her thoughts—well, some of them—that afternoon at Amelia's. "It's Tuesday, and we're sewing, aren't we? Just like all the other women in the district."

"All the other women in the district are sewing *Kapps* and pants and things their households need," Emma pointed out.

"We'll finish the borders today," Amelia said from behind her treadle, the needle beginning its march up several feet of green border in tiny steps. "It might be slow, but it's coming together. And I don't know about you, but I can make shirts and pants for the boys and *Kapps* in the evenings."

"Your *Mamm* would think all this time we're taking is a disgrace," Emma said. "I know mine does, but she's too kind to say so in case she offends one of you."

Amelia mumbled something about not everyone being so considerate. Then she said more clearly, "As you say, getting this quilt done isn't the point. The point is that we're together doing it. And if you need to do some mending or make a new *Kapp*, you bring it along and go right ahead."

"I'll tell you what I did bring along." Emma took out the second letter from New York and read it aloud. "So that's that. It was fun while it lasted, but now it's done."

"At least you had a few weeks of knowing your work was among the best," Carrie offered.

"It still is," Amelia pointed out. "What was that part about having merit?"

"They were just being nice." Emma folded up the letter and put it back in her pocket. "It doesn't mean anything."

"Maybe not, but it was good of them to say it." Carrie could find something positive in a torrential downpour on a stormy day. "I wonder what 'the usual channels' are?"

"No idea." Emma didn't want to talk about it anymore. "Amelia, have you heard from Eli this week?" Eli had gone up to Lebanon to visit his family.

The march of the needle stopped. "I have. He's coming back soon. Sometime in the next ten days. He says he needs to find an *Englisch* man with a backhoe."

"When are you two going to announce your engagement in public?" Emma asked. "I mean, you're planting a bigger garden, he's here every other week, and now he's hiring equipment...to do what?"

"What do backhoes do but dig foundation trenches?" Carrie's eyes were big and blue and guileless. "Do you know, Emma?"

Amelia shot her a look that plainly said, *Who do you think you're fooling?* "Very funny. There will be no digging up my front acre yet. Eli just wants to be prepared for when the day comes."

"I think a wedding day had better come before anybody starts digging anything up," Emma said dryly. "What will the neighbors think?"

"You *are* the neighbors," Carrie said. "What do you think?"

"I am shocked and appalled that anyone would even *mention* a backhoe before asking a certain question," Emma said firmly, trying to keep her lips from twitching. "It's positively indecent. What kind of example is that for the children?"

"Well, he did say he had something to talk about besides backhoes." Amelia looked down at her seam and blushed scarlet.

Carrie gasped while Emma fought down a pang. It was not jealousy. It wasn't. It was simply the knowledge that Amelia would not need her friends as much once everything was settled and she had Eli to make a family with. They would still be neighbors, and would still see each other all the time, but it wouldn't be the same. Amelia would have new priorities, which was just as it should be.

God was healing Amelia's heart even as He healed her body, and a good friend would rejoice with her in the happy times just as she'd cried with her in times of despair.

Emma crossed the room and gave Amelia a hug as soon as Carrie released her, fervently hoping that Amelia would not see that despair was her own struggle, now.

Emma loved the smell of freshly cut grass and baking bread. Now she had a third favorite smell: the scent of newly cut planks on a finished porch.

She wouldn't need to walk circumspectly up to her own doors anymore, for sure. She sat on the back step and gave an experimental bounce.

Nothing moved. Solid as a rock. The workman was truly worthy of his hire.

As if she'd conjured him up out of the late-afternoon air, Grant came around the side of the house, looking up at the clapboard and eyeing the trim. A hummingbird shot past his ear—she would have to get the feeder back up soon, before they got cranky and abandoned them—and when he turned to follow its flight, he saw her.

"Hello, Emma. Taking it for a drive?"

She gripped the edge of the sun-warmed plank, set evenly next to its neighbors and perfectly on square. "*Ischt gut.* Think I'll keep it."

"Glad to hear it. Careful you don't get a sliver. The boys and I are going to paint tomorrow." She nodded, and he looked up again. "We should do the rest of the house or it will look bad. When was this place last painted?"

A good question. Karen had been pregnant, but with which child? "Nine years ago, maybe? I think Karen was expecting Maryann, and she's eight now."

Grant nodded. "Coming up on ten years, it's probably time. I'll check with John and make sure it's okay we do the whole thing."

Here was a chance that wouldn't come around again for another ten years. "If he agrees, maybe we could paint the trim green instead of blue?"

"Don't you like blue?"

It had been a bad mix that someone had refused at the warehouse store. Pap had consequently got it for cheap, and the color always reminded her of bread mold. "I like blue just fine, but I think green would be better. It's a cheery color, to match the trees and the lawn."

Mamm adored color, which anyone could tell by the orange day lilies and the roses and snapdragons she'd planted over the years, but to paint one's house and outbuildings anything but white was unheard of. Even green trim was pushing the district's *Ordnung* just a bit; Daniel Lapp painted his black in a pointed reminder to the *Gmee* about his standards of plainness. And if you wanted red or burgundy, you were plumb out of luck.

"I used green for mine," Grant said, still scanning the sills and trim boards. Emma felt a tiny burst of pleasure at having that decision in common. "I'll check with John, then, and get some more white and a gallon can of green while I'm in town. I hope you're not fussy about what shade." He smiled, and even if the sun hadn't been spiking through the trees in broad rays, she would have felt the world had burst into light. "If you ever had a hankering to write graffiti on the walls like the city kids do, now's your chance. Tomorrow we'll cover up all the evidence."

What on earth—? The insanity of such a thing startled a laugh out of her. "Honestly, the things you say."

"Just don't do it in blue. That will show through, no matter how many coats of white we put on it."

"I won't do it in any color. I'm not going to vandalize my own house." Technically it was John and Karen's house, but still.

Smiling now that he'd got a rise out of her, he gestured over his shoulder. "I've got a couple of cans and the other stuff in the wagon. I'll just leave them here until tomorrow, unless you want them out of the way in the shed."

"Here is fine."

While he brought the paint cans, she helped him by carrying the milk crates full of the brushes and rollers, well used but well cared for. When they'd lined everything up on the new porch, she dusted off her hands on her kitchen apron.

"I'll see you tomorrow."

He nodded. "If we do the whole house, my crew will be here another couple of days."

"I'll have breakfast ready at seven, same as usual, then."

A small silence fell.

"You're a good cook."

She looked up, surprised. Another compliment. For a woman who had been starved of them, these were riches indeed. "My teacher sits at the same table. I would hear about it if the eggs weren't fluffy and the biscuits light."

"And a good writer. You can't say your teacher is responsible for that."

"I'd better, if I don't want a head so big I can't get in the door."

"No danger of that." He shot her a look. "Did you ever have a little time to write that article?"

Guilt arrowed through her. "I've been turning it over in my mind. I'll put something on paper tonight and send it this week."

He nodded. "I know it's a lot to ask."

Not in comparison to everything he had given. Going to the police must have been awful for a man as private and quiet as this one. Even asking her for this little thing had to have been difficult. "What are friends for, if not to help?"

"You're a *gut* friend. I thank God for my friends in these difficult days."

Remembering her foolishness, her secret thoughts, her silly pleasure at his compliments, Emma felt worse than ever.

* * *

The moon hung low over the horizon, and beyond the gentle hills and farms of Whinburg Township, the first wash of gray lightened the night sky.

Emma crept down the stairs. She hadn't slept much. After writing the article and folding it into its envelope, she'd stared at the ceiling. Lavina had left of her own free will. But when the article was published, people would hear of her again. Yes, she was under *die Meinding*, so by the letter of the law she did not have a voice. But Emma would speak for her. Grant would speak for her. Would people hear? Would Lavina herself hear the voices calling her name?

Would she come back? And if she did, what then?

Finally, toward two o'clock, Emma had fallen into a fitful sleep. Her eyes had opened a couple of hours later with the certainty of what she was going to do . . . as if she'd dreamed it.

Quietly, she put on a dress so old she'd only used it to feed the cows when Pap had kept them, and slipped downstairs barefoot. With a screwdriver from Pap's toolbox, she opened the can of white paint and carried it around to the side of the house that faced the fields. No one would see from the road, and Mamm was not in the habit anymore of rambling around the yard. With a shim from the construction debris that someone had forgotten to pick up, she stirred the paint, then chose a nice wide brush.

Her whole body got into the work, bending and stretching and slashing stroke after stroke. It didn't take long.

She put everything back where she'd found it. Even if John said no, the house could go another couple of years before it needed painting, it would be a while before anyone saw. And even longer before they figured out who was responsible.

When Grant arrived in the morning, his two helpers riding in the back of the spring wagon with their feet swinging, it took him a few minutes to realize that something was different. She watched from her bedroom window, standing to one side of the frame so he wouldn't look up and see her.

She saw him spell out the letters, painted white on white and four feet tall on the side of the house.

L-I-S-T-E-N

Chapter 6

May 10, 2012

Dear Ms. Stolzfus,

I am the literary agent who read your entry, *Inherit the Earth*, in the Commonwealth Prize fiction contest. Since the contest was seeking the next voice in literary fiction, and yours had a more down-to-earth, accessible tone, I was unable to award it the point score it deserved—*deserved* being the operative term. Ms. Stolzfus, your writing has a lyrical voice, humor, and the kind of penetrating but compassionate insight into the human spirit that certain markets are desperately seeking.

Are you already represented? If not, I would very much like the chance to speak with you. My phone number and email address are below. Please give me a call. Or, if it's more convenient, let me know your number and I'll call you. I look forward to hearing from you.

Sincerely,
Tyler West
West & Associates
Literary Agency

May 12, 2012

Dear Tyler West,

Thank you for your letter. I am Amish and have no phone except for the one in the shanty out on Edgeware Road, and I don't have enough quarters for a long-distance call to New York. I hope you will not mind.

I appreciate all the nice things you said about my writing. I'm not sure what you mean about insight into the human spirit. In my experience, the human spirit does better when folks don't know what's going on in there. But it was kind of you to be so encouraging.

I'm also not sure what you meant about representation. I don't plan to publish the story. My bishop would never allow it. Even though the *Ordnung* doesn't include anything about publishing books (that I know of), it has plenty to say about women speaking up in public and drawing attention to themselves.

Thank you again for your letter. I'll keep it always.

                              Sincerely,
                              Emma Stolzfus

May 14, 2012

Dear Ms. Stolzfus,

Your letter was the best thing to happen to me all week. Thank you for your speedy reply.

I know you said you don't plan to publish the story, but I hope I can convince you otherwise. What representation means is that I would take your manuscript to several editors that I know. Once you give it to me and

I have your permission, you don't have to do a thing. The editors will read it, and if someone likes it, they'll offer you an advance against royalties—in other words, an up-front payment. Then they'll publish your book and you get a percentage of every copy that sells.

I know several editors right off the top of my head who would kill for this book. The Amish are very popular right now. Please don't do your book a disservice by putting it in a drawer. People will love your characters and your town—and you.

Let me know what you would like to do.

Best,
Tyler

May 16, 2012

Dear Tyler,

Please don't let anyone kill for my book. It isn't *that* good. I'm sorry, but I can't let you represent it. Popular or not, an Amish woman can't be published, and that's all there is to it.

I'm sorry if I misled you when I entered it in the contest. I only wanted to see how it would do. I never expected to be a finalist. What I've gained from my experience was more than good enough for me.

Thank you,
Emma

May 18, 2012

Dear Emma,

Maybe you can help me understand a little more about this *Ordnung* thing if we meet in person and talk it over. I really feel you have a bright future in fiction, and it would be a shame to...not sure what the expression is. Hide your light under a basket?

I'm informed by my assistant that the Amish do not fly in planes. Enclosed please find a business-class ticket on the Pennsylvanian from Lancaster into Penn Station. You'll be met and after that I'd like to take you to dinner, talk this over, and show you around a little. I'll also put you up in a hotel close to the office and you can go home the next day. Don't worry about anything. This one is on me.

As you can tell, I'm serious about this. I hope you will take me seriously.

Plus, I'd love to find out if the person on the page is the same as the person in real life.

My best,
Tyler

The person on the page? What on earth did he mean?

Emma fingered the train ticket. Never mind her, what about him? She had never heard of a man so forward. Did he do this all the time—invite women he'd never met on overnight trips? She had half a mind to rip his presumptuous letter and ticket into tiny pieces and mail them back to him.

But that would be a waste of eighty dollars, not to mention a stamp, said the other half of her mind. *Think of how much he believes in your book, if he would go out on a limb like this to convince you.*

Actions spoke louder than words, everybody knew that. His words had been wonderful *gut*, no doubt about it. Her vanity had been stroked as smooth as velvet during the last several days. What were this letter and the ticket but more of the same, puffing her up and making her think she must be somebody? Bad enough she had allowed this correspondence to go on so long. It would be a sin of the most dangerous sort to go to New York and hear these blandishments in person—especially having accepted the man's money.

Yet...under the compliments and the temptation was a truth that she couldn't avoid. He had read her book. He believed in it. He was listening, and he had the ability to make other people listen.

And that was the most powerful temptation of all.

Communion Sunday was at Karen and John's, a case of perfect timing as far as construction went. Not only was the *Daadi Haus* sparkling with its new coat of pristine white—her graffiti painted over with not one word spoken on the subject—but a couple of days before, there had been a painting frolic at the big house. The crew hadn't had time to do the barns, but Emma had no doubt that was number one on Karen's list.

Emma tried to quiet her mind on this, one of the holiest days of the year. As Bishop Daniel tore a piece from the loaf of bread in his hands, she focused on the sacrifice of Jesus, and the community of believers that it had made. They had all been brought together in unity. There were no individual grains of wheat left in this loaf; each one had been ground to powder so that it could contribute its essence to the whole.

Her determination to do nothing that would make her

seem like a grain of wheat sticking in the community's teeth lasted until after the all-day service ended. Then, Amelia and Carrie separated themselves from their men and walked over to the *Daadi Haus* with Emma to see the new porches.

At which point she made the mistake of showing them Tyler West's letter and the train ticket, large as life.

Amelia was rendered speechless. Carrie took the letter and read it a second time, her eyes huge as she lifted her gaze to Emma's. "This is amazing—and a little shocking," she managed. "Are you going to go?"

"Of course she's not," Amelia finally got out. "I hope you haven't told anyone, Emma. If anyone hears, you can only imagine the fuss."

Amelia was no stranger to fusses, after last winter. And she'd been sensitive about people's opinions before that.

"No, I haven't. Not even Mamm."

"Have you answered him?" Carrie asked. She pulled her sweater tighter and folded her arms. It was cool out, with clouds piling up in the east. If they were in for a storm, it was good that the paint had had time to dry.

"I just got it yesterday. There hasn't been time. And I—" *I don't know what to say.*

No, that wasn't true. She did know. At least, she had up until she'd broken bread, when God had clearly pointed her in the way she should go.

"What are you going to tell him?" Amelia wanted to know. "I know what I'd say."

Did she have to sound quite so positive? "Seems to me you were in this very position not so long ago. Knowing what you wanted to do, yet knowing that if you did it, you'd put your soul in danger."

Amelia flinched, and turned to look back down the lane.

"It's not the same. This isn't life and death, and you don't have two little boys depending on your decision."

Emma breathed in a lungful of air scented with cut grass and the vigorous plants coming up in her garden. "That's true. I don't."

"But what an experience it would be," Carrie said on a sigh. "I've never been outside Pennsylvania, not even for vacations. At least you've been to Florida, Emma. I would love to take a ride on a train all the way to New York."

Emma held out the ticket and Carrie snatched it away, dimpling. Quick as a chicken yanking a worm from the soil, Amelia whipped it away from both of them. "Neither of you can be trusted with this."

"Careful, you'll tear it," Emma protested, reaching for the slip of paper. Thank heaven for Carrie, who could lighten a mood the way the weather changed.

Amelia handed it over with a big show of reluctance. "It would be better torn, and then it wouldn't tempt you."

"What wouldn't tempt her?" Emma turned to see Mamm leaning on Maryann's shoulder, making her slow way up the path to the front door.

She went to her side. "I'll look after her from here. *Denki*, Maryann."

The girl nodded and ran off in the direction of the creek, where distant shouts told her the children were trying to resist the temptation to play, and failing. Karen would have a wash basket full of muddy pants tomorrow.

"What's tempting you?" Lena asked again as the younger women followed her and Emma into the house. Her sharp eyes hadn't missed the letter and the ticket.

If only she'd shown them inside, in the privacy of her room upstairs. But it was too late now.

"A literary agent from New York thinks he can sell my book," she said, when Mamm was comfortable in her chair. "Do you want some tea while I get supper?"

"I do not. I want you to tell me how a man in New York even knows you have a book when I don't. What book? Is that what you clack away on that typewriter for at all hours of the night?"

Emma nodded. "It wasn't a secret."

"A secret is something you don't talk about. And you don't talk about that book." Her mother's logic was infallible. "I can't believe you didn't tell me you did such a thing."

Emma had expected her to be angry. But what was this? Could she possibly be...hurt?

"I—" *Didn't want anyone to know.* "I—" *Thought you would make me burn it.* "I've told you now."

"Did you girls know about this?" Carrie and Amelia had settled uneasily on the new burgundy couch like a pair of birds on a power line in a high wind.

Amelia shook her head. "I know Emma writes articles, but up until recently I didn't know anything about a book."

"What's it about, Emma?" Trust Carrie to try to steer the conversation onto a less rocky road.

"It's about...us. The *Gmee*. Well, one I made up. It's about this woman and her friends and their man problems and...oh, never mind. That's not the point. The point is, do I go to New York and talk to this Tyler West or not?"

"Amelia, may I see that letter?" Wordlessly, she handed it to Lena, who scanned it rapidly. When she lifted her head, Emma swallowed and prepared herself. "He seems very thorough."

"*Ja.*"

"Very forward, too. This ticket is for Tuesday, coming

back Wednesday. As if you had nothing in the world to do but drop everything and go to New York."

"*Ja.*"

Lena folded up the letter with the ticket inside and handed it back. "So you had better go and see your sister. I think I'd like Maryann to stay with me instead of asking Katherine to leave her family and come all the way here from Strasburg."

"*Ja*— What?" Emma took it with fingers that hardly knew what they were doing.

"There's no sin in talking with the man. A trip would do you good."

"But—" She must be hearing things. Either that, or her mother's mind had finally given way.

Lena's gaze softened. "Emma, *Liewi*, don't think I don't know what it's like for you. If this man is willing to pay for something so crazy, without expecting anything in return but a conversation, I think it is safe to do it. You don't have to give him your book. That would open up a whole new can of worms, and I have to believe you've already counted the cost of it."

"*Ja*," Emma whispered. She could never be published while she was a member of the church. It was foolish to even toy with the idea. Then why was Mamm so bent on her not only toying with it, but taking it and throwing it in the air and playing with it?

Carrie stared at Lena as if she'd never seen her before, but Amelia's face held the slow light of recognition. "Lena Stolzfus, you radical," she said softly. "Didn't you sit in this very room and tell me I ought to throw caution to the winds, as well, when everyone else thought I should stay home and do as I was told?"

Lena reached into her knitting basket and settled a half-finished shawl on her lap. "I might have."

"That was different, you said so yourself," Emma told her friend.

"Maybe. But if it's advice you're looking for, you've had mine and Carrie's."

"And it's left me right where I began, where two ways meet, and me without a clue which way to go."

"The colt didn't worry about which way to go," Lena told her. "It let the Lord decide."

Emma sank onto the couch next to her mother, who even at seventy-eight and a half could still surprise her—and then bring her to her knees.

"You're absolutely right. This colt had better do some praying, whether that train leaves from Lancaster on Tuesday or not."

CHAPTER 7

Emma had been in the Lancaster train station only twice before—once to go to Florida, and once to go to Mamm's mother's funeral when she'd been a little girl. The Stolzfus family, needless to say, did not believe in traipsing around the country. A tiny girl, she'd stood in this very spot on the platform, watching a train roar down the track, thinking it was going awfully fast for something that was supposed to stop and let her and her family get on. With an explosion of wind as cruel as a blow, it had flashed past, the sound of it louder than ten thunderstorms all at once. It had taken Mamm ten minutes to stop her screaming, hands over her ears, her *Kapp* blown down her back and its straight pins irretrievably lost.

Emma stepped to the concrete lip of the platform and looked down at the track. They were probably still there, buried in rocks and cinders. Then she moved back, gripping the overnight bag Karen had lent her. "Just you keep an eye on it," she had told Emma. "You never know when someone could walk by and steal it right out from under your nose. And keep your money in your skirt pocket, under your apron, where no one can see it. You don't want to invite someone to rob you in that dreadful place."

To Emma's knowledge, Karen had never been nearer to New York than Lancaster herself, so how she had become such an authority was a mystery. Still, under the bossy exterior, she saw the concern, and had merely hugged her in reassurance.

But being Karen, her sister was more than concerned. She'd spent half an hour closeted with Mamm, trying to ferret out all the details of why on earth Emma should need to go to New York, and when that didn't work, she'd settled for going to the source. "It's business, Karen," was all Emma would say, no matter how many ingenious ways Karen found to ask the same question.

It was kind of fun knowing something that Karen wanted to know. It lessened the sting of her attempts at matchmaking.

But this morning Karen had got the best of her. When she heard the *Englisch* driver's car crunching up the drive to the big house, she'd gently hugged Mamm good-bye. "Remember, medicine at six o'clock without fail, and make sure she takes it," she told Maryann. Then she picked up her bag, touched the pocketbook in her skirt pocket for the twentieth time, took a deep breath, and walked down the lane to meet the car.

"You're heading to the Lancaster train station?" The *Englisch* woman—a friend of Amelia's who worked at the Dutch Deli—shook hands and opened the front passenger door.

"I am." It wasn't until Emma slid into the car that she realized she was not the only one traveling more than ten miles this morning.

"*Guder Mariye*, Emma," Joshua Steiner said with enough cheer to fill the back of a spring wagon. "It's a *gut* day for a journey, wouldn't you say?"

Astonished past the point of speech, Emma turned to gape at him before the *Englisch* woman reminded her about the seat belt. Since the woman wouldn't go unless Emma was buckled in, she had no choice but to turn and face the front. "What are you doing here?" she finally managed by the time they got to the end of the drive, having gotten herself secured. "Do you have business somewhere so early?"

"*Ja*," he'd said, grinning as though he'd put one over on her. "I'm taking you to the train."

That was when she'd realized Karen had outsmarted her. And once they'd reached their destination, he wasn't satisfied with waving from his window when she got out of the car, either. Oh, no. He'd come into the station, and now here he was on the platform with her, waiting as though he meant to see her to her seat. She hoped that between the two of them, Karen and Joshua had enough money to pay the *Englisch* lady to wait.

"Carrie would have taken me to the bus," she told him for the third time. "Truly, you didn't have to put yourself out like this."

"Still as humble as ever," he said in a tone that made her wonder if he thought she was humble at all. "Besides, if you'd taken the bus you'd be on it yet. This way, we have a little time to visit. I wonder how long it took them to paint all this woodwork white?"

She didn't want to talk about the woodwork. Or the odd way the square blocks of the station gave way to all this painted fanciness on the platform for no apparent reason. She wanted him to go so she could savor the novelty of traveling alone for the first time.

"As long as it would take Grant and his crew to paint two

houses, a barn, and a bunch of outbuildings, I bet," she said. "Look, Joshua—"

"Ah, Grant." He didn't seem to realize he'd interrupted her. Men seldom did. "How is he doing?"

"As well as can be expected," she said. "You know him. He doesn't show much."

"I wouldn't say that. He did a good job on the *Daadi Haus*?"

"I thought so. Mamm is pleased—and so is Karen."

"It seemed to take him a long time, in my view. He took extra care, painting all the trim, for instance."

She squared him in the view allowed her from under the brim of her away bonnet. "Nothing wrong with taking care on a job. I suppose that's why he has a reputation as a good workman." Unlike some people, whose reputations could use more than a coat of paint.

Emma felt a sudden plunge inside, as if the train platform had dipped and swayed like the floating wharf in Moses Yoder's pond. What would happen to *her* reputation when it got out that Joshua Steiner had gone all the way into Lancaster from Whinburg to see her off at the train? Oh, goodness. People were going to have a field day—her destination would take a pale second place to who her companion was on the journey. Next time he went to town for feed or seed, the *Gmee* would decide he was there to buy an engagement clock.

"I'm not so sure."

She reined in her galloping thoughts and tried to remember what they'd been talking about. Paint. Grant. Yes. "What do you mean?"

He gave her a teasing glance, then gazed up the line as if he hadn't a care in the world. "I mean that a busy man doesn't hang around a place doing what the ladies of the house could do if he doesn't have a reason."

What on earth was he nattering about? Had he been this aggravating when they were *Kinner*? "Speak plain, for goodness sake, Joshua. You're making me tired and it's not even noon yet."

"Don't be so coy, then. I think Grant had a very good reason." He paused. Grinned. "You."

Had the man lost his mind? They might have been friends close enough for teasing a decade ago, but not now. "I think your mouth works faster than your brain, and always did. Grant is a married man and it's wicked of you to say such things."

"It's not just me. When your sister let me know you'd be traveling, and asked if I had any business in Lancaster— which I do; she's a very considerate girl, Karen—I'd already heard a little bird or two peeping on the subject."

"Most birds don't know a fact from an earthworm."

"They've got sharp eyes, though. So I told myself that I'd better hitch a ride with your driver, because if I didn't, I'd miss the train in more ways than one." When she didn't dignify this with an answer, he lowered his voice even though the nearest people were a tourist couple twenty feet away, trying to take a picture without looking like they were doing it. Emma turned her back and gazed up the line as well.

"I hear there's a get-together on Friday evening at Lehmans' for Eli Fischer's birthday. Would you care to go with me?"

Her cheeks cooled as the blood drained out of her face. That would be making such a statement that she might as well go and buy the clock herself. "I can't leave Mamm."

"You're leaving her this morning."

"Maryann is looking after her, as you know very well if you've talked to Karen."

"Maryann can look after her again."

"She's not a child, Joshua, to be babysat every time her parents want to go out."

"And you're not a child, either. You're a woman who deserves all the joy life has to offer."

Oh, the vanity of the man! "And going to Lehmans' with you will bring me joy?"

"I hope so. I know it will for me."

The laughter had faded from his hazel eyes and in them she saw not vanity, but the shadow of the boy he had once been. Before bad decisions and too many years had changed him. The boy who was still standing on the outside, looking in.

Like her.

And just like that, her temper, which had been approaching a rolling boil, calmed as though someone had turned off the flame. "That's the first sincere thing you've said all morning."

In the silence, below the rushing of the wind and the sound of traffic from the other side of the building, she heard him swallow. "I mean it, Emma." He turned to her. "I miss you. I miss our friendship. I would like to have it again."

She answered the boy who had gone tubing with her down the river, not the man who had left the district in disgrace. "Then I'd be happy to go to Lehmans' with you. But let's not arrive in a buggy and make a big show of it. Let's walk across the fields together, as we used to."

The train rolled into the station with a roar and a rattle, and she didn't hear his reply. Since the stationmaster had told her it would only stop long enough for passengers to get off and on, she counted cars and got onto the one that had a placard on it saying Business Class. In the door of the car, she turned.

"Good-bye, Joshua. Thank you for waiting with me."

"Hurry back," he called.

When she found a seat, settled her bag in the rack, and looked outside, he was still there, still smiling, as the train pulled away from the platform.

And his smile was not the mocking one that he used with other people. It was the boyish one she had not seen in sixteen years.

Did the people of New York realize that when you entered their city on the Pennsylvanian, it was like coming up from the underworld? Did they really mean their welcome to look like the gates of hell?

Comfortable in her cushiony seat, Emma gazed out the window, seeing black walls and tunnels that vanished into night, even though it was only five in the afternoon. Her journey had been uneventful, and she had even taken out her notebook and written an article for *Family Life* about backsides. Not of people, mind you, but of places. Traveling by train, you got to see the backside of everything—yards, towns, fields…and now an enormous city. The backside really told the truth about a place. The dark lightened enough for her to see the underside of a bridge; then the track seemed to rise and they came up out of the dark and into the city proper.

How ugly it was! Goodness, you'd think with all the money people had in cities that they would take a little care with where they lived. But no. It was all metal and tumbled buildings and miles of traffic and concrete and junk. A few trees struggled on the sides of roads, but there wasn't a flower to be seen anywhere.

The train pulled into the platform and stopped, and when she stepped out, Emma was whirled into a rush of humanity that pushed her up a set of stairs whether she wanted to go or not. She emerged into a set of tunnels that looked like a shopping mall, with people scurrying hither and yon—hundreds, maybe thousands of people. And the noise! It was as bad as the train from her childhood—and she'd left the real trains somewhere below. Clutching her overnight case, Emma took refuge in an eddy of the current of people, next to a sign advertising a movie of some kind.

How on earth was she to find where she was supposed to go? Here half a dozen ways met, and they all looked exactly the same—tunnels packed with the same noise and craziness. Tyler West had told her she'd be met. Foolish Emma. She should have written to ask by whom. Or where. Or when, even.

All around her, people ran headlong, rushing under signs with the names of streets on them. She had no map to tell her what street she should wait on. She had nothing. And the people who weren't striding as if sheer determination would take them where they were going were walking past slowly, staring as if they'd never seen a woman in a cape and apron and bonnet before. Now they were pointing. Now someone was getting out a camera. Emma whirled, the too-bright, unnatural colors of the movie poster blinding her.

Stupid. Stupid. You should never have come. A whole day spent to accomplish what? You could have been working in the garden or getting milk or—oh, woe, you've missed the quilting frolic. Carrie and Amelia probably went on without you, together, enjoying each other's fellowship, and what do you have? Nothing. Just a lot of noise and confusion.

Noise and confusion and loneliness so acute its edge cut her self-confidence to pieces.

Tears burned into her eyes. This was what she got for all her vanity.

"Ma'am?" It took a moment to realize someone was speaking to her. "Excuse me, ma'am?"

"I do not pose for pictures," she told the movie poster. She would not look. They would snap the camera in her face and she could not bear it.

"Pardon me, ma'am, but is your name Stoles Fuss?"

She turned to see a huge man with skin as black as coal. He was dressed in a black suit that must have had an acre of fabric in it, and his shirt was blindingly white in contrast. Someone knew what they were doing with the bleach.

"I am Emma Stolzfus." At his expression of relief, she went to pieces. "Please, please, I beg you to take me out of this insane place. I didn't know where to go, I'm so confused, and those people want to take a picture and—thank you, Tyler West, for coming to get me. I've never been so glad to see anyone in my life."

Something in his eyes made her babbling mouth stop its flapping.

"Ma'am, excuse me, no, I'm just the driver."

"The driver?" This was not Tyler West, the man who had said all those lovely things in his letters about her work? "What driver?"

"I'm here to pick up an Emma Stolzfus—" This time he pronounced it correctly. "—and take her over to Fifty-eighth.

You're her, right? 'Cause I don't see too many other Amish ladies down here. You're kinda hard to miss."

The driver. Hot color rose in her face and for two cents she would have fled back down the tunnel and climbed back on the train.

"Yes, I'm Emma Stolzfus," she repeated feebly.

"Great. Here, let me take that for you."

"No, no." She wasn't about to let a stranger make off with her case, even though it held nothing but a dress, some underthings, a hairbrush and some extra pins, and a toothbrush. "I'll carry it."

"Suit yourself. Follow me, ma'am, please."

She should tell him not to call her ma'am, that plain folk didn't hold with honorifics. But instead, she merely obeyed with a relief so sweet it was almost a blessing. Someone who knew where he was going. *Denkes, lieber Gott.*

Down the tunnel. Across an underground plaza and up some stairs. On the other side, a river of people was so thick it rippled and moved like a waterfall down the stairs. She would never again think that a writer who referred to a "river of humanity" was exaggerating. Then outside to a cacophony of car horns, screeching brakes, loud music, and the hum of millions of people.

"Is it always this loud here?" she shouted to the driver as he opened the door of a car parked at the curb.

"Loud?" He looked blank. "Watch your head, ma'am."

She slid inside and the car took off like a spooked horse. She rocked back against the upholstery, which pushed her bonnet down over her forehead. By the time she'd righted it, they were swimming through traffic at a rate that would make her sick if she thought about it.

So she didn't think about it. She prayed instead.

They surfaced in front of a glass building and the car rocked to a standstill. "Just in there, ma'am. Eighteenth floor. You can't miss it."

"*Denk*—I mean, thank you." She fumbled in her pocket. "How much was it?"

"Don't worry about that, ma'am. It's taken care of."

She'd barely got the door shut when the car whipped away from the curb and vanished into a stream of yellow cars and black ones just like it. Then she turned to face the building. A door. There. She could do this.

"Emma?"

She couldn't remember a time when the sound of her name had been so welcome. Turning, she saw a whip-thin young man who looked about as old as Alvin Esch coming toward her, hand outstretched.

"Emma Stolzfus, right? I was in the lobby making some calls while I waited for you, and saw you get out of the car."

She took his hand. Better ask this time, just to make sure. "Tyler West?" His handshake was firm, his hair curly and brown, and his green eyes full of merry intelligence. She would overlook the pink shirt and the cherry-and-gray striped tie. Perhaps he didn't have a wife to choose his clothes for him.

"That's me. You look just how I pictured you, only younger."

Younger? What had he been expecting—someone's mother? "We all look much the same."

He laughed as if she'd told the best joke all year. "I knew there was a reason I was looking forward to this. Come on up. Let me take your case." She surrendered it to him. "Do you want to talk a few minutes first? Our reservation's not until seven-thirty."

"Reservation?"

"Yes, for dinner." A glass wall whooshed open and he ushered her inside. The doors closed and her knees nearly buckled as the floor rose under her feet. "Oops, steady there."

"This is an elevator." Her ears popped and she swallowed.

"Sure is. Never been in one?"

"There are no buildings this tall in Lancaster County."

"Good point. We wouldn't survive without elevators around here. Eighteen flights of stairs four times a day? No thanks. Anyway, we're going to Eleven Park West. Ever heard of it?"

The door opened and he indicated she should get off. Her legs still felt a little wobbly, and she swallowed again. "I've heard of parks. Those we have."

Another laugh. "This is a restaurant. It's kinda different. I hope you like it. Anyway, here's where I earn my keep." He showed her into an office that, like his building, was all glass and metal. Outside the window, the world fell away into empty space, punctuated by buildings as tall as this one, some of glass, some of concrete, all rather forbidding and gray.

Emma's stomach still hadn't recovered from the elevator. The view out the window did not help. When he waved her into a chair, she didn't protest, and focused on the piles of paper standing in heaps all over the place and the colorful spines of other people's books on a big wood shelf.

Which was *gut*, because then she didn't have to meet his eyes as he took her in from top to bottom. With her, there was a lot to take in. Emma didn't think she could bear the part that inevitably happened next—the polite smile and the dropping of the gaze beneath the hat brim as a man turned away to go and find the girls who were prettier and livelier.

Tyler West noticed the direction of her gaze. "Those are the books of the people I represent," he said. "Someday maybe I'll see *Inherit the Earth* there."

At least he was still talking. Because this was a business meeting, and he was not a boy at a Sunday singing, looking for a girl to ride home with him. *Keep that idea in your head, Emma.*

"That isn't likely." Kind as he had been, sending a car for her and paying for the train ticket, she had to make him understand before he spent another dime. "It's not our way to publish books. Especially not a woman." Imagine if it were, though. Imagine people paying cash money to read her words. They would not turn away to find someone more interesting. They would listen to what she had to say—listen *voluntarily.*

Nei. That was the devil talking, doing his best to tempt her with the thing she wanted most.

"I've been doing a little research." He reached over and poked a big book on top of one of his stacks of paper. On the front of it was a woman from Ohio, from the look of her *Kapp*, walking down a road and holding the hands of her *Kinner.* "I understand about the *Ordnung* and about *Gelassenheit* and all that."

"Your pronunciation is very good." Surely he hadn't grown up plain. Not a man who wore a shirt like that.

"I took German in college. The thing is, I could make it part of any book deal that you wouldn't have to do promo. That you'd write the books and maybe have a Facebook page, but that's it. No book tours, no TV, no radio—though that might be tough to get past Marketing."

She stared at him, helplessly. "What is promo? And a book of faces? Are they anything like *die Bekanntmachung*? Or maybe *es Pickder*?"

He stared back. "It's—they're—"

Unbidden, she felt a smile coming. She tried to fight it, but the look on his face was so identical to the one she no doubt had on her own as they both tried to translate the other's language that she finally gave up and let it go.

At her hoot of laughter, he relaxed and stopped staring. His gaze lost the quality that made her think of people looking in shop windows, and became the kind that one person gives to another when they meet among friends. "I'm so sorry, Emma. You're absolutely right. You don't know about any of that stuff—and it's exactly why your work is so different and appealing."

He got up from behind his desk and came around to fold his long body into the other guest chair. "So now that we've got that cleared up, tell me about yourself. I want to know about the woman who wrote that book."

She'd wanted someone to listen, hadn't she? Well, here he was…and Emma couldn't think of a word to say. "It's—it's not seemly for me to talk about myself."

Tyler didn't miss a beat. "Tell me about your family. What does your house look like?"

That was easy enough. "I live in the *Daadi Haus* with Mamm—with my mother. It's on my sister Karen's—I mean, my brother-in-law John's farm on Edgeware Road."

He nodded. "I have to confess that I cyberstalked you. I checked out the address on Google Earth."

She shook her head at him. "You're doing it again. Speak English."

"How about I show you?" He pulled a thin computer off the desk like the librarians had in the Whinburg Public Library, and tapped a few keys. He spun it around so she could see the screen.

She blinked. "That's our barn."

"A bird's-eye view. So this little building here—" He made the world zip sideways. "—this is the grandfather house?"

Goodness. There was hers and Mamm's washing on the line, for the whole world to see.

Literally the whole world.

Blushing, she looked up. "How does it do this?"

"Satellites, up in the atmosphere, taking pictures."

"Hmph." She sat back, giving his computer a dirty look. "They shouldn't take pictures of us. We don't like it."

"It takes pictures of everyone. Any address you want, you can have a look."

"It isn't right."

"Maybe not, but it's there. I hope you don't mind I floated over your farm to see what kind of world you live in."

"The starlings do it and there's nothing I can do about them, either, except throw a rock."

He threw up his hands. "All right, I promise I won't do it again. So you started to say 'Karen's farm.' Who's Karen?"

She told him, and before she knew it, she was telling him about Mamm and Maryann looking after her and Pap's funeral and the quilting frolic she had missed. And he told her about his apartment in the Village, wherever that was. It must be a long way away, because there was nothing but city for miles, and finding a place with a bit of grass around it couldn't be easy. He had two sisters, both married, and his parents lived in Florida. And that took them into a discussion of whether it was better to swim in the ocean or in a river, and then he was looking at his watch and saying they'd be late for dinner if they didn't get moving.

At the restaurant, she realized it was possible to be surrounded by flowers and beauty and space, and still be so uncomfortable that she could hardly sit still. Did everyone she met have to call her *ma'am?* A man in a suit pulled out her chair and she stared at him, wondering why she could not sit there. Once Tyler resolved that, the menu was another puzzle. Tyler explained that she could choose one thing from each row on a card, and they would make a dish out of it. She finally told him to order two of everything, and eleven courses later, wondered how such tiny, pretty little bites could make a person feel so full.

"I'd love to take you to a show," Tyler said as they waited outside for a yellow taxi.

"A show? Do you mean a movie?"

"No, a Broadway show. A play, usually with music."

She shook her head. "I would not go in any case. Paying for food is one thing. We all have to eat. But paying for someone to entertain me is just frivolous."

He waved an arm and a cab swerved over to the curb. Emma wondered if she could make one do that.

Probably not.

He pointed out one thing after another—Times Square, lit up as bright as daylight, the crowds waiting in line outside theater after theater—as if he expected her to know landmarks from his roaring city. Maybe this Empire State Building was where he turned to go home, the way Moses Yoder's fence told the horses. Or that enormous television on the side of that hotel, as big as Amelia Beiler's new garden—maybe that one told him he was close to a friend's house.

"Is there nowhere green in this place?" she finally asked. "Nowhere quiet?"

For answer, he leaned over and spoke into the little window to the man driving. "Central Park."

And within minutes, there they were in the midst of trees and lawn and flowers—even a lake. With huge relief, she climbed out of the taxi and allowed Tyler to take her bag.

"We should have dropped this off at the hotel, but never mind," he said. "It doesn't weigh anything. Is it empty?"

"A change of clothes doesn't weigh much. It's not as if I was going to be gone for a month."

"My sisters would be amazed. They can't go away for a weekend without the van being stuffed to the gills."

"Do they have big families?"

"One has a baby. The other one doesn't plan on kids."

No children? On purpose? "I have a friend who would thank the good *Gott* on her knees if she could have a baby."

"Not my sister. She made good and sure her husband felt the same way before she married him. And, you know, whatever. It's a personal choice."

"We believe each child is a blessing from God."

"And what does Emma believe?"

Unaccountably, her throat closed up, and she paused to look across the lake at a little restaurant all strung with white lights. "It doesn't matter, does it? Without a husband, there's nothing to talk about."

"One of the girls in foreign rights adopted a baby girl from China. She's single."

Emma began to walk again. It was dark, but the paths were brightly lit and full of people. There must certainly be stars up above, but she couldn't see a single one. The lights of the city drowned even God's handiwork.

"It's possible in Whinburg, too, that a woman could adopt if there were children in need. A woman will raise the children if something happens to her sister. The family will step in and help, no matter what happens. I know a man whose wife left him, and his family is helping to raise his girls and the baby."

Tyler huffed a breath, almost as if he didn't believe her. "That's what I call a support network. The girl I was talking about has a nanny. She must be independently wealthy—she sure isn't dishing out a thousand a week on what the agency pays her."

"A thousand a week? To look after one baby?"

"Plus room and board."

"Goodness. I'm in the wrong business."

She'd surprised another laugh out of him. "Me, too. I guess that's the advantage of your big families, though. Lots of hands to help. So what's he like?"

They were passing under an arched bridge, so she couldn't see his face clearly. "Who?"

"This man you were talking about whose wife left. Is he a nice guy?"

"Why do you want to know?"

"Oh, I don't know. I guess it's a roundabout way of asking if there's anyone in your life. See, I get what you're doing. We've spent a whole evening together and you've told me everything there is to know about Whinburg and your family and the church, and nearly nothing about what I wanted to know, namely Emma Stolzfus."

"That's not true." But the simple fact was, she and her community and everyone in it were one and the same, or as good as. Talk about one and you talked about the rest.

"I make my living keeping my ear to the ground. I can tell what a person means by listening to what they don't say."

"You're a rosebush in a field of hay, then," she muttered. All she wanted was someone to hear her when she spoke. This man was listening even when she didn't. It was enough to make a woman want to hang around this awful place, just to lap up some more of it.

"So let me guess. He's a hardworking Amish man who wants to put a roof over his kids' heads, so he does, but meanwhile, the kids need a mom, right?"

"I think I pretty much told you that. And it's wrong to be thinking that way. Their mother may have left with that *Englisch* boy, but they are still married in the eyes of God."

"Oooh. I smell a scandal."

"Poor Grant. If not for the Yoders standing around him like a fortress, the gossip would have been even worse than it was." It felt so freeing talking about Grant like this. Chances were zero that it would ever get back to Whinburg from this source, even with the picture-taking satellites.

"Not a lot of wives leaving their husbands where you live?"

"No. We do not believe in divorce. It is still hard for me to believe she would do it. And with three little children, too."

"What *did* she do?"

"All I know is that she lives in Springfield, Missouri. And we heard recently that she is missing."

He pulled out the slender wafer of glass and metal that he called a phone, and tappity-tapped on its surface. "What was her name?" When she told him, he tapped some more. "Hm.

Even Google can't find anything. That doesn't happen much anymore, with everyone putting their lives up for daily consumption."

"It doesn't matter whether she is on your phone or not. She'd have done better to appreciate the gifts she had and not run after those she didn't."

"Emma Stolzfus, I think you're jealous."

In a sudden spurt of temper, Emma snatched her case out of his hand and marched away down the path. She was as tall as he, and her legs were toned from years of walking country roads. It wasn't long before she'd left him in the dust, calling pathetically after her in the dark.

Presumptuous, arrogant man, calling her names! She'd just show him!

In the end, though, when her little tantrum had burned itself to cold ash, the joke was on her. She stood in the middle of acres of dark, with frightening shapes of people brushing past and not a familiar landmark or face to be seen. She would be robbed. Someone would hit her on the head and the police would find her in the morning, and people with their little phones could read all about her. None of them would know the truth of why she'd been in New York.

"Emma!" She turned as Tyler West loped up behind her. "Look, I'm sorry I offended you. I didn't mean it. Please don't do that again—this place can be a little dicey after dark if you're a woman alone."

Talk about pathetic. She was so glad to see him she would hug him if she knew how. "I'm sorry, too. My pride got pricked and if I had been knocked over the head by a thief, it would have been my own fault. How did you find me?" It was a miracle he had.

He nodded toward her hair. "The bonnet. Even in the dark, it's hard to miss."

She swallowed the lump of gratitude in her throat. "It's called a *Kapp*. I'm glad I put my away bonnet in my case, then."

"Come on, let's get you to the hotel. You must be tired."

She should have been. But she wasn't. "You were right, Tyler West." She picked up her steps to match his as they headed toward a glow of light.

"That's unusual. About what?"

"I am jealous. Lavina Weaver has nothing, not her family or her husband or even the truth. And yet I'm jealous of her."

"Because...?"

"Because she had Grant Weaver for twelve whole years. And I would give twelve years off my life if I could have him even for one."

CHAPTER 8

Don't look out the window.

Emma brushed her teeth and braided her hair, keeping her back to the two layers of drapes that hid the brightly lit skyscrapers sprouting up out of the dark. One look had been enough—she'd stay on the far side of the room, thank you very much, just in case the building decided to shrug and flip her out into twenty stories of cold space.

She chose the bed closest to the sparkling modern bathroom, warm and toasty from the luxury of a shower that had lasted at least thirty minutes. She'd never taken one that long in her life, mostly because the hot water tank in the *Daadi Haus* wasn't big enough for two people taking ten-minute showers consecutively, never mind thirty minutes.

So there was one good thing about New York. The shower in the hotel room.

When she woke at six the next morning, she'd discovered a second good thing. The mattress. It was like waking up in a cloud, rested and happy.

You got a new couch. How difficult would it be to get a mattress like this?

Maybe not so difficult in a practical sense, but very difficult in every other way. A person was meant to mortify the flesh, not loll in fluffy, luxurious mattresses pampering herself just because she could.

She was to meet Tyler West in the lobby at eight, and he had promised to take her to breakfast. So, on the dot of eight, she stepped out of the elevator with her case in hand, her away bonnet inside it so he could find her by her *Kapp*.

Maybe he would have forgotten the words she'd blurted at him in the dark—words she would give nearly anything to take back.

She tried not to notice people staring at her, keeping her gaze instead on the elevators going up and down the enormous central column of the hotel like so many hummingbirds. No wonder her stomach felt queasy.

"Emma." She turned to see Tyler coming toward her, his hand held out.

She shook it. "*Guder Mariye.*"

"*Guten Morgen,*" he replied in *hoch Deutsch.*

"Try it my way."

But his tongue stumbled on the simple syllables, which only made him laugh. "Come on, I'm starving." He guided her into the revolving door and out the other side. They turned away from Times Square, moving west. "I tried to clear my calendar for this morning, but no luck. I have to be in the office for a meeting at ten, but I'll put you in a cab to Penn Station before I go."

"You don't have to do that. I can walk." The fewer trips in those crazy yellow cabs, the better. "Just point me in the right direction."

He still wasn't convinced by the time he'd located the restaurant and the waitress had shown them to a table. "I don't want you getting lost, Emma. I still have hopes that you'll let me rep your book. For all I know, you might wind up on the front steps of some other agent's office, be taken in, and I'd never see you again."

"You'd get along with my friend Carrie," she told him, sipping coffee that tasted better than anything except the little bites at Eleven Park West. "She's always saying whimsical things."

He ordered pancakes. She wasn't about to have anything she could make at home, so she picked the most foreign thing on the menu. The problem was, she had no idea what it was, never mind how to say it.

"*Huevos rancheros,*" Tyler told the waitress, following Emma's pointing finger. "Good choice. They make their own salsa here. I meant it, Emma. I still hope you'll give in about the book."

"You're more persistent than my nephew Nathaniel. And I'll tell you the same thing I tell him. *Nei.* It can't be done."

"So why did you enter it in that contest?" He buttered a tiny muffin the size of his thumb with short, precise strokes. Imagine feeding her painting crew with such muffins. They would climb back in their buggies and leave for greener pastures. "It said right in the rules that the winner would be offered a book deal. If you didn't plan to take the deal, why waste your time?"

Why waste the judges' time? she heard. "It was a contest. I wanted to see how it would do. I never expected to win, and I didn't."

"You should have. But there are other ways to win. The advance the contest winner got was only five grand. We could do better."

"It doesn't matter. Why won't you understand that what I have is enough? People read it and thought well of it and it went to the final round. I don't need any more than that."

"Maybe I do," he mumbled around the muffin, and did not meet her eyes.

Oho. He wasn't the only one who could ask painfully personal questions. "What do you mean? Do you think it will make money for you?" He'd told her that he would get 15 percent of whatever money came to her. As far as she was concerned, 15 percent of five thousand dollars was nothing to sneeze at.

"I know it would. This kind of book—heartwarming but bone-scraping honest about people—would fly off the shelves. But that's not what I meant." He took a sip of his coffee. "You don't have a way to make a living, do you?"

The waitress brought two piping hot plates of food, and Emma waited until she'd filled their mugs and gone. Then she tasted her eggs, lying on top of squished-up beans in a blanket of melted cheese, with—what had he called it?—*salsa* running down the sides.

"Oh, my." Hot chile exploded in her mouth, the flavors of fresh tomato and cilantro twisting with the beans and melted cheese.

"Chiles too hot for you?"

She shook her head. "*Ischt gut. Aich gut.*" Her eyes were like to roll back in her head in sheer ecstasy. They sure knew how to cook here in New York. That made four good things.

"I'm glad you like it. But you didn't give me an answer about making your living."

"Has anyone ever told you you're nosy?"

"They don't have to. I already know." She expected him to lift his gaze and twinkle at her, but his eyes were somber.

It never occurred to her to give him anything but the

truth. "No, of course not. I keep house for Mamm. I've already said so."

"And what happens when Mamm shuffles off this mortal coil?"

"If you mean what happens when she dies, I imagine I'll move back into the big house and help Karen with the children." She ate the egg and half the beans, but they no longer had the intense flavor they had in the beginning. Or maybe more than just food was losing its flavor.

"Is that all you want?"

"It is not. But it's what I'll get, if God wills it."

"Emma, if you sell that book, you'll have an independent income. It may not be much at first, but since you're not likely to blow it on liquor and gambling and cruises around the world, it would probably keep you until you write another. And you wouldn't have to depend on a room in Karen's house. What if Karen decides she needs that square footage for something else?"

"She'd sooner double up the *Kinner* in their rooms. She won't turn me out, if that's what you're worried about. She's my sister. We both grew up in that house."

Instead of nodding and finishing off his pancakes, he took another sip of coffee, as if the caffeine were fortifying him somehow. "So. You're just going to move into the family home, then, and let Grant marry someone else?"

The shock of hearing her worst nightmare spoken into the world took her breath away. "He will never do that. I told you, he's married already. So I ask you to forget I ever said anything about him."

"It's forgotten. As soon as you tell me."

It took a whole egg and the rest of the salsa to regain her balance. "It's foolish and wicked even to think of it. I had my chance over a decade ago when we had a buggy ride together, and he chose someone else. I don't need the humiliation—I'm capable of that on my own."

"I thought the Amish valued being humble."

"There's a big difference between being humble and being humiliated." Even though there were some who might not make that distinction.

"I don't see why the poor guy has to be alone for the rest of his life if his wife left him. It's not his fault."

"The Bible says, what God has joined together let no man put asunder. Period. Until death do you part."

"Well, say death did part them. Then what? Would he give you a do-over on that buggy ride?"

Goosebumps broke out on her arms, and she rubbed her sleeves briskly. "Don't say that. Besides, he wouldn't."

"He'd be crazy, then. Heck, if you didn't have to catch that train, I'd take you over to the park again and give you a buggy ride myself."

She'd seen the fancy carriages with their tired horses. "I wouldn't go. I couldn't resist telling those drivers how to care for their animals."

"You know what I mean." She eyed him. "Any man would be proud to have you in his buggy, Emma."

Hot color flooded her cheeks, and she couldn't blame it on the chiles in the sauce. "Even if he was single, it wouldn't matter. He still loves Lavina. He's been corresponding with her ever since she left, probably begging her to come back. And now he's trying to find her and get her to come home."

"You're doing it again. Deflecting. We were talking about you, not him. I have sisters, you know. I know how it's done."

"Then stop being so personal, Tyler West. You mustn't say such things to me."

"It's only the truth. You're an attractive woman with a good mind. If the men in your town don't see that, too bad for them."

If he didn't stop, her face would spontaneously combust. She had never been called attractive in her life. She was tall, plain, big-boned Emma who did what had to be done without complaint. Who never set a foot outside the *Ordnung*, never did the unexpected.

Except for those letters painted on the side of the house.

Ja. Except for those. And her book. That was definitely stepping outside the *Ordnung*. And look what it got her. A holiday in someone else's world and the companionship of an *Englisch* man whose merry eyes saw far too much.

"I'm sorry, Emma. I didn't mean to embarrass you. Do you know how many years it's been since I saw a woman blush?"

"It can't be that many. You have to be five or six years younger than me."

"I'm thirty-six."

Goodness. "Are you married?"

"Not I. Haven't found anyone who would settle for me."

Thirty-six and not married. "And here I thought I had problems."

"Mostly because I haven't got time to date. I work long hours, and on the weekends I read people's manuscripts. It's all I can do to get to the gym three times a week."

"You need to come to Whinburg. John would have you out in the fields tilling the corn. You wouldn't need to find time to work out then."

He grinned at her, making him look even younger. "Maybe I will. Maybe I'll do more than stalk you on Google Earth."

"You'd better not. Bad enough I'm going to have to explain my trip to the city. I couldn't explain you at all."

"Maybe I'll give the guys out there some competition. That should open their eyes."

He expected her to laugh, but unaccountably, her own eyes filled with tears. She tried to hide behind her coffee cup, blinking furiously, but it did no good. *Ach*, this was why a woman should wear her away bonnet out in public—so she could use modesty to keep the whole world from intruding on her emotion.

"Emma, I'm sorry." Tyler moved to the chair next to her and pulled her napkin off her lap. He handed it to her. "I feel like I'm spending all our time together apologizing. I didn't mean to make you cry. It was thoughtless. Forgive me."

"You're f-forgiven."

But it was not his words that had touched her on the raw. It was the certainty that even if someone did give the men of Whinburg a little competition, it would do no good at all.

To Emma's enormous relief, Carrie waited on the other side of the barrier at the Lancaster station. She had been shaken so far out of her normal self that she hugged her hard, surprising both of them.

"Emma? Are you all right?"

She swallowed the lump in her throat before it got big enough to push out tears. "I'm fine. I'm just glad to see you and not—" She stopped.

"Not Joshua Steiner?"

Emma sucked in a long breath and gripped the handle of her traveling case as though it were a life raft and she a swimmer trying to climb out of the water. "How did you know?" Carrie's cheeks had turned pink—the very shade of Emma's.

"Look at us. Please don't tell me the whole *Gmee* knows he rode up here with me yesterday."

"The whole *Gmee*, plus every relative outside it who might have gotten a letter from someone today." Emma closed her eyes and resisted the urge to scream while Carrie went on, "Honestly, I offered to come with you. You should have let me." Carrie waved at one of the cars in the parking lot, and the driver started the engine. "We'll talk more later."

So Emma had time to cool off during the drive down to Whinburg. Carrie chatted about inconsequential things, like what progress she and Amelia had made on the quilt yesterday, and the vegetables the two of them had planted now that the weather had finally committed itself to spring.

When they reached Whinburg, Emma leaned forward. "We'll drop my friend off first, please. I'll walk from there."

Carrie gazed at her in surprise. "Are you sure? It's three miles. And you have to cross the county highway."

"After Times Square, the highway is not a problem. The walk will be good, and I need the time." Time to come back to her real life. Time to appreciate the silence. Time to slow down. With all this whizzing from city to train to car, she'd hardly had a moment to catch her breath and thank the good *Gott* for bringing her back in one whole piece.

Mostly whole, anyway.

They crunched down the Miller lane, the driver going at a crawl. "I'm afraid I'm going to hit one of these chickens."

"Don't worry," Carrie reassured her. "They know what cars and buggies are. They'll move."

They got out, and Emma paid him while the chickens crowded around Carrie as if she were the one who had left them for the big city. "Can you come in for some coffee and cake?"

"Think I can do that, walk three miles, and get home in time for supper?"

"Only if you don't have to make it."

Emma followed Carrie inside, and closed the door on the disappointed hens. Silly things. Did they think she was going to let them in the house?

"We're going over to Karen's, where no doubt she'll spend the entire evening grilling me like a pork chop."

Carrie spooned coffee into the pot and set water on the stove to heat. "If you wouldn't go gadding about the countryside with a man, she wouldn't have to."

"He wasn't the only one."

It was a second before Carrie could speak. "What do you mean? Did you meet a man on this trip?"

"Sure. The man who wrote those letters. Tyler West. The man who sent the train ticket so I could go and see him."

"What was he like?" Carrie asked cautiously, as if Emma would spring another man out of her pocket at any moment.

"He's thirty-six and unmarried. He's a literary agent and he spared no expense to convince me to let him have my book to sell."

"And did you?"

"Of course not. Bishop Daniel would never allow it."

"The way everyone is talking, you could say you flew to the moon whether he allowed it or not, and people would believe it."

"You'd better tell me, Carrie. I don't want to be ambushed by Karen when I walk into the kitchen."

"Maybe you should tell me what Joshua Steiner was doing taking you to the train station in the first place," Carrie said. "How did all that come about?"

"Karen arranged the whole thing behind my back. I came

out of the house and there he was in the car. He said he had business in Lancaster, and it was not my place to tell him he could not come." She took a deep breath and committed herself to the plunge. "And then he asked me to go with him to Lehmans' for Eli Fischer's birthday supper on Friday."

Carrie dropped the spoon, and the sugar she'd meant for the coffee went all over the counter. "He asked you for a *date?*"

"Don't sound so surprised. Not after all that talk about Aaron King this winter."

"Yes, but I knew that wasn't true. This is different." Carrie scrubbed at her spotless counter with the dishcloth.

She couldn't leave her best friend with such a look on her face. If she'd said she'd gone to a Broadway show with an *Englisch* man, Carrie couldn't have been more shocked. So she told her what had happened on the train platform in Lancaster, and when she was done, felt drained. Even the journey itself had not taken this much out of her.

"Do you care about Joshua?" Carrie finally asked, as carefully as if each word were a bird's egg, liable to break at a breath. "Is that what's behind this?"

It was on the tip of Emma's tongue to say, *No, but if he cares about me, I'd be tempted to settle.* But deep down, it would be a lie. She could not settle. If she couldn't have the man who held her heart in his hand, she'd learn to accept being single. There were worse things.

So instead, she said, "Is that so bad?"

Carrie brought two mugs of coffee and slid into her chair. "No, not if you—I mean, if he's—" Why was she blushing? "He—he doesn't have the best reputation, that's all. And you...well, you're not very experienced with men and I'd hate for you to..."

Ah. No wonder Carrie's fair skin was the color of a beet-root. It wasn't easy to say words like that, even to your best friend. "You're sweet to be concerned. I mean that, *Liewi*." She laid a hand on Carrie's work-worn one and squeezed. "But I've known Joshua all my life. I know what he used to be, and I know what he is now. If he wants to amuse himself by walking me to Lehmans' and starting up more gossip than any man needs, then that's fine with me. But my eyes are open."

Carrie's shoulders relaxed, and she turned her hand over and squeezed back. "I should have known better than to believe you would be carried away by a handsome face and a pair of eyes that don't belong on a good Amish man."

"You think he's handsome?"

Carrie blushed again, just when she'd managed to get her color back to normal. "I may be married, but I have eyes."

"And hopefully, so do the other girls. Though if he decides on someone, I may have to have a little talk with her before she gets in deeper than she should."

"He could have changed, Emma."

She nodded, and sipped her *Kaffi*. "He could. With God, all things are possible. Even the reformation of Joshua Steiner."

Carrie put her mug down with a clack. "Do you think he could be—no. Of course not. That would be terrible unfair to you."

"Could be what? Come on, you can't start a sentence like that and not finish it."

"Do you think he could be...using you to put a shine on his reputation? Because yours is so good, I mean. There isn't a person in the settlement who doesn't think well of you, and how good you've been to Lena."

"Mamm deserves nothing less than my best, after spending her life giving her best for us *Kinner*." Emma's voice felt a little scratchy in her own throat at the thought of Mamm darning endless piles of socks for the boys and sewing dresses for her and Karen when Pap was getting the farm going and money had been tight, and meanwhile her own dresses faded in the sun and she patched and mended seams, all hidden under cape and apron.

"Of course that's true, but that's not what I meant."

"I know what you meant." But Emma didn't think so. The man whose eyes had lit up when she'd agreed to go with him had been sincere. He had been her friend again, not some schemer who would use a woman to give a fresh coat of paint to a badly built barn.

She was sure of it.

CHAPTER 9

At the age of six, Emma had been chosen to play one of the sheep at the school Christmas pageant. She and her two companions were to wear woolly ears and sing to the Christ Child (played by William Esch, Alvin's oldest brother, who had been not quite two) in his straw-filled manger. They had rehearsed and rehearsed until they had their song pitch perfect...and then when they'd finally mounted the steps to the manger, Emma had looked out at the sea of people filling the schoolroom and had her first attack of stage fright. Pap had had to take her outside to the porch, bawling at the top of her lungs, and Christina Yoder and Esther Grohl had sung their song without her.

If dinner at Karen's had been the rehearsal, then surely this was the command performance. All that remained was the attack of stage fright, and Emma could feel it building in her stomach with every step she took.

"Why so quiet?" The sun had just set, but the twilight had enough light in it yet to let Joshua Steiner see her face as they crossed the field. "Nervous?"

"Of course not. Amelia and I have been best friends since third grade, and her parents have welcomed me so often that their house is practically my second home."

"I didn't mean about them or the get-together. I meant about *uns*. About being seen together."

"Joshua, there isn't any *uns*, and don't you go around saying there is."

"Because if I say it, that will make it true?"

"In the ears of our friends, it will." And there was no truth harder to break than one that had its roots in the grapevine.

"I'm more concerned about *your* ears."

What was he getting at? "My ears are just fine the way they are, *denkes*." She nudged him out of the way of an enormous cow pie. Moses Yoder had clearly been pasturing his herd in this field instead of the one that lay between the Stolzfus place and Amelia's little white house.

Had Eli had supper with Amelia and the boys before coming over to Isaac and Ruth's? No, probably not. If he were staying at the Martin Kings' place, she and Matthew and Elam would either go there or wait until they saw him at Lehmans'. There would not be any talk about Amelia Beiler. She wouldn't allow it, as concerned about the appearance of evil as she was.

Emma just didn't seem to have the knack.

Joshua stepped over the cow pie and held two strands of barbed-wire fencing apart wide enough for her to slip through, since her hands were full. Down at the bottom of the southeast-facing slope, nestled in trees that had leafed out at top speed in the warmer weather, they could see the lights of the Lehman place. The yard was packed with buggies, and the boys had already started parking them at the bottom of this field, on the level part before it dropped off into the creek bottom.

Joshua touched her arm. "Wait a moment, Emma."

She moved her elbow away just enough to break the contact. "I don't want to be late. This layer salad won't improve for waiting, either."

"I won't keep it long." He made her look at him. "If there was an *uns*, would that be so bad?"

Impossible as it is, I don't want that word to ever mean anything but Emma and Grant. Together. One word, one couple, one home.

How could so much be packed into three little letters?

But he was waiting for her answer. If only she could figure out what he wanted it to be. "Joshua, we're good friends. I'm happy that you're home, and happy to be your friend. But I don't know what you want from me with all this talk of *uns*."

"Isn't that pretty obvious? I didn't walk you over here to help you through fences, or to make the old ladies gossip. I asked you to come with me so that we could spend the evening together and get to know each other…as we are now. Not as we used to be."

We. There you go again. Joshua was awfully fond of plural pronouns. "Which will make the old ladies gossip. And everyone else."

"Let them."

And Grant would hear, and then what would he think of her?

Oh, who was she fooling? The man had liked her cooking, and had given her permission to paint graffiti on her own house. He was Lavina's faithful husband, and when he saw her, he probably just thought, *Oh, that poor old maid. What a life she must have.*

Well, she had a life, one for which she thanked the *gut Gott* daily. But maybe God wanted more than that from her. Maybe He had sent Joshua—soiled, tattered, and chastened as he was—to do more than see her off in train stations. Maybe she was the blind one.

God had not seen fit to open any other man's eyes to her. But maybe He was doing His level best to open her eyes to Joshua. Maybe she should pay some attention to the bird she had in her hand, and stop pining for the one so busy looking after its nest in the bush.

"Is that what you want, truly, Joshua Steiner?" This time, he didn't have to peer into her face. She gazed at him squarely in the fading light, while the sounds of a houseful of people drifted up the slope, ready to welcome them. "You want me to be a part of your *uns*?"

"I do," he said without hesitation. "I like you, and you always liked me, even when it wasn't the prudent thing to do."

"But we're not children anymore."

"I know it. What I don't know is whether I'm husband material…or even courtship material. But I figure, if I were to give this a try, I'd want it to be with you. My steady, sensible Emma. You'll keep me on the straight and narrow, won't you?"

She didn't much like the sound of that. "A man needs to keep himself on the straight and narrow, or he's not a man." She narrowed her eyes, wishing she'd brought her glasses if she was going to be looking into men's faces in the near dark. "I'm not going to be your conscience in a *Kapp*."

"And I wouldn't want you to be. Already you're setting me on the right road." With a chuckle, he reached out and took the salad in its big, cumbersome bowl from her. "Let me take this the rest of the way for you."

She was only too happy to let him. Because it was everything she could do to wrap her mind around the fact that here, at last, was someone who wanted to be with her—for herself.

* * *

Emma had never been as sensitive to people's emotions and feelings as Carrie, but even she felt the wave of astonishment and speculation that washed up against the door as she stepped into the Lehmans' front room with Joshua beside her. And when she turned to take the salad bowl from him and he pretended to hang on to it to keep the whole thing for himself... well, they might as well have sold tickets and called it a show.

How could she have let him carry the bowl? Arriving with a man could be written off as coincidence—a chance meeting on the porch—but arriving with a man who was carrying your contribution to the supper was a *statement*. How could she have been so stupid?

She practically fled into the kitchen, holding the salad in front of her, leaving Joshua to shake hands and brave the surge of visiting couples and families. Amelia stopped her mad rush by the propane refrigerator, otherwise she might have flown straight through Ruth's compounding room and out the back door, salad and all.

"Emma! Where are you going in such a hurry?"

"Anywhere but in there," she blurted. Thank goodness for Amelia. "He must be crazy to make such a display."

"He who? What display?"

"Oh..." Emma struggled for words and finally gave up. "You'll hear, probably sooner rather than later."

"I'd rather hear now, from my friend who is so *verhuddelt* she hasn't even taken off her gums."

Oh. There they were on her feet, probably bringing some of Moses Yoder's cow pies into Ruth's spotless kitchen.

"Is that your layer salad? Give it to me and slip those off in Mamm's compounding room. She won't mind. With all the strange things that get dripped and spilled in there, no one will know the difference."

Emma had no sooner done so, and handed her shawl to Amelia to put on the downstairs bed with the others, when Ruth bustled back in. "Well, Emma Stolzfus, if you don't take the prize. Joshua Steiner, of all people. When did that happen?"

About ten minutes ago. "It—I—"

When Amelia came back, it was obvious from her face that someone had stopped her to tell her the news. Her eyes were huge. "I thought…didn't you tell us…does Carrie know?" Emma nodded. "But when…?"

"That's what I just asked," Ruth said, while the two older ladies and half a dozen matrons helping uncover dishes watched, smiling in anticipation at details of the happy news. "Is that why he went all the way to Lancaster with you?"

"He had some business," Emma managed weakly. How could he have put her in this position? Why hadn't he talked it over with her yesterday, or the day before? Couples weren't supposed to make a big splash like this. They were discreet. Modest. Kept themselves to themselves until—well, usually until the announcement was made in church and they were published.

But she and Joshua weren't getting married.

"So when is the big day?" Erica Steiner, who hadn't been married much more than a year herself, adjusted her sleeping baby on her shoulder and smiled at Emma. "Are you going to wait until fall?"

"We—"

"The nice thing about the two of you being more...mature," Ruth put in, "is that you don't need to wait until fall if you don't want to. You'd want to keep it small and modest."

"We're not—"

Amelia stepped bravely into the breach. "Listen to yourselves. You'll have Emma and Joshua married off before they've even had their supper. I think it's a little too soon to be asking all these questions. Joshua has barely been in town a month."

Denki, *my dear friend*. Emma found her voice. "More like two, but you're right. He only walked me over here. That's all."

"It's a start," Ruth said.

"And I'm happy for you." Erica's voice was soft. "He seems like a good man."

"He does now." Kathryn Esch had a warm heart, but a voice like a rusty gate. "There was a time when no father would let him anywhere near his girls. Remember when he and that gang of his hoisted Boyd's new washer up on top of the barn the morning of his wedding?"

No one was ever going to forget that.

"I heard," Erica said with a laugh. "And all the wedding linens to wash the next day."

"That wasn't the worst of it." Did Kathryn realize Emma was still in the room? If they'd just been published, would she be raking up all Joshua's dirty laundry? "You'd best be careful, Emma." That answered that question. "I'd have a stern talk with Joshua and ask him what really happened with that *Englisch* girl."

"I'm sure it was only gossip," Emma said, hoping she'd get the hint. What was Kathryn up to? She was usually much kinder than this. Had she found out about her son Alvin's correspondence packets coming to the *Daadi Haus*, and this was her way of punishing Emma for it?

No, it couldn't be. That wasn't the Amish way. You could be brought into line by hints and the older ladies' critical gazes if your hems were too short or you wore your *Kapp* too far back on your hair so it left your ears uncovered, but for something as serious as those packets, she would have found Will and Kathryn on her doorstep to correct her in person and in private.

"I'm sure Joshua has been honest in all his dealings since he came back," Amelia said. "Just as Emma has been honest with him."

"Let her speak for herself, Amelia Beiler."

Emma could take any number of busybodies' noses in her business, but she would not tolerate that tone of voice being used on her best friend. "I don't choose to speak of Joshua Steiner anymore," she said firmly. "This is Eli's birthday party, and it's him and Amelia we should be thinking of." The gentle stress she'd put on *thinking of* had turned Erica's cheeks a faint shade of pink, but Kathryn was made of sterner stuff.

"I don't mean to speak ill of anyone you've chosen, Emma. I just hope that your man is as honest and decent as you are."

"And I hope that since Bishop Daniel has welcomed him into the *Gmee*, the past will be put where it belongs. If God has forgiven him, then it would be presumptuous for us to bring these things up again. Don't you agree?"

Kathryn could do nothing but nod, and Emma turned to Amelia. "I have a question for your Eli. Is he in the house, or did he go out to the barn with the men?"

"He's probably out in the barn. I'll go with you."

They hurried down the back steps without their shawls, but Emma wouldn't have gone back into that kitchen even if there had been a foot of snow on the ground.

"What's got into Kathryn, I wonder?" Amelia asked. "Did she find out about your little evening classes?"

"I wondered that myself. You've never said anything, have you?"

"Of course not. That's a confession for you to make, not me. Maybe one of her sisters was one of Joshua's conquests, and she wants to warn you away from him."

"I don't think so. Joshua didn't go for the girls from the plainer families. He had a taste for the fancy back then."

"Things have changed." They'd almost reached the barn. "What was it that you wanted to ask Eli?"

Emma grinned. "If he truly loves my friend."

"Emma Stolzfus! You did not."

"I just needed to get out of that kitchen."

"Well, now that we're here, you'd better come and say happy birthday."

Amelia leaned through the opening in the barn doors and called Eli's name, which resulted in a babble of good-natured ribbing about who should come when who called. When he stepped outside, he was grinning, and took Amelia's hand in his with such a look of love in his eyes that Emma's throat closed up.

This was what her heart yearned for. Not the kind regard of friendship that Joshua offered, tinged with need and the faintest hint of desperation around the edges. But this...this all-encompassing love, the kind that surely Christ must have when he looked upon His Church and saw them all waiting for His return.

Are you going to settle? Can you? Is it better to wait for what may never come than to live with what has already arrived?

Her brave determination of half an hour ago, that had carried her through the front door and the resulting sensation, now seemed less about God's will for her and more about her own foolishness. Why would God send second best for her partner?

Ach, Emma. Aren't you just as proud as can be to label a good, God-fearing man such a thing?

As Emma smiled and wished Eli happy birthday, then asked him some nonsense question about the shed he planned to build, she wondered in despair if the whole subject of waiting for God to reveal His choice of mate was supposed to be this difficult. How did girls like Mandy Lapp and Lavina Weaver make up their minds when they were so young—just teenagers yet. They met a boy, they decided to marry, and they were published, just like that. Did they simply not think? Or was Emma thinking far too much, and letting her human reasoning elbow out God's choice?

Thinking about it all was exhausting.

Amelia squeezed Eli's hand and shooed him back into the barn, where apparently he was talking over a business plan for his mechanical conversions with Moses and Bishop Daniel and a bunch of the younger men.

"Ready to brave the kitchen again?" Amelia bumped her shoulder with her own.

"*Ja.* And I plan to find the biggest, fattest piece of pie in the whole house and eat it all by myself."

One thing about getting together with her friends and neighbors...there would be no shortage of comfort food.

When nine o'clock came, Emma whispered to Amelia that

she needed to get back to Mamm, collected her clean salad bowl, and tried to slip out quietly. But Joshua materialized out of nowhere and stuck himself to her side, so that they left as a couple. At least they'd walked over, so there would be no jokes about taking deserted side roads and stopping the buggy in someone's field to canoodle.

Emma welcomed the dark, cow pies and all. After the cheerful teasing and gradually increasing volume of conversation as people got to eating and visiting, the silence of the fields and the nighttime scent of green things springing from the earth were a relief to her soul.

"Did you have a good time?" Joshua asked at last, when she'd made it clear by her silence that she wasn't going to be talking anytime soon.

"*Ja*. But it would have been better if we'd come separately."

"If we're going to be seeing each other, why shouldn't we come together?"

"Because we're not engaged. We're not even courting. After tonight, seeing what a fuss people made, I think we should be more discreet if we're going to see each other as friends."

"Too late now." He sounded far too cheerful. "There was such a crowd I never got the chance to really talk with you. Maybe it's a good thing we're walking."

Kathryn Esch's warning rang in Emma's memory. "I have something I'd like to ask you."

"Anything. Ask away."

There was no way to make this sound good, so Emma plunged in before she lost her courage. "Is it true that you got an *Englisch* girl in...in the family way?"

The outline of his hat turned in her direction, but on such a moonless night she couldn't see his face. "Is that what they're saying? No wonder some of the matrons are giving me the cold shoulder."

"Well, is it?"

He was silent a moment. "It pains me that you even need to ask such a question."

"It pains me to ask it. But I would still like to know the truth."

"The truth. Well, here it is. *Ja*, I was seeing an *Englisch* girl up there in Shipshey. I was seeing lots of girls, and come to find out she was seeing more guys than me. But I was not..." He paused. "It feels strange to talk of such things with a single woman."

"I asked."

"*Ja*, you did. Here is the truth, then. I'm not—not inexperienced when it comes to women. That girl did get pregnant. But not by me. When she had her baby, he had skin the color of Mamm's good cocoa, and she subsequently married the father. I sent a nice pair of glass salt and pepper shakers as a wedding gift."

Emma did not want to know what "not inexperienced" meant. But she got the drift. When Joshua came to his marriage bed, he would not be as shy and ignorant as—as his future wife, whoever she might be.

Her mind shuddered away from that faceless woman before her features became recognizable.

"Here we are at the fence," she said instead.

"Let me." He held the strands of barbed wire again, and slipped through after her. "I'm sure you have more questions."

She almost wished she hadn't. "What do you plan to live on here in Whinburg? Melvin Miller's fields aren't in such good shape, and harvest is a long way off."

"I have a little in the bank, and I'm in my old room at Mamm and Daed's. They don't charge me rent, but I contribute what I can to the grocery bill. I have to say, though, that bringing Melvin's fields back to health might take more than one summer."

"He's no farmer, it's true. Going in with the Steiner boys on Amelia's pallet shop has to be better for him."

"They were talking out in Isaac's barn about him becoming a kind of traveling salesman. Some of the men laughed at the idea—how far can you travel in a buggy, anyway? All the folks within a day's ride already know about the pallet shop. But it might have merit."

"Amelia says he's always talking to people, and has even brought in some business that way. But I hope he doesn't go through with it. Carrie has been alone enough since they got married, with him off trying to find work."

"Carrie. She's the blond one? The one who's so slender she could turn sideways and not cast a shadow?"

"That's the one. But she has a spirit as big as Moses Yoder's barn."

They walked into the yard and Emma ran a practiced eye over the house. All the windows were dark, except for a single lamp burning in the kitchen. Mamm would have gone to bed an hour ago and left the lamp for her.

"*Gut Nacht,*" she said, turning to face the shadow that was Joshua. "*Denki* for walking over with me."

"What, no more questions?" The laughter was back in his voice.

"I think those two were enough, don't you?"

"My character and my prospects. I suppose those are the most important."

He stood there, as if he were waiting for something. Good heavens. Did he expect her to kiss him good night? As if she'd been goosed by an impertinent dog, Emma scooted up the front steps of the *Daadi Haus*. "I need to check on Mamm. See you next Sunday, Joshua."

"If not sooner."

When he turned to go, she closed the door behind her and sagged against it in relief. Without a doubt, this had been the longest evening of her life.

CHAPTER 10

"You just need a few more evenings like that to get comfortable being with a man," Carrie said from behind her sewing machine on Tuesday afternoon. "It takes a little while, but before you know it, you'll be *wanting* him to kiss you."

"It will take more than a little while." Emma's shears sang against the green fabric as she cut the last panel of their quilt top. After Carrie sewed it on, the piecing would be finished and they could begin quilting. Already the big roll of batting sat on the metal shelf in Amelia's washroom, and they'd pieced a nice big star shape out of scraps for a backing that would show their quilt patterns nicely.

"Why do you say that?" Amelia wanted to know. "If you don't want to kiss the man, maybe you shouldn't be courting."

"That's the trouble." A final snip, and the big panel fell to the table, arrow-straight. "What if I want to kiss a man who wouldn't dream of kissing me, and don't want to kiss the one who does?"

Carrie's foot stopped its motion on the treadle. "Emma Stolzfus. Did something happen between you and that *Englisch* man in New York?"

They had no inkling about who her heart had really chosen, because she had not done much more than hint about it. But

Amelia and Carrie wouldn't judge her for giving away her heart to someone who didn't want it. They would give her sympathy and kindness, not ridicule. What was she afraid of?

She could make a choice, here and now. She could let them think that the man who haunted her was Tyler West without saying much at all. Or she could be honest and tell them the truth.

These are your friends—closer even than sisters. You know the secrets of their hearts. It isn't fair for you to keep yours back.

As she took a breath, the decision wasn't so hard to make, after all. "It's not Tyler West. It's Grant Weaver."

Silence fell in Carrie's sunny front room as both she and Amelia spooled back over the past few weeks. Emma could see understanding dawn at about the same rate as the blush rose in her face.

"You really meant it," Carrie said at last. "You really care. Oh, Emma."

In those two words, Emma heard pity and understanding. "I know it's foolish and wicked. I know he's married. I know it's a sin. And I still can't help it." Now that her secret was out, the words fell out of her mouth as though she'd pulled a stopper from a drain. "He worked around our place for those weeks, eating in my kitchen, joking with Mamm, asking my opinion, and I feasted on all of it like it was Christmas dinner. And then, when the work was done, he drove away without a backward look." She pulled herself together. "He had no reason to look back, of course."

"He's building Mandy and Kelvin's house on the acreage Daniel Lapp gave them," Amelia said. "It's good he has work to take his mind off this mystery about Lavina. He must be working hard, because we haven't seen much of him."

"He wasn't at your folks' on Friday?" Carrie asked.

"Neither were you. We missed you—especially when Emma and Joshua made such a grand entrance. People are going to be talking about it for weeks."

"I heard about it, never fear. I wish I had been there, but I didn't feel well." She got the needle going again. "Cramps."

It would have been more than cramps. It would have been confirmation that, for one more month, there was no possibility of a baby. The ache in Emma's heart deepened to include empathy for Carrie. It was bad enough to be bereaved once or twice in a lifetime. But to wait every month, only to find out that the little life you hoped for had been taken away yet again...that would be ongoing. A relentless, unending bereavement.

Amelia caught her eye and Emma brought the conversation back into the safer, clearer shallows of her love life. "Yes, Joshua made sure we arrived as a couple, and I let him. But oh, my friends, I've been going over and over it in my mind and I can't get any further. Maybe you can help me if we talk it out."

"Is it so hard to care for him?" Carrie asked softly. "Joshua, I mean."

"Imagine if he were courting you when all the time you cared about Melvin. How would you feel?"

Carrie nodded. "If Melvin didn't care, that would be a problem. What's that saying about the bird in the hand?"

"That's exactly what it is. Do I take the bird in the hand, because the one in the bush will never love anyone but his wife, no matter if they're separated or not?" Emma hated the way her voice trembled. But her whole heart was in this conversation. She couldn't help it if all her emotions were involved, too.

"Emma," Amelia said gently. "You must put Grant aside

and not think of him anymore. God has closed that door, and it's wrong to keep knocking on it."

"You're right." Emma sighed. "I know. I have to stop nourishing these feelings."

"Give someone else a chance," Carrie said. "You may find that God knows what He's doing after all."

"There's nothing wrong with Joshua Steiner liking you," Amelia said. "I can't blame him a bit. And who knows? There may be other people out there who like you, too."

Carrie finished the seam and snipped the threads. "There's nothing to make a man take notice like another man taking notice."

"Thus speaks the voice of experience," Amelia said to no one in particular.

"I'm just telling the truth."

Emma laughed. It was all so unlikely, as if they were talking about someone else altogether. "Well, now I'm prepared, anyway."

"Emma." Carrie got up and gave her a hug. "If there's one thing I've learned, it's that love is the *last* thing you can prepare for."

May 30, 2012

Dear Emma,

It was great to meet you here in New York and I hope you had as good a time as I did. I appreciated getting to know you a little, and learning about life in your world.

I know you don't want to publish the book, but things do change. If you ever change your mind, I hope you'll think of me.

In the meantime, please let me know if you're in the city again. I'd really like to see you and catch up on your news.

My best to you,
Tyler West

Emma pushed open the door of the bulk goods store with her rear end, gripped the three carry bags in each hand, and maneuvered her way out. When the door finished its arc without the help of her posterior, she nearly lost her balance and did a quick dance step before she found it again. Jerking her head up, she found herself face to face with Calvin King, one of Martin King's four brothers. She couldn't remember if he was the one who farmed with Martin or not. In fact, he was lucky she remembered his name, she was so surprised.

"*Wie geht's*, Emma?" He held the door until she got herself and her bags out of it, then bent down to take the right-hand load. "Here, let me get those for you."

"*Denki*, Calvin. But you don't have to. I've had lots of practice." She struggled to hang on to the bags, but then stopped herself. If he wanted to lug that heavy bag of purple onions over to her buggy, she'd be a fool not to let him.

"How have you been keeping?" He put the onions in the back of her buggy, then took the other bags from her, one by one, stowing them with the efficiency and ease of long practice. "You and Lena? She's well?"

"She needs to rest a lot, but she sews and reads as much as ever." Goodness. She hadn't exchanged much more than a *Guder Mariye* with Calvin King since he'd graduated from school three years ahead of her. Amelia had had such a crush on him when they'd been little girls—back when he'd been slender and handsome. He wasn't so bad to look at now, give or take fifty pounds. Before she died, his wife had fed him well, and no doubt she'd trained her girls to do the same.

"And the girls? I saw them on Sunday, playing with my niece. They must be nearly eleven, aren't they?"

"Eleven in February. But before I know it, they'll be out of school and running around, and I'll be needing to keep a close eye on flashlights lying on windowsills."

Emma smiled. "No girl in her right mind would leave a flashlight any such place, for fear her father would do just that. They'll come out at night, though, just you watch. Goodness knows the boys will be."

"Let's not get ahead of ourselves." He laughed, and when he didn't wave and walk away to tend his own horse, who had lifted its head and was regarding him with an "Aren't you coming? I want to go home" kind of look, she shifted her weight and wondered if it would be rude to just take Ajax's bridle and start backing him up. Calvin cleared his throat. "So, Emma, I'm a plain-spoken man with no skill at beating around the bush."

Now she was really at sea. Did he need something? "I know that, Calvin. There's nothing wrong with saying what you mean. It saves a lot of time."

Oops. She hoped he wouldn't take that as a hint that he was wasting hers. She was happy to visit with anybody who wanted to, but all the same, they were out in a paved parking lot and it was lucky she hadn't bought ice cream.

"I'm glad you feel that way. You're a sensible, direct woman yourself. I've always liked that about you."

Really? The echo of what Carrie had said at the quilting frolic yesterday skittered through her head, and she shook it away.

When she didn't reply, Calvin went on, "I just...that is to say...well, I'll just come out and say it. Is it true that you and Joshua Steiner are courting? I heard you came together to the do at Lehmans'."

That is none of your business. The words trembled on the tip of her tongue, but instead of letting them fly, she took a deep breath. She had never snapped at anyone in a public place—with the possible exception of Karen—and she wasn't about to start now. Besides, a carload of *Englisch* folk had just pulled up in the row of spaces behind the buggy parking area, and even though they wouldn't understand *Deitch*, they would understand tone of voice just fine.

"It is not true that he is courting me," she said as steadily as she could. "But we are good friends."

He let out a breath, as if he'd been holding it. "*Ischt gut.*"

She raised one eyebrow. "It is?" And why on earth would he ask her such a personal question?

"*Ja*, it is. Because if he's not courting you, then he won't mind if I buy you an ice cream across the road." He beamed at her. "If you'd like one, that is."

Carrie had been right. Holy smokes, as the *Youngie* would say. She had been right, and Emma had laughed and dismissed it, and now she was in for it. Oh, how Carrie would tease!

But telling Carrie all about it later was not going to get her out of this now. "Calvin, I—my goodness, I—"

"Don't you like ice cream?"

"Well, sure, but—but I have to get home with these groceries."

"They'll wait. You don't have anything perishable in there, do you?"

Who knew that a bucket of melting ice cream would have made such a good escape? It looked as though she was going to get some anyway, though, unless she could come up with a reason not to in the next five seconds.

Calvin seemed to sense her hesitation. "I'm going about this all wrong, aren't I?" It was bright out, but not terribly warm, yet his temples under his hat were shiny with perspiration. "I don't mind telling you, Emma, it's been a long time since I asked a woman for...for ice cream. It's not an easy thing for a man to do, young or old."

"Why me?" came out of her mouth before she could stop it. "Why now?"

His cheeks reddened. "I thought you might like some chocolate or vanilla, is all."

The poor man. She couldn't keep this up. Much as she didn't care to eat ice cream when it was barely sixty-five out, she couldn't stand to see a man in such discomfort, either. "I'm more a lemon coconut person."

"Shall we go see if they have such?"

"All right." At least maybe she'd find out what on earth was going on.

And so it was that when Mary Lapp clattered by in her buggy with the newlywed Mandy, obviously fresh from shopping themselves, there was Emma sitting opposite Calvin King on the picnic bench outside the stand, licking coconut ice cream like a pair of children. The look Mary gave them pretty much guaranteed that it would be all over the district by suppertime.

It would have been funny if it weren't so...embarrassing.

"So I hear you were in the big city recently?" Calvin

seemed to be enjoying the coconut ice cream, which by his own admission he'd never tasted in his life. "What for?"

"I had business there."

"What business does a plain woman have in New York?"

A fair question. One that she had no intention of answering. "My own." Emma crunched up the last of her waffle cone and took the bull by its figurative horns. "But there's business here that interests me more. I'd like to know what you're about, asking me out for ice cream when either of your girls can make it for you at home."

"Anyone might be able to make it, but convincing you to come over and eat it is a lot harder. I thought it would be better in a public place."

He obviously hadn't seen Mary Lapp.

"The truth is, Emma, I've often thought of you. I wonder, have you ever thought of me?"

"I've thought that it must be difficult, losing Rose Ann to cancer with the girls so young," she said carefully. "But you have the boys to help you on the farm, so that's a blessing."

"The girls need female companionship. I'm sure they'd like to see you if you came over sometime."

I'm sure they'd rather see Maryann or Amelia's boys or any number of the young couples with children who are already their playmates.

"There I go again, beating around the bush when I said I'd speak plain. What I mean to say is, I'd like to see you. My girls and I could whip up a pretty fine supper if you'd come to share it with us."

"Calvin...I..."

"You asked why you, why now, and those are fair questions. The truth is, you're like those little flowers Rose Ann used to keep in her garden, the ones that lie close to the ground so you don't see them blooming right away, next to the showier ones. But they last a good long time and they smell sweet."

Emma remembered Rose Ann's rock garden and the carpets of flowers it used to have. Calvin hadn't been able to keep it up, and the last time they'd been there for church, the flowers had died away and the thyme had begun to take over.

"The primroses, you mean."

"*Ja.* You're not a showy woman, but anyone with eyes in his head can see from the way you care for your mother that you're a giving woman. An enduring one. Those are qualities a man can only admire." She could feel the heat creeping up her neck, her cheeks, even her forehead. "Aw, now, I've embarrassed you and I didn't mean to do that."

He tried to take her hand, but she gripped her handbag so hard there would be crescent-shaped marks in the leather later.

"I guess what I'm leading up to is, if you're free and you're interested, would you mind if we saw each other now and again?"

She had gone for a decade and a half wishing to be asked on a date even once, and now within the space of a month, she'd been keeping company with no less than four men. If it hadn't been so awful she would have laughed.

"Calvin, I…much as I like you and your family, it… well, it would be difficult. To begin when there might not be any future in it. No matter what happens, I can't leave Mamm."

He nodded, his big hands clasping and unclasping on the picnic table. "I know it. But you could get away for an evening once in awhile, couldn't you?" He turned his head, looking up at her from under the brim of his hat. "My girls need a woman's influence. Their grandmother has been wonderful, and their aunts and cousins, too, but it's not the same, is it?"

The same as what? Rose Ann? Oh, if only her heart hadn't already made its crazy, futile choice! "It's more than just Mamm. It's me." What was it the *Englisch* said? *It's not you, it's me.* Again, she choked down the urge to giggle. Or to cry. She was no longer sure.

"You don't think you could learn to care for me?" His voice was so low it roughened with emotion.

"Oh, no." Stricken, she put a hand on his arm. "You would not have any trouble finding a woman who would care for you the way you deserve."

"It doesn't sound like it."

"It's just that I—there's someone who—"

"You have feelings for already?" She let out a long breath and nodded. "But not Joshua Steiner."

A shake of the head, this time.

"So I waited too long?"

"It was too late ten years ago, I'm afraid," she whispered. Why did it have to be Calvin King, of all people, who had winkled her deepest secret out of her?

"You've been waiting for him to take notice for ten years?" When the color rose in her face again, he said, "Emma, I'm not going to say anything one way or another. But when I heard that Joshua Steiner might be courting you, I woke up and realized that maybe I hadn't even seen the flowers closest to the ground, and only realized now that they might have the most to offer. But if you've been waiting for this man for ten years, maybe you should look around you, too." He paused. "I don't want to hurt you, but sometimes the crabapple that won't let go of the branch isn't the one you want to pick. Sometimes the windfalls can be good fruit. You just can't wait too long to appreciate them."

"I know," she said softly. "But Calvin?"

"*Ja?*"

"No matter what happens, I want to say thank you. For the ice cream. And your friendship. And for...for appreciating flowers wherever they grow." Rose Ann had been a much luckier woman than the folks in the district realized, she saw now.

When she dared to look at him again, she saw that he was smiling.

And she finally had the courage to smile back.

CHAPTER 11

Maybe some might feel sorry for her for spending the best years of her youth caring for Lena, but Emma never saw it that way. With Pap, it had been different. Pap's mind had begun giving way when Emma had been around twenty-two, and by the time she hit thirty, the only person he really recognized was Karen. He even thought Lena was Karen, and Emma figured that had hurt her mother much more than it did Emma.

It wasn't until God had called Victor Stolzfus home that Emma had realized that He took care of each of his children, and if His will was for her to live quietly with Lena, it also included a new kind of freedom.

One of those freedoms was in conversation. Emma could say nearly anything to her mother; after working side by side for all these years, some things came naturally. But these days, some subjects—men, for instance—were buried so deeply that a comment might only glance off the surface, disappear, and not come up again, like a skipping stone.

As she climbed the steps of the root cellar after emptying the bag of onions into their basket, the pressure under her breastbone increased to the point that Emma knew she must talk to someone about Calvin, or burst. Carrie would get the biggest charge out of it, but she was three miles away and might not even be home. Amelia was at the shop today signing papers with Melvin and the Steiner boys. But really, who better to talk with than Lena, who had seen nearly as much life as all three of them put together? She didn't need to bring up specific names, but surely she could find some way to introduce Calvin into the conversation?

In the end Lena did it herself. She put her teacup down in its saucer with a clink. "Emma, *Liewi*, what is going on with you? You just put the cream pitcher in the cupboard and the sugar bowl in the fridge."

Jolted out of her mental fog, Emma opened the refrigerator door. Sure enough, there sat the sugar bowl, getting nicely chilled. She pulled it out and swapped it with the cream, then sat at the table with a sigh and took another butter tart. "Good thing you said something," she said around the caramel sweetness. "Nothing I hate more than cold sugar in my coffee in the morning."

"I've done it a time or two myself." Lena took a sip of tea. "Usually when I've got something on my mind."

Her mother was so graceful. She would give you an opportunity, which you could take at face value and move on, or you could open it like a door and step in.

"I do have something on my mind. I've turned it over and over and I still don't know what to do."

Lena sat a little straighter. "Have you been to the doctor?"

"For man trouble?"

"Man trouble? Is that all?" Lena's spine wilted again and Emma saw too late that she had really frightened her.

"Mamm, I promise, that's all it is. You didn't think I was sick, did you?"

"I've seen you moping around here with a long face since

you got back from New York. You don't hear when someone talks to you, you go for hours on end without saying a word...and I haven't heard that typewriter of yours going at night since you came home. All this tells me you're either in love, or you're sick. Up until now, the second option is what I would have thought."

"Up until now?"

"Well, I've been hearing things about the first option, but I don't usually make diagnoses on the basis of talk around the *Kaffi* cups. Though I have to say, your sister is having a better time with this than you seem to be."

"She would. She's the one who started it."

"So it's true, what I'm hearing, then? That you and that Steiner boy are courting?"

"He's not a boy anymore, Mamm."

"He is to me. In fact, he'll always be that drowned rat who got dragged out of the river ten miles away, grinning his fool head off, and not caring one bit that my girl could have been swept away to wind up who knows where. Mississippi, maybe."

"I can swim. And I was just as guilty as he was. Maybe more."

"Be that as it may, I hope he's improved. Karen seems to think he's the catch of the county. I wonder what John thinks of that idea."

"If Joshua had a new strain of hardy wheat growing out of his ears, John might be interested. Other than that, I'm sure he's used to Karen and her little dramas."

"Do you think he's the catch of the county? Especially as you seem to have caught him?" Lena twinkled at her over the rim of her cup.

"I haven't caught him, Mamm. We're just good friends, the way we have always been."

"And good friends who haven't seen each other in twelve years take one another to train stations, of course."

"I had no idea he was in that car, much less that he'd decided he was going with me. But when he asked me to go to the Lehmans' the other night, that was different. He asked if he could court me, but that is too much, too soon. I told him it would be better if we see each other as friends."

Lena was silent a moment. "And what did he say to that?"

"What could he say? He knows he will have to prove himself to any woman's family, given his reputation."

"Interesting he chose to start with you."

"We were good friends once. Maybe he feels safe with me."

"Safe? Do you feel safe with him, is the question."

"Safe enough for friendship. I don't know about more." Her voice trailed away, and Lena's gaze sharpened.

"Because...?"

Emma took a breath and dove in. "What would you say it meant if a man stopped you outside the grocery store and asked you to go have an ice cream?"

"A man like, say, Calvin King?"

Emma practically dropped her cup. As it was, tea slopped as she put it down and she had to go and get a cloth to wipe it up. "Don't tell me. Mary Lapp came for a visit this afternoon while I was running errands."

"She did indeed. And since it was as much a surprise to me as no doubt Calvin was to you, Mary found it very rewarding. And there sat Mandy beside her, prim as a prune, like she'd never done a thing in her life to make people talk."

"I don't think she has. Who could, if you were the bishop's daughter?"

"I bet she's done plenty and her parents just don't know

about it. So how was it? Calvin was always a nice boy. Rose Ann was a lucky woman."

Emma nodded. Then she told Lena all about it, including the parts about the low-growing flowers and the windfall apples.

"The man is a bit of a poet," Lena remarked when she was done. "Though I'm not sure I see him as a windfall. The *gut Gott* may have seen fit to take his wife, but others have suffered as much and not rotted on the ground. Grant Weaver, for instance. Though I wouldn't say God took Lavina, exactly."

Emma gripped her cup to stop herself from leaping through that conversational door headfirst. But even that heroic self-control didn't fool Lena for a moment.

"*Docher*, don't think that because I don't speak of certain things I don't know how it is with you." Emma's lips trembled at the softness in her mother's tone. "I saw how you looked at him when he was here for the construction."

"He is married, and I was wrong to look," Emma managed. Her throat felt as if it would close after every word. "And now here I am with a man on either hand, and neither of them is the one I really want."

"What we want and what God wants for us are two different things. You might spend some time in prayer trying to reconcile the two."

That would be the right thing to do. Some might even say that a spinster over thirty shouldn't be so particular, that she should take that bird in the hand before it flew off and left her alone again.

"I'm so *verhuddelt*, Mamm," she said on a long sigh.

Lena's gaze was soft behind her spectacles. "If you were writing a story about it, what would you have the girl do?"

"Well, she'd be Amish, so she couldn't move away and start over somewhere else while she tries to forget the first man. I suppose I'd have the men try to get her attention somehow—you know, compete for her. Eventually the best man would rise to the top."

"Nothing wrong with a little competition," Mamm said. "Is there any more tea?"

Emma topped up her cup, then put the pot down slowly. "But this is real life, not a story. Who's going to compete over me?"

"Why shouldn't they? You're as godly and capable a woman as any in the district. More, probably, since you know how to work all this machinery." Lena indicated the oxygen tank next to her chair.

"Those aren't the qualities that a man looks for."

"They should be, if he's a good plain man."

Lavina got further in two weeks with her eyes and smile than I did in ten years with all my godliness and capability.

"Besides," Lena went on, "we're not talking about twenty-year-olds. We're talking about a man who has been married and is raising his family. A man who has seen a bit of the world. These men are looking for something different than they might have a decade ago. You can't tell me that some giddy eighteen-year-old is going to offer more than you do, Emma."

I'm good enough for seconds, but I'm no one's first choice.

Nei. That was self-pity, and dissatisfaction with the path God had chosen for her, and if she voiced those words Lena would slap them down the way she swatted flies—with efficiency and deadly accuracy.

"*Ach*, it doesn't matter anyway. I'm not going to leave you."

"If a good man wants you for his own, what kind of mother would I be if I kept you here?" Lena shook her head, her hair silvery white under her *Kapp*. "If one of these men shows the sense God gave a goose, I will go and live with Katherine. We talked about it at Christmas when everyone was here."

"Mamm." Emma gazed at her in shock. "You can't leave the farm. You've lived here for sixty years."

"And been happy. That's not to say that I wouldn't miss it. I would. But Katherine's only over in the next township, not the other side of the country. And there's a *Daadi Haus* attached to their place already. I would only be a wall's width away, and no time to be lonesome."

Emma had seen the *Daadi Haus* at Katherine's. It was tiny—only a kitchen and a bedroom and a sitting room—but those were the only rooms Mamm used now, anyway. She'd had no idea Mamm and Katherine had been hatching up plots the way the hens tried to hide their eggs in the barn. Did Karen know? She needed to be the one in charge, so Emma had a feeling she didn't. Karen felt Lena was her responsibility, even though they didn't see her much and Emma was her caregiver in the eyes of the county hospital. She probably wouldn't take too kindly to having her younger sister steal Lena away.

But goodness, Karen had been the one to start all this, inviting Joshua to lunch all those weeks ago. It would serve her right if she lost her mother and her sister all at once.

Lena wasn't finished. "I love our little life here, Emma. But don't you even think about telling one of those men no for my sake. If God has brought good men into your life, it's not your place to turn them away because you think you need to take care of me."

"I'd be happier if God had made up His mind and only brought one." Emma's chin rested on her hand as she gazed into the milky depths of her tea.

"It's what's called an embarrassment of riches. You've never been one for running around after the men. It's about time the Lord saw to bringing them running after you." Lena paused. "You mind what I say. A little competition is good for a man. And having lots of friends is good for a woman. Give them both a chance until God points you to His choice."

Emma lifted her head and sat back in the chair. "I'll be giving folks a lot to talk about, with all this running around and eating ice cream and whatnot."

"You never mind them," Lena said. "God's opinion is the only one you should listen to."

CHAPTER 12

Emma sat on the edge of the bed and gazed at her Smith-Corona, which waited patiently for her to roll some paper into it and put it back to work. Mamm was right. Despite the notes in her little book, she hadn't typed up a thing since her return from New York City, not even that article on backsides for *Family Life* or an editorial for the *Whinburg Weekly*. In fact, she hadn't looked at the *Weekly* in days, she who had read it cover to cover just in case something in there triggered an essay of her own.

What was wrong with her?

Was it true, what people had hinted in the past? *You need a home and husband to keep you busy, then you wouldn't have so much time to waste on writing.* Had she buried herself in the worlds in her mind so that she wouldn't have to face actually going out there and making a world of her own? Could it be that her spinsterhood was less about her looks than about her self-confidence?

Had she brought spinsterhood on herself?

Now, that was a terrifying thought.

It was no good blaming the men when she'd been hiding in her room writing instead of going to the singings or to volleyball games. A whole decade had passed that way, and what did she have to show for it? A few articles, a few essays, and a book she couldn't publish. If she hadn't been so afraid, so crushed by rejection all those years ago, maybe she would have had a flesh-and-blood child of her own by now, instead of a lot of little paper substitutes.

You said you wanted people to listen, Emma Stolzfus, but did you ever actually open your mouth and speak? Did you ever have a conversation with a young man, or smile at a visitor, or go to a band hop when you were running around? Did you even bother to go on Rumspringe?

No. You hid in your room and let your writing speak for you, and if no one heard, it's your own fault.

"I'm not so sure about that," Carrie said the next day at their quilting frolic, when Emma had summoned her courage and haltingly put some of these things into words. Carrie knelt on the Stolzfus sitting-room floor with the big silver shears as Emma and Amelia rolled out the batting. The quilt back lay under it, wrong side up, where its seams would be hidden inside. "Pull a bit your way. There. I'll cut it even with the backing. Do you really think it's being afraid, or was it a case of God guiding you?"

"Would God guide her away from a home and family for all these years?" Amelia objected. "Careful, it's traveling. Let me pull it this way."

"Why would He do that?" Emma asked. "Every Amish girl prays He will guide her to the man meant for her. And children are a blessing."

"Maybe..." Amelia hesitated, as comfortable on her knees as some people were in a chair.

"Maybe what?"

"I don't want to say something hurtful."

"Amelia, my dear friend, you couldn't say anything nearly

so hurtful as some of the *Gmee* have said to me on this subject," Emma said. "Besides, we tell each other the truth, no matter what."

Amelia nodded, sliding backward on the plank floor as Carrie passed her, snipping carefully. "Maybe in your desire to be heard," she said quietly, "you forgot to listen."

Emma was silent. Then, "Do you know how many nights I have prayed about this? And mornings, and noons, hoping God would hear?"

"But that's just it. Hoping He would listen. But were you listening to Him?" Amelia's voice was as gentle as if she were speaking to little Elam before turning down the lamp.

Carrie made the last cut and Emma shook out the pieced quilt top. Each of them took a corner and laid it on the batting, smoothing it from center to edges, then Emma moved to the last corner and did the same. As her hands did what they had done many times before, she faced Amelia's gentle reproof, trying not to flinch away from it.

"I don't know," she said at last. "I wonder if I even know how."

Had she really treated the Lord of Heaven the way people treated her? Asking for everything under the sun, but not listening for a reply?

Maybe God had been ready to show her His will, and she'd been up and away to can bean pickles, or off to her typewriter, or going somewhere else to do goodness knows what, and His counsel had blown away on the wind she kicked up as she bustled hither and yon.

Emma took a box of safety pins and began to pin the back, batting, and top together at small, even intervals, beginning near the middle and working out. Amelia started on the other long side, while Carrie settled at one end.

"Tonight, when you pray, just take a few extra minutes to listen to the silence. Or open up the Bible and see what it tells you," Amelia suggested. "An answer might not come tonight, or the next night. But God is faithful. It will come."

"And in the meantime, Lena is right." Carrie spoke around the row of pins between her lips, her hands moving quickly. "God has already made His choice for you. You just have to find out who it is."

There was the sound of feet on the porch, and Karen stepped inside, her chest heaving and her *Kapp* strings hanging down her back. Emma sat back on her heels in astonishment.

"Karen, what's wrong? Is it Mamm?" Lena had gone over to the big house for a visit, being not so obvious about leaving Emma alone with her friends to talk.

"John just came in from the field. Amos Yoder stopped to tell him that they've found Lavina."

Emma couldn't have spoken if it meant her life.

"Where is she? Did she come home?" Amelia said.

"No. That's just it. The poor girl has been dead for nearly half a year and nobody knew it. If it wasn't for Grant searching for her, they would never have known. The *Englisch* cremated her body, so Grant and Amos are going down on the train to Springfield to get her ashes."

"But how?" Emma's voice came out in a squeak. "How could a woman die and nobody know?"

"Apparently she went to a convenience store to get something for her Christmas baking, and somebody tried to rob it. The robber shot the proprietor and her, too. I don't know why. I don't know why that man she was living with didn't do anything. Grant had to look at a photo, so he could tell them for sure it was her." Karen shook her head. "It's all over now."

"How awful," Carrie breathed, "to have to tell your little *Kinner* that their mother will never come back."

"The little boy has never known her," Karen said. "Grant sure has had a hard row to hoe. I doubt she would have come back anyway."

"We can't know that," Amelia said gently. "God could have been working in her heart and softening it again."

"He could have been," Karen allowed. "I hope it's so. What I do know is, Amos will let the *Gmee* know when the funeral will be. There won't be a service, of course, since she died outside the faith. But some might want to go to the graveside."

When the sound of her shoes on the porch stairs faded, Carrie, Emma, and Amelia looked at one another.

"It's hard to settle to sewing after news like that." Emma looked down at the quilt. "I've lost my heart for it."

"It would probably be good for us to concentrate on something useful." Carrie moved the box of pins and began on another row. "That poor, poor girl. To go out for something as harmless as baking things and then..." Her voice trailed away.

Emma couldn't concentrate on work. She felt as if she had been struck by something heavy. "Remember the time she went to the drugstore for that fancy perfume and her mother made her dig a hole in the garden and pour the whole bottle out?"

"And she'd worked as a *Maud* for an *Englisch* woman for weeks to buy it, too."

"How could she have imagined she would get away with it?" Amelia wanted to know. "It's not like you can hide the smell of perfume. That's why someone would wear it. To be noticed."

"She sure never had any trouble with that," Emma said on a sigh.

"She was baking. Somehow I never imagined that. And…" Amelia trailed off.

And God chose that moment to take her. Probably wearing Englisch *clothes, living who knows what kind of* Englisch *life.*

They all thought it, but no one said it.

Only God knew the condition of her heart—and whether her soul was safe.

That night, after she turned down the wick and extinguished the flame, Emma didn't kneel by her bed to pray, as usual. Instead, she padded barefoot across the hardwood floor and opened the window to the soft early summer night. She curled up in the wicker chair next to it, wrapped her shawl around her shoulders, and gazed up, past the barn and the trees and the fields of her neighbors, up over the horizon to a sky spangled with stars. The breeze played in the leaves of the maple, and somewhere in the distance, she heard the clop-clop-clop of someone coming home late.

Lord, for once I'm not going to bother you with a list of my needs. Only watch over Mamm, and bring her safely through the night. Be with my family and my friends, who are not afraid to tell me the truth if it means bringing me closer to You. Please let me know Your will for me. Help me to hear You and not the fearful yammerings of my brain.

Oh, Lord, please be with Grant tonight as he travels, and with the children as they sleep. They will be grieving, maybe not for the loss of their mother, but for the loss of the hope that she would come back. Give him strength from Yourself, Lord, so that he can be strong and wise for them.

She tried to empty her mind, to listen as intently as she

sometimes had to when Lena was short of breath. In the hedge, something rustled. The creek at the back of Amelia's place, all the way across Moses Yoder's pasture, chuckled and rushed. How amazing that she could hear it.

This was how prayer should be. She would come again and again, and invite the quiet into her soul. And one of these times she would hear the still, small voice she loved, telling her which way she should go.

Dear Grant,

I was so very sorry to hear about Lavina's passing. I can't imagine how difficult the circumstances must be for you. Please know that while we may not say much, all of us feel for you, and are praying that God will heal the hearts of you and the children. We will do everything we can to help you.

I remember once when Lavina made root beer floats for all of us after a singing. She forgot that you put in the ice cream after, not before you pour in the root beer. What a mess! But she just laughed herself silly and slurped up the root beer in her hands until all of us joined in. She loved life, and I'm glad for the time you had together when your hearts were full of love.

Remember those times, Grant, and tell the *Kinner* about them. I have to believe that will make it easier.

Your friend,
Emma

The sun shone from a brilliant, clean-washed sky as the small crowd gathered in the cemetery on Saturday to lay Lavina's ashes to rest among the Yoder graves. Since she had left the church, there had been no funeral service attended by the entire *Gmee*, which Emma had to believe was a relief to Bishop Daniel. After all, he couldn't exactly expound on the reward to the faithful soul, but neither could he hurt Grant and the Yoders by dwelling too long on the terrible price a soul risked by leaving the people of God. In the end, the prayer at the graveside was brief, as was the hymn, and only family and close friends were present.

Emma watched from a distance but did not go into the cemetery. She was not what you could call a close friend, though she and Lavina had been in the same gang and everyone in the congregation had known one another most of their lives. But out of consideration for the family, she would not add to what amounted to a silent spectacle. She had written her letter and that was that.

How Grant planned to go on with his life was none of her business. Not now. It was clear to anyone with a pair of eyes that he would never stop loving his wife, had done everything he could to find her and bring her home. No woman could compete with that, and Emma saw exactly how foolish her dreams had been in the face of such devotion.

It was time to stop going down a path that led nowhere, and start hiking up a different one.

So, at an off-Sunday get-together at Brian and Erica Steiner's little place, when it seemed Calvin King or his girls were everywhere she looked, she decided to pay attention to the Lord's hints on the subject. The two youngest Steiner boys owned the cabinet shop next to Amelia's pallet shop, and had now officially bought into Amelia's place with Carrie's husband, Melvin, now that it seemed to be settled between Amelia and Eli Fischer. Because their father had already divided up the farm among their three older brothers, Brian and Boyd had had no choice but to buy five-acre "hobby" farms on the edge of town, just as Amelia and her first husband, Enoch Beiler, had done several years ago.

Not that planting and raising a couple of acres of vegetables and selling or preserving them was any kind of a hobby. It was months of work, and Erica was already sunburned from weeding.

Working off the sweets from the outdoor lunch, children ran and chased each other around the house and through the garden, including Calvin's eleven-year-old twin girls. Mollie and Barbara, they were called. His boys were older— thirteen and fifteen—so they were probably off with their friends who were also in that awkward age between when they left school at fourteen, and sixteen, when some parents gave their children more freedom to run around and try their wings.

As if her thoughts were a magnet, one of the twins dashed up—she had no idea which one. "Hullo, Emma," she panted, her eyes the bright King blue, just like Calvin's.

"Hullo yourself," she said. "Which one are you?"

"I'm Mollie."

"Does everyone ask you that?"

"Everyone who doesn't know that I'm the one with freckles."

"Aha." And so it was. Blond she might be, but there were freckles dusted across her nose, as pretty as you please. "Did you make ice cream last week?"

The blue eyes widened. "How did you know?"

"Because your *daed* and I had ice cream at the shop across from the bulk food store, and I wondered if he would go home and decide it was a pretty good idea to make some more."

"Are you and Daed courting?"

Emma barely managed to keep her gaze on the child, and not look around to see who was listening. "Is that what it means when you eat ice cream?" She raised her brows in mock horror.

"My brother Kenneth says you are."

"Your brother Kenneth ought to ask his father."

"Ask me what?" boomed a voice just behind her, and Mollie bounced around her to give her father a hug.

"Noth—"

"If you're courting Emma," the child interrupted, standing on the tops of his feet and looking up, her arms around his waist. "Kenneth says you are."

The flush burned into Calvin's skin at about the same rate Emma could feel it burning into hers.

"Then Kenneth has it wrong, and you should tell him so," he said with admirable steadiness. Emma felt like running helter-skelter across the fields until she could see the silos of home. If she hadn't been driving Mamm in the buggy, she might just have done it. But since she had to stand there, she liked that Calvin answered his *Docher* seriously, and didn't try to put her off or tell her to mind her own business. "We are good friends, and good friends can have an ice cream every now and again."

Mollie shot Emma a look that left Emma at a loss as to its meaning, and when one of her friends called to her from behind the chicken pen, she ran off, the loose strings of her little *Kapp* flying behind her.

"I wonder where your boy heard such a thing." Emma felt awkward saying it, but it was one thing to hear it from one's father, and quite another to hear it from the grapevine.

"Not from me. If it had been, he would have had his facts

straight. I'm afraid we need look no further than our bishop's wife and daughter."

"We knew it would happen." It felt strange and far too intimate to be using the plural pronoun with him.

Calvin tugged on his black vest, as if he found it confining. "We could always make the rumors true."

"Calvin..." People were already beginning to look at them sideways, and look, there was Esther Grohl leaning over to whisper something behind her hand to Erica Steiner.

"I know. I won't pester you. But that offer of ice cream is still open. We made some again the other night and it would be no trouble at all to drop off a pint for you and Lena."

"Mamm would love it."

"I hoped that you might, too."

"It depends on the flavor." Plural pronouns or not, he was so kind she didn't have the heart to discourage him. And if this really was God's will, she needed to do just the opposite. "What did you make?"

"We took some canned peaches from last year and cut them up. It turned out pretty well, if I do say so myself."

"Peach is almost as good as lemon coconut."

"Maybe I could bring it by this evening, and we could go for a ride afterward?"

Oh, my. Oh, my. A date. This was a date. Emma's breath backed up in her lungs and she struggled to find words, struggled for calm...and then she saw Grant Weaver over by the hawthorn hedge, pointing out something in the branches to one of his little girls.

Oh, the brave man, to come out in public the day after his wife's funeral. Probably he was doing it for the sake of the girls. Striving to be normal. Which made him even braver.

She dragged her gaze away and found Calvin looking at her, hope and trepidation in his eyes. "You are so kind," she said a little breathlessly. "That would be—be very nice. *Denki*."

She might as well have given him a Christmas present, he looked so delighted. "I'll come by after supper, before it gets too dark, then."

If you put a toe in the pond, you might as well just go swimming. "Why don't you come for supper, and we'll have the ice cream for dessert? I have a lemon poppyseed cake on hand, with lemon frosting."

"That sounds mighty *gut*. Around five?"

When she nodded, he smiled again and walked off in the direction of Brian's workshop behind the house, where the men had gathered to talk.

"And what was *that* about?" Amelia sidled up to her and spoke out of the side of her mouth.

Breathe. "Calvin asked me to go for a ride this evening. After he comes to supper bringing some ice cream for Mamm." *Breathe.*

"Did he, now? And I notice that Grant is over there, looking undecided about whether or not to join us."

"He's showing his little girl something."

"Emma, he's staring at you. No, don't look."

"Oh, for goodness sake, you sound like a teenager. The man just went to his wife's funeral. He's not looking at anybody."

Grant seemed to make up his mind and ambled in their direction. Before he reached them, Eli came up behind Amelia and put a hand on her waist.

"I thought you went to see what Brian has going on in his shop," she said softly. "Back already?"

"I had something important to do."

"And what was that?"

"See you."

They locked gazes. Three was definitely a crowd, right there on the lawn in front of two dozen people, chatting in groups under the trees. Would it be too obvious if she gracefully stepped away? But no, there was Grant coming up on the other side. If she turned and headed for the house, it would look as if she were deliberately avoiding him, and that was the last impression she wanted to give.

Lawn lunches never used to be this complicated.

Eli dragged his gaze from Amelia's face. "Grant Weaver. We are very sorry to hear of your family's loss." Grant nodded, and the two men shook hands. "I was hoping to get a moment to speak with you."

"Here I am."

"The township has approved our drawings and it seems we might have a permit soon. What is your schedule like?"

"It's pretty busy, but I knew this project was coming, so I saved some space for you."

"Maybe you could come for supper and talk it over, if you feel up to it?"

"There's always room for one more." Amelia smiled, her gray eyes warm with pleasure at the prospect. "Eli has to go back to Lebanon first thing tomorrow, so you won't get a chance to talk unless it's tonight."

Eli smiled at Emma. "What about you, Emma? Would you like to join our little party?"

Amelia's eyes widened and she bit her lip to keep from speaking. Emma felt as though the ground had fallen out from under her feet.

"I—I think Grant might not prefer a social visit," she said, and risked a glance at him. "It wouldn't be seemly to—I mean—"

"We have had a few hard weeks, but knowing that it was God's will has helped the healing to begin," Grant said slowly, saving her from more stammering foolishness. "I think the girls and Zachary would like an evening making puzzles with your boys, Amelia. It would make this more a normal Sunday. So Emma, if you wish to come and visit, too, you should do just that."

Where was a sign from God when she needed it? He had allowed Calvin to ask her for a date instead, and she couldn't get out of it without hurting a good man's feelings and looking heartless and inconsiderate on top of it.

"I would have loved to," she said slowly, "but we already have company coming and Mamm isn't able to manage on her own."

Grant nodded, his hat tilted down as he studied the ground. Eli looked from her to Amelia as if he knew he'd missed something, but didn't have the first idea what. And before she knew it, Grant had melted away, leading little Sarah by the hand back to her Yoder cousins.

"He seems at peace," Amelia breathed. "I'm so glad."

He had nothing to reproach himself with, Emma thought. "Mamm will be getting tired," she said. "I'm going to tell her I'm ready to leave, and get the horse."

"Let me do that," Eli said. "He's the black gelding with the star and three socks, *ja*?"

Emma nodded, thanked him, and headed for the house.

Between man's will and the will of God, it seemed, there was a great gulf fixed. All she wanted in the world right now was to go to that little supper party. But it would be pointless. In his heart, Grant would be married to Lavina forever, so the presence of a single woman in the kitchen would mean as much as her presence in church or any other place.

Besides, only a blind woman could miss the precision of God's timing, which had caused her to accept one invitation just in time to make it impossible to accept the other.

CHAPTER 13

When Calvin's buggy rolled up the lane promptly at five o'clock, Emma knew that every eye in the big house would be on it once it made the right turn through the trees over to the *Daadi Haus*. She and Lena hardly ever had company; Lena just wasn't able for it. Instead, Karen and John entertained a couple of times a week, and they would walk over to join in, sometimes both, and sometimes just Emma.

She had changed out of her Sunday black into a newer everyday dress in a shade of green that Amelia had once told her matched her eyes. Not that she was trying to impress Calvin King. Far from it. But company deserved more than a kitchen dress, and if it happened to be a nice color, that was a bonus.

At the sound of boots on the porch steps, she opened the door. "*Guder Owed*, Calvin. *Willkumm*. Where are the girls?" She'd expected him to bring them, at least, even if the older boys had other plans with the *Youngie*. But here he was, all by himself, his face shining as if he'd scrubbed it before he left.

"*Die Maedscher* are over at Martin and Anna's for supper and an evening of games with their cousins, and the boys will probably sneak over to Grohls' for the singing, even though

I've told them they're too young and the older ones will just shoo them away. In case you get the wrong idea, I was invited to Martin's, too. But I told them I was booked." He handed her a plastic tub. "Better get this into the freezer."

She took the ice cream, already sweating from its ride over, and hustled it into the freezer unit in the top part of their propane fridge. At least she could cool her scarlet face for a few moments, and try to regain her composure.

He had come alone. Not with his children, as a good friend might do, but alone, as a courting man did. Goodness, for fifty cents she'd pack them both into the buggy and drive over to Martin King's herself, so that Calvin would have no doubt which she preferred.

Calvin sat across the kitchen table from Lena, who was shredding lettuce for the salad. "And how are you, Lena? Keeping well?"

"*Ja, denki*, Calvin. It's good to see you. I would have liked to have seen those girls of yours. We made supper for six at least."

"Sorry about that. We spent the afternoon there and they were having such a good time they begged me to let them stay. I'm hungry enough to eat their share, though."

"Not much for them to do here, with me and Emma, I suppose," Lena said. "But Karen's *Kinner* would have been glad to see them. Little Maryann and your Barbara are good chums, I think."

"Two peas in a pod, those two, studious and good helpers in the house. They'll likely be in the same buddy bunch eventually," he allowed. "But that's a ways off yet."

"And Mollie?" Emma asked as she took the kale off the stove, simmering in chicken broth and onions, and dished it up along with the mashed potatoes. "Is she not so studious and helpful?"

"Mollie is different," he said on a sigh. "Always staring off into space and doodling on pieces of paper. Her teachers say she's smart enough, but she doesn't pay attention."

"I remember someone very much like that," Lena said with a smile. She pushed the salad bowl, now decorated with carrot curls and enticing circles of tomato, into the middle of the table.

"I can't think who." Emma put the roast beef in front of Calvin. "Would you do the honors?"

He carved the meat while she turned buttermilk biscuits into a bowl and folded a clean tea towel over them. After they said their silent grace, dishes clattered and cutlery got busy while Emma did her best to keep the conversation off herself and on his family, on how high the corn was getting after such a wet spring, and whether Karen was hoping for a boy or a girl. That carried them all the way through dinner, and during dessert it was easy enough to keep him talking about the fun the girls had had making the ice cream.

And then it was time for the buggy ride. Even if their laughter and conversation had lasted twice as long, it still would not have given her enough time to prepare for this.

The buggy dipped under her weight as she climbed in on the left side. Since it was the family buggy and not an open courting buggy, he had slid the doors open and rolled the back flap up to let in the evening air and make it seem as though they were not seeking privacy.

It didn't help, though. As he made the turn into the lane, Emma glimpsed Karen and Maryann rocking lazily together on the front porch swing, and rolled her eyes toward heaven. It would be as plain as daybreak that only the two of them were inside the buggy, and Karen would know exactly what was going on. It would be all over the settlement by lunchtime tomorrow that she and Calvin were more than merely friends.

But there was no help for it. No matter what her intentions were, appearances would fuel gossip, and there was nothing she could do about it now.

Calvin shook the reins over his horse's back as though there was nothing more to the evening than soft air and an empty road. "I thought we might take a look at the river and see if it's dropped any."

She nodded and did her best to smile. "I haven't been over there in a long time. Did you hear the story about the time Joshua Steiner and I floated down it? We were nearly ten miles away by the time Daed got wind of it and came after us."

"I didn't hear that one, but I have heard a thing or two about Joshua Steiner."

Silence fell, punctuated by the clip-clop of hooves and the rattling thrum of the wheels on asphalt. Since when had the bench seat of a buggy become so small? She was no fragile flower, and Calvin was a good-sized man. She had to keep her legs pulled all the way to the left to keep their thighs from bumping against each other in a very immodest way.

Was this the romantic buggy ride that all the girls had been so anxious to be asked for, back when they were teenagers? Or did the romance bleed out of it as you got older, until all you were left with was discomfort and awkwardness while you tried to calculate how much further you had to go?

Stop thinking about yourself. He has been very kind. The least you can do is make this ride a good use of his time—something worth giving up an evening with his Kinner *for.*

A swallow dipped and swooped right in front of them as they turned into the river road. "Look," she said. "He's catching bugs. It's nesting time again. I love the swallows. They're so companionable once they get used to you."

"They make a mess on my barn floor, but the ceilings are too high for me to sweep them out. The girls just have to scrub a little harder when our Sunday rolls around."

"Daed didn't used to like them, either, but John doesn't seem to mind. I think he's so used to having nesting females around that whether they have wings or not doesn't really matter."

"What about you, Emma? Did you ever have the urge to nest?"

Did he have to phrase that in past tense? "Sure. Most women do, I think." Except Lavina Weaver, after she had her children.

"There's still time."

"What, to nest? I suppose, but since I'm *leddich* yet, it's not likely."

"It might be more likely if you were to let me court you." The horse felt the slackness in the reins and slowed. "I'm not sure I want to merely be good friends with you, Emma. I thought as much before, but this evening made me sure."

Emma wondered wildly if she would hurt herself leaping out of a moving buggy, even at this slow a pace.

"I didn't bring the girls along for a good reason. I wanted to spend some time with you, just the two of us. I had a fine time at supper, and I think you did, too."

"Calvin, I—I told you already that I...that my heart was..."

"That you had feelings for someone else. *Ja*, I remember. But Emma, I've given it a lot of thought, and what I said before is true. If he has shown no interest in all this time, he's not likely to. And here I am, ready to court you, with a family who would love you if you gave them a chance. Don't you think I might be the better bargain?"

But you are not a pair of shoes in the half-off bin. She reined in her galloping thoughts. "It's very soon, Calvin," she said in a low tone, then spoke more firmly when she realized he was leaning in even closer in order to hear her. "We've only really spoken, um, in a personal way twice. That's not enough to base a—a marriage on."

"I'm not rushing you to marriage, though I'll tell you, it's in the back of my mind. Every time Mollie comes home from school with a note from Hannah Holstetler, I wish her mother were here to help her. Rose Ann always understood my little dreamer much better than I seem to be able to."

Emma could understand her, too, having been a little dreamer herself, thinking up stories and imagining wonderful things in a mind that was miles away from a one-room schoolhouse in Whinburg, Pennsylvania. But that was neither here nor there. Understanding a child was a much different thing than beginning a relationship with her father. And Emma had seen it happen often enough to know that even though he said he wouldn't rush her, second marriages often happened much quicker than they had the first time around—as if the parties realized that life was short and happiness not so thick on the ground that you could waste it.

Emma, listen to yourself. Is that what you're doing? Letting the chance of happiness slip through your fingers while you moon after what you can't have? If the swallows did that, there would be no nests and no young swallows, either.

"I feel as if I'm standing in the door of the hayloft," she said at last. "It's only one step, but if I take it, I won't be able to stop or change my mind."

"At least I'll be there to catch you at the bottom," Calvin offered. He flapped the reins, and the horse picked up its pace. Emma couldn't hear the river over the sound of the wheels, but she could smell it from here—a rich, damp smell that held green weeds and mud and wet stones.

But did she want someone to catch her at the bottom of the drop? Or did she want someone to hold her hand and jump with her, knowing that, come what may, he would never let go and they would take the journey together?

As Calvin tied up the horse at the rail in the little parking area, then handed her out of the buggy, she was no closer to answering his question than she had been the first time he'd asked it.

If only she could go back in time to that lunch at Karen's. If she had known what would happen afterward, she would have stayed in her own room and locked the door.

The county kept a walking path maintained beside the river, wide enough for two people. In the spring it was too muddy to stroll on, but the good weather lately had dried out all but the lowest spots close to the water. Tree branches nodded over their heads, and to the left, a pair of ducks chivvied their little ones, as fluffy as kittens, into a clump of grasses for the night.

Everything, it seemed, was pairing off and having children.

Spring must be a terrible time for Carrie, who would see babies everywhere except in her own home.

"Did...did you enjoy your ride on the train when you went to New York?" Calvin asked at last, when the silence could no longer be filled by the rush of the river and the sound of birds settling in the trees. "I went to Florida on the train a couple of times to see family, and once to upstate New York to see my cousins, who moved out there a couple of years ago."

"I did enjoy it. It was very comfortable, and the trip was faster than I thought it would be."

"Anytime you ride in an *Englisch* vehicle, that's the case." He chuckled, as if he'd made a joke. "What about boats? Do you like those?"

"I've never been in anything but a rowboat on this very river. And the inner tubes, that day with Joshua."

"Ah. Joshua." He fell silent again. Then, "I don't want to impose, Emma, but if it were to get about that you and I were seeing each other—" *If? I think you mean when.* "—it would look bad, what with the rumors that he is courting you as well."

"But the truth is that I'm courting neither of you." Oh, dear. She hadn't meant that to sound quite so abrupt. "The grapevine will say what it wants," she said more gently. "I know the truth, and so do you."

"Yes, but I wouldn't want it to get back to Mollie and Barbara that their father was seeing a woman who was—who wasn't—I mean—"

Emma stepped away from him out onto a big rock that jutted into the water. It was clear from the way the grass and undergrowth had been trodden down that this was a popular diving place in the summer. "You mean you wouldn't want your girls to hear you were courting a loose woman, *nix?*"

He frowned, as if her bluntness pained him. Best he get used to that. "I just meant that if you made it plain to Joshua that you wouldn't be seeing him anymore, it would be better for all of us."

"He is my friend, as you are," she said slowly. "How would you feel if I said such a thing to you?"

"It's not the same, Emma. A friend is someone you shake hands with after church. A man who brings in the dish you made to a potluck is something different."

So was a man who bought you ice cream in public. "People make too much of that. He is trying to establish himself here. I think a misstep or two is forgivable."

"I don't think it was a misstep. I think he was using you. Using your good reputation to—as you say—establish himself."

This very fear had been lurking in the shadows in the back of her mind, and it made her angry that he would reach in, turn up the lamp, and force her to look at it. If Lena had done so, or Amelia or Carrie, she would have humbled herself and let them help her face it. But not Calvin, who had shouldered his way into her life and was now telling her what she should do as if they were already married.

"How can you say such a thing of *ein Bruder?*" was all she could manage without lashing out and giving him the rough side of her tongue.

"If you are honest with yourself, you'll see that I'm only trying to give you good counsel, even leaving myself and my girls out of it. He has always been a problem, has Joshua. You said yourself he led you to ride those inner tubes away down the river, putting both of you in danger and putting your *Daed* to a whole lot of trouble."

"We were ten!"

"But it was a sign of things to come. A character that was set even at ten has not changed much. You were lucky he didn't lead you astray in other ways. I've heard some very bad things since he's come back to town."

"Those things happened before he joined church. He told me about them himself." She clutched at a straw of fact. "Besides, if Bishop Daniel has forgiven him and welcomed him back into the *Gmee*, then you shouldn't put yourself above him and keep bringing up the past."

"Are you defending your childhood friend, Emma?" He gazed at her, but the twilight had deepened to the point that she couldn't see his eyes clearly, and once again she'd left her glasses at home. At this rate she would need to wear them on the top of her head, to keep them handy while talking to men. "Or the man he became?"

"I'm not defending anyone. I'm setting the facts straight about a brother with full membership in the church."

"If all these things are true, then why is he deceiving the *Gmee* by pretending to court you? And if you do not intend to marry him, why do you permit it?"

What was he, the voice of her conscience? "He has been my friend for many years and I enjoy his company," she said lamely. "There is nothing wrong with that. No one is being deceitful."

"I feel deceived."

Between the rasping of her conscience and his relentless worrying of the subject, the ends of her temper were beginning to fray. "Why should you? You are doing exactly the same things with me as he is—coming to the house, being seen together in public. What makes you different from him?"

"Because he is using you as a shield, and I am trying to court you." His voice sounded patient, but under it all she heard the beginnings of exasperation.

"Why me, Calvin? Why now, and not years ago, when we were all running around together?" *If you're going to make me face the truth, then I'll make you do the same.*

"Because…when I met…why would you ask me such a thing?"

"I want to know why I'm good enough to be mother to your girls now, but I wasn't back then. I'm the same woman. I've lived in the same place, and seen you in the same church meetings all my life. Why would you not choose me then?"

He stared at her, his mouth opening and closing. "*Ich— Ich wisse nichts.* Perhaps I did not know you so well then. And you were younger than me. I met Rose Ann before you were of age to marry." His voice got stronger as the current of his thought swelled into a stream. "I've seen you with your family, and especially caring for your *Mamm* and *Daed.* As I said before, I've seen your tenderness of heart and your uncomplaining service to your parents. Those are qualities I want in a wife—qualities my girls would do well to have in front of them."

"Uncomplaining service?" Was that what he wanted? Whatever happened to being partners in this life, helping one another and lifting one another up? "I serve my mother out of love."

"And hopefully you would do the same for me and my *Kinner.*" He smiled, but Emma ducked her head and focused on getting off the rock and onto the path, heading back to the buggy.

"How do you feel about a woman who writes, Calvin?"

"Writes?" He quickened his steps to keep up with her. "Most women write their letters back and forth. Rose Ann always did, and the girls write to their cousins and aunts all the time."

"I don't just mean letters. I mean articles. Essays. Letters to the editor."

"Editor? As in the newspaper? Writing for that?"

"Yes."

"Emma, my dear friend, women don't write to the papers."

"My articles and letters to the editor are printed in *Family Life*, the *Budget*, and the *Whinburg Weekly*."

He stopped, but when she didn't, he hustled to catch up with her. "Emma, this is not right. Our women have no public voice. Their voices are to be heard in the home."

"This one is heard in both places."

"Does our bishop know of this?"

"I think so. Mary Lapp has my recipe for pickled beans in her recipe box, and she cut it out of *Family Life*. I recognized the print."

Either he was out of breath, or he was huffing with indignation. "Emma, you must stop this. You are setting yourself up for exposure. Putting yourself out in public, where people can ridicule you and bring the wrong kind of attention on you—and therefore on God's people."

"For pickled beans?" She couldn't help herself. If she gave him enough rope, he would hang himself with it, figuratively speaking, and then she would know for certain what to do.

"You know that's not what I mean. You are setting yourself apart. Bringing attention to yourself, not just by our people, but by the *Englisch* readers as well. It's not right."

"What it brings is a little money, which we can certainly use."

"Even worse, then, to be paid for setting the wrong kind of example."

Now, wait just a minute. "Back there you said I would be the right kind of example to your girls."

"Back there I did not know of this writing. Promise me that if we keep seeing each other, you'll stop."

"I can't promise that." She'd better keep quiet about Alvin Esch and the correspondence courses, that was for sure. "I've been writing for most of my life. Except lately. Mamm says she hasn't heard my typewriter going late at night so much, and I suppose she's right."

"Your mother knows of this and permits it?"

"Calvin, settle down. It's not like I'm fomenting unrest in the streets of Whinburg. I write essays about spring, about caring for hens, about—about the dingle-dangles the boys hang in the storm fronts of their buggies. Nothing harmful. Nothing very interesting, really, except to people who like pickled beans and spring flowers."

"It's not the content, it's the fact that you do it at all, Emma. That is what bothers me. Please say you'll give it up."

"I already told you. I won't. I can't. Even if I were never published again, I would still write." And then there was the book. All the more reason to be glad she had never told anyone except Mamm, Amelia, and Carrie the reason she had gone to New York.

"I could not have this in my home." He sounded so distressed that her heart melted a little.

She climbed the bank up to the parking lot, now deserted except for the horse, who whickered at them. "Then I cannot be in your home, I guess," she told him gently, standing by the horse's head and patting its nose as Calvin untied the reins.

"You would give up a chance at marriage and a home of your own for this—this foolishness? I cannot believe this of you, Emma."

"I don't see it as foolishness."

"Then I'm very sorry. More sorry than I can say. Because I do enjoy your company, and I thought you enjoyed mine."

"I do, Calvin. But if you want me, then you must take all of me, typewriter included."

He helped her into the buggy and did not answer.

The river sounded very loud in the silence on the way home.

CHAPTER 14

Emma and Carrie knew what had happened the moment they walked into Amelia's house. Carrie grabbed Emma's hand, swinging the door shut behind her with the other. "Emma, look at her face. She's glowing. Amelia, are you—did he—?"

Amelia came forward to take their away bonnets and somehow they all wound up holding each other's hands. "Yes—I am—Eli proposed Sunday night, before he went away."

With a squeal of delight, Carrie pulled them both into a hug, and Emma let her own cares go on a flood of happiness. Amelia's eyes sparkled as she said, "Such excitement. Were you like Mamm, and beginning to think he would never speak?"

"I knew he would speak." Emma rescued her bonnet and hung it by its ribbons on the peg by the door. "Any man who looks at a woman the way Eli looks at you is going to ask. It was only a matter of time. I'm so happy for you, *Liewi*."

"And it's not as if he hid his intentions, what with all this coming and going and getting ready to build your new shop," Carrie pointed out. Amelia led them into the front room, where the quilt was laid out on the floor, ready to be marked. "Are you going to have it announced in church on Sunday?"

Amelia nodded. "And Eli will have it published in Lebanon. It will seem strange, hearing such a thing at this time of year."

"But... the shop is going to be built this summer, isn't it?" Emma took off her shawl and draped it over a chair, then dug in her bag for her collection of plastic marking templates. "Aren't you going to wait until November to be married?"

"I would rather not. When Eli comes back on Friday, we're going to visit Bishop Daniel to see if he's available before the end of June. Since it's the second marriage for both of us, there is no need for a big wedding. Most of the men won't be able to come, anyway, since the fields won't wait for me to be married. It will probably be here, with family and close friends only."

"Does that include us?" Emma tried to keep her face straight and serious.

"If it doesn't, I'm not going," Amelia shot back, and laughter rang through the house. If anyone had been passing on the road, they probably would have heard it all the way out there. "I hope you will both stand up with me and be my *Newesitzern.*"

Of course they would. "I was wondering if there would be more than one wedding late this spring," Carrie said slyly. "I hear *someone* was riding in a buggy and going very slowly on the river road the other night."

"Who on earth would you hear that from?" Emma demanded.

"Oh, a little bird."

"Little birds would do better to pay attention to their own nests and not chatter about other people. Gossip is a sin."

"Goodness," Amelia put in mildly. "This must be serious to get you so worked up, Emma."

"I think it must be." Carrie brought her marking pencils to the edge of the quilt. "Amelia, if we're going to plan *two* late-season weddings, you'd better—"

"Carrie," Emma choked out. "*Schtobbe Dich.*" She blinked, but it did no good. Her eyes flooded with unexpected, ridiculous tears, and she dashed them away with her sleeve.

Carrie's mouth hung open on her unfinished sentence, and then her eyes filled, too. "Emma. Oh, Emma, *Schatzi*, I didn't mean to—you know I would never hurt you for the world." She stepped over the corner of the quilt and took her in a fierce hug—so fierce that Emma could feel the bones of her arms. "Please, please forgive me."

"Of course," she whispered brokenly, the organdy of Carrie's covering soft against her cheek. She pulled her hankie out of her sleeve and mopped her eyes and nose. "I don't know what is wrong with me. We're supposed to be celebrating with Amelia, not getting water spots on this quilt."

"Celebrations include laughter and tears," Amelia said quietly. "Why don't you tell us what's going on?"

So she did. All of it—the disastrous walk along the river, Calvin's ultimatum about her writing, even his poor opinion of Joshua Steiner. At this last, Carrie bristled, but Emma couldn't tell if it was indignation on her behalf, or Joshua's.

"But Emma, I don't understand," Amelia said when Emma's voice finally trailed away into the silence of relief—the way the body relaxes after a boil is lanced. "How did it get this far with Calvin? Do you mean to say that he actually proposed?"

"*Ja*...I mean, *nei*, he didn't actually say the words, 'Will you marry me?' It's more like he was—he was plowing the ground, getting it ready for seed. Except that he ran into a couple of great big rocks, and that was the end of that."

Now it was Amelia's turn to try for a straight face, until her dancing eyes gave her away. "Poor Calvin. I bet his plow will never be the same."

"Emma put a good bend in it, that's for sure," Carrie agreed, and they broke into giggles.

"You girls, try to be serious for two minutes," Emma begged, digging for her handkerchief again. Her stomach hurt from laughing, and her eyes stung from tears. How upside down was that? "Poor Calvin doesn't deserve this."

"He doesn't deserve you for a wife, either," Amelia said. "I don't know why he's trying to court you, when it seems he wants to change nearly everything about you. He should try someone who's already perfect."

"I think Eli beat him to it." Carrie bumped her with one shoulder.

"I'm a long way from perfect, and don't you say anything different." Amelia bent and fanned out her plastic templates, dropping some of the smaller ones in the middle of the quilt's plain blocks. "The good *Gott* made Emma just the way she is, and it makes me tired that a man can't see that without giving in to the temptation to chip off the bits he doesn't like."

"I don't doubt that there are bits that *should* be chipped off," Emma said.

"Then that's God's work, over the course of your life," Carrie said. "Not some man's. And what is Calvin doing talking about marriage with you, anyway? I thought you cared for Grant Weaver."

"I do," Emma moaned. "God is punishing me for coveting somebody else's husband."

"He is no one's husband now," Amelia told her. "Come now, and let's decide on patterns."

Carrie knelt at the end of the quilt and laid patterns on it, switching them back and forth, trying different combinations. But Emma couldn't let it go. She had to get this off her chest once and for all. "He may be widowed, but he is still Lavina's husband. He's still in love with her."

Carrie gazed thoughtfully at a stylized flower pattern, and centered it in a plain block. "How do you know?"

"From his actions. He kept in touch with her those two years she was gone. He filed that missing persons report. He went all the way to Missouri to fetch her ashes. Not even her family would do those things."

"But he and the children had dinner with us on Sunday, and he seemed just the way he always is," Amelia said. "Quiet. Kind. You have to remember, some men do things just because they are the right thing to do."

"Maybe you have a chance now," Carrie said.

"I don't have a chance with anyone," Emma confessed. She could not let her heart turn in that direction, like a shivering child to a warm stove. She had burned herself quite enough already. "I'm not sure I can even have a friendship with Calvin now. He thinks I'm the worst sort of sinner."

"Imagine. A woman who speaks in public. I bet he went home and started reading the papers, looking for things signed E.S.," Carrie said.

"And I hope he enjoyed every one," Amelia said stoutly. "There is nothing wrong with the things you write—or with the fact that you write them. He's only being very—"

"Stodgy?" Carrie supplied helpfully.

"—plain. Maybe it's just as well. I wouldn't want to live

with someone whose standards are so high he can't see over them."

"Me either," Carrie agreed. "I like this rose in the unpieced blocks, don't you? Are there roses in our green fields?"

"Only if we want them." Relief was trickling into Emma's heart with every word her friends said. Maybe she wasn't such a bad person, despite what Calvin thought. Maybe God wasn't pointing her to Calvin after all, and that giant block of resistance in her chest that had made her blurt out the fact that she wrote had been put there by a greater hand than she knew.

"Listen to your gut," Pap used to say to her brothers when they had to make some big decision. "Use your head, but listen to your gut."

But that didn't mean she could look in the direction of that warm stove.

Carrie's quick hands sifted out all the floral motifs in their collection. "I think we have enough for a different flower in every row. What do you think?"

"We could," Amelia allowed. "Then your butterflies could dance among the flowers in our green fields." She slid a glance to Emma. "What's your opinion, Emma?"

She dragged her thoughts away from her own sorry situation and tried to focus on their quilt for her friends' sakes. With all the time they were putting into this, the least she could do was offer an opinion when it was asked for.

"I like the rose," she said. "But if it were me, I would use just that one pattern in the unpieced blocks. Otherwise it will look too busy. We want it to speak a clear message, don't we, not babble."

Amelia smiled at her. "That's so like you. All right, then, if Carrie agrees?" Amelia's tone carried an odd emphasis, and

Carrie nodded quickly. "Do you still like the idea of the feathers on the borders twining around a central pillar?"

Emma could just imagine it. "I'd like to see that most of all. It will be the most beautiful thing—especially as I don't think one has been done that way in our district. I've only seen them up Bird-in-Hand way, in that big quilt store."

"Done." Amelia sounded so satisfied you'd have thought *she* was getting the quilt.

Wait a moment. Oh, my, yes, what a good idea. How could she not have thought of this before? This quilt should not go to the auction. It should go to Amelia and Eli for a wedding gift. As soon as she and Carrie were back in the buggy and heading home, she would suggest it and see what Carrie thought.

Carrie knelt and smoothed a hand over the piecing. "We could do simple diamonds on the pieced blocks, and stitch in the ditch. That would make the rose medallions stand out even more."

Amelia and Emma nodded, and they got to work with the marking pencils. The twining feathers were sure to be a challenge, so they left that until later. Meanwhile, the rose medallions went into each plain block—and there were a lot of them. It took every minute of their two hours, and on the way home, Carrie chattered almost without stopping about men and chickens and where Melvin was this week, flushing customers out of the bushes for the pallet shop.

Emma couldn't get a word in edgewise about making their quilt a wedding gift.

Which was all right, she supposed. Because she'd had just about enough talk of courtship and weddings for one day.

* * *

Amelia and Eli must have made good use of their time, because on Sunday, after the preaching on the subject of Pentecost but before the final hymn, Bishop Daniel made public the news that they planned to marry on the first Tuesday in July.

Amid the handshakes and congratulations out in Carrie and Melvin's yard afterward, only one sour note was struck. Instead of coming over and greeting her as he had done the last couple of church Sundays, Calvin King made sure there was always a crowd between himself and Emma, and when she finally did manage to catch his eye and smile, he looked down and away, as if whatever his brother Martin had been saying just then was vitally important.

Maybe it was. Much more important than the death of a friendship. How little it took to make someone feel invisible once again. Emma sighed and went into the kitchen to give Carrie a hand with the lunch.

The state of the cupboards in the Miller household had improved in recent months. Since Melvin no longer had to depend on his skills as a farmer to earn his bread, the bread coming in these days not only had butter on it, but sometimes jam as well. Carrie was beginning to put on a little weight. Her figure might still be wand slim, but at least her collarbones and elbows didn't stick out quite so gracelessly.

The women of the district silently pitched in to help with the food when it was the Millers' turn to host church. Today Carrie's *Buhnesupp* was supplemented by a raft of pickled beets, dill pickles, cold sliced meat, canned peaches and cherries, jars of jam, and loaves of bread. No one would leave the Miller house hungry, but first everything had to be set out on the tables in the basement.

One thing about their farmhouse—it was big. Too big

for the two of them; as Carrie had once told them at one of their quilting frolics, the sound of emptiness where there should have been the squeals and laughter of children was the thing she found the hardest to bear. But maybe things would be different now that Melvin had steady work, even though it took him around the county talking to people. If Carrie could put on some weight, maybe her poor little body could stop worrying about its next meal and turn its attention to fertility. Some folks thought they should have moved back to Melvin's home district, so that his extensive family could see them through, but that would have brought its own set of problems.

Emma sent up a prayer of thanks that she was the daughter of Lena Stolzfus and not the daughter-in-law of Aleta Miller.

No one would have expected Amelia to join the helpers to-day of all days, but she appeared at Emma's elbow not five minutes later. "I thought you would be with Eli." Emma took one plate of cold sliced ham from Amelia and a second from six-year-old Elam, who had carried it down the stairs with such care it might have been made of crystal. She set them out on a table that had no meat yet.

"He's gone out to the barn to talk with the men. One of Young Joe's boys is moving back to Whinburg as a harness maker, and they're all excited about having one so close. He'll be scheduled for six months out from the sound of it."

"They'll be back. Lunch is nearly ready." She surveyed the table. "Everyone pitched in. It looks nice, doesn't it? *Denki*, Elam, for bringing that ham. It's exactly what this table needed."

"We're going to have a new *Daed*," Elam confided as Emma bent to hug him. "Bishop Daniel said it, right out loud in church."

"I heard him myself. And are you happy with that?" she asked gravely, as if the fate of the wedding hung on his answer.

He considered the question with equal gravity. "I think so," he said at last. "Eli made me a wooden horse, with legs that go back and forth."

"Did he?" Emma raised her eyebrows, impressed. "That's a good sign in a *Daed*, I would say. And what did you make him?"

Elam gazed at her, distress filling his eyes. "I didn't make him anything."

"Just think how happy he would be to know you're as glad he will be your *Daed* as he is that you will be his son."

Elam nodded, then looked up at Amelia with urgency in every line of his face. "Mamm, can I go to the barn? I have to ask Uncle Melvin if I can make something for Eli."

"On a Sunday?" Amelia shook her head. "Tomorrow after the washing is hung, and you're home from school, I'll take you to the shop and Uncle Melvin can help you. And if he's not there, Brian will be. You know..." She paused, looking thoughtful. "Only yesterday Eli mentioned to me how much he needed a nice round drawer pull for his dresser. The top one fell off one day and he hasn't seen it since."

"But I don't know how to make a drawer pull."

Emma hugged him again. "You will after Uncle Melvin and Brian show you. I bet you could make a whole mountain of drawer pulls and sell them at a stand at the end of your lane. I bet the tourists would pay a dollar apiece for something you made."

Elam looked amazed and a little nervous at the prospect, and Amelia took his shoulders and turned him toward the stairs. "Go and find your brother and tell him it's time to eat."

When he'd run upstairs, Amelia gave Emma a fond glance. "Someday you will make a wonderful mother. You're always so encouraging, and you have *wunderbaar* ideas for the little ones."

"Melvin may not think so if he has a full day on Monday."

"Melvin is like you. He'll make time for Elam and his little project, never fear."

"Did Eli really lose a drawer pull?"

"He did. If he had a cat, I'd say it might have batted it out of the room, but he doesn't."

"It sounds like he's not paying attention to what happens in his old life. Too busy looking forward to the new."

"He's not the only one. And *denkes* for teaching my boy that it's not what others do for us that makes us love them, but what we do for them."

Emma's mind flashed to Grant, working on the *Daadi Haus* and making porches so solid they would last for fifty years. But that was silly. He had been paid for the job. It wasn't the same thing at all. But the meals she had fed him and his crew? Ah, now, there was a labor of love. Luckily, she'd done it with no thought of any return, or she'd be even more hopeless than she was now.

The men began to come in, and the women after them, separating themselves on either side of the room. After they'd said a silent grace, Emma moved between the tables with a pitcher of water, filling glasses and seeing that everyone had what he or she needed. She would eat afterward, along with Carrie and the other ladies acting as helpers today.

And every moment, she was acutely aware of Grant Weaver sitting under the window at the end of one of the men's tables. He kept an eye on his girls, even though they were being well looked after by their Yoder aunties. His little boy sat on his knee, a napkin tied around his neck, as he shared food from his father's plate with chubby fingers.

Emma refilled the pitcher and made her way down the aisle. A bar of sunlight fell through the window and illuminated father and son. Grant looked up, and she couldn't help but smile at the picture the little boy made on his *Daed*'s knee, face happily smeared with bread and jam, with a bean from his soup stuck to one cheek. Grant's gaze met hers, and the light struck his eyes just enough to make their color more brilliant against his tan skin and brown beard.

And then he smiled, too.

Emma had not seen him smile fully before. All those breakfasts across from him and she had never seen that light on his face, never seen the humor dancing around the edges of his lips. As Karen said, he had a hard row to hoe, and real, open smiles were probably more costly for him than other men. But oh, what a gift it was to her—a gift beyond price!

"Emma."

Above the clatter of cutlery and conversation, his voice struck her heart like a gong.

"Emma, the pitcher."

At that moment, one of the Yoder nephews laughed and leaned away from her, and she realized with a jolt that the pitcher had tipped and ice water was cascading down onto her skirt and the young man's shirt.

"Oh, my goodness, Myron, I'm so sorry." She grabbed a napkin and began to dab at his shoulder and arm.

"It's no trouble, Emma," he said, apparently not one bit concerned. "I didn't get that spot during my bath last night anyway."

The men laughed and Emma couldn't get away from there fast enough. Every time a man laughed during the rest of the meal, she was convinced it was because someone had told him about absentminded Emma Stolzfus, so busy mooning over a man's smile that she'd poured a pitcher of water on Myron instead of in his glass.

That smile had been costly, all right. If her pride had been money, she'd have paid a heavy price.

And it would have been worth every cent.

CHAPTER 15

It took so little to feed a woman's heart, even though in the long run—as with the doughnuts and pastries she loved—no growth or nourishment would come of it. And yet, during the next two weeks, as Emma threw herself into preparations for Amelia's wedding, the vision of Grant and his little boy sustained her. Maybe it was the *gut Gott* reminding her that He provided moments of beauty and love to His children. Carrie and Amelia seemed to find these moments daily, but for Emma, it was harder. Was it because she was too practical? Or because she was too busy and self-absorbed?

Maybe she should be like them, and open her heart a little more to the simpler gifts. That was a way to ward off disappointment, wasn't it? Gratitude was a sure cure for a number of human failings.

The Friday before the wedding, friends and neighbors descended on Amelia's house for a work frolic. Her brothers and their wives all came—even the brother from Smicksburg who was set to move onto the home place sometime this year. Melvin and Carrie rolled into the yard with a buggy full of linens and carpentry tools, and David Yoder from her pallet shop came as well with a bucketful of paintbrushes.

While the men organized a painting party for the house, chicken coop, and barn, the women divided into teams and tackled windows, floors, carpets, and furniture. If it had a surface, it was scrubbed and polished. If it had a nap, it was cleaned or washed. Smokey, Elam's little gray cat, vanished through the back door when the brooms came out, and Emma didn't see him for the rest of the day.

What she did see, as she polished panes of glass in the upstairs bedroom with vinegar and newspaper, was Grant Weaver driving in about midmorning in the familiar spring wagon, loaded with his own tools and a few lengths of lumber. Not one of the ladies busy scrubbing floors and doing windows in the other bedrooms knew what it cost her to stay and finish what she was doing and not dash downstairs to ask Amelia what was going on. Surely he wasn't going to break ground for the new workshop, and make a big mess at the front of the property before the wedding? That didn't seem like him at all.

She polished a little faster, though, and when she went into one of the other rooms to help the window washer there, she made sure it was one where she could look out and see the wagon parked next to the barn.

Ah. Mystery solved. He was replacing a couple of boards on the north side, where the worst of the weather tended to wear on buildings. He would get the job done well before the painters finished with the house and moved on to the barn.

She didn't have much time for more than a glimpse, though. Ruth Lehman directed the work parties with the skill and keen eye of a traffic policeman—even Amelia meekly submitted to her mother's firm suggestions, probably because it was safer to do what she said. It was a fine day, so at lunchtime Emma and Carrie set up tables outside on the lawn for the food that everyone had brought. Salads, fried chicken, thick slices of ham with pink-rimmed cinnamon apple slices, bread, rolls, and half a dozen different kinds of pickles disappeared as hungry helpers wolfed it down.

"*Denki* for helping me serve," Amelia whispered as she passed Emma with another tray of cut vegetables. "And don't forget to eat—I'm saving the best of the desserts for you and me and Carrie."

"What would Eli say if he knew he didn't get your best?" Emma teased.

"The laborer is worthy of her hire," Amelia shot back, and then she was off to the kitchen with two empty trays.

"Watch out, here comes Emma with the water," Joshua Steiner said from a seat just ahead of where she was pouring. "Anybody got an umbrella?"

In the smattering of laughter, Emma's face burned. Try as she might to keep her hand steady, some of the water slopped over the edges of the glass she was filling. Thank goodness they were out on the lawn. It hid a multitude of sins.

"There's no call to embarrass our sister, Joshua," Grant Weaver said from across the table. Emma's heart swelled with gratitude. Not only had he seen she was there, he had come to her defense as well.

In public. This was a first.

"Aw, Emma knows I don't mean any harm." As if to prove it, he held out his glass. "I'm just glad it's not coffee."

Again, chuckles filled the air, but Emma had regained her composure. "I wouldn't say any more, Joshua, since I'm the one with the cold water and you're the one trapped in his seat."

Now the chuckles were a little louder, and she risked a

quick glance at Grant. He was drinking from his own glass, but she could swear she saw the beginnings of a smile. All the same, she made quick work of the rest of the row, and pulled an empty tray to take it into the kitchen, where she could savor the moment in relative privacy.

There she found Amelia, Carrie, and Ruth with their plates, leaning against the counters and eating during the lull while everyone had what they needed outside.

"The house looks nice with a new coat of paint, Amelia. Is this for me?" She tucked into the full plate that waited on the kitchen table.

"I can't believe they have the house done already. The outbuildings will be finished by supper at this rate, and Eli and I can do the trim tomorrow."

"And you have your dress done? I didn't see it anywhere while we were cleaning."

"It's in the bedroom closet, in a plastic bag. I got it finished Wednesday night."

"Did you pick the blue or the purple?"

"Blue. Purple is for the mourning I'm leaving behind. Besides, blue is a wedding color."

"And the white cape and apron are with it?" Ruth asked. "Lucky thing they accommodate all sizes. After two children and ten years, they will still fit."

Color burned into Amelia's cheeks. "I made a new cape and apron, Mamm, out of fresh organdy. I'm not using the ones from my wedding to Enoch."

Ruth shook her head. "It's a waste of money. Those things have only been used once, and I know for a fact they haven't so much as a water spot on them. Mostly because you hardly ate anything that day."

"We have all new clothes to be married in, Mamm,"

Amelia said quietly. "Eli is content to live in a house another man provided, but I want to come to him in clothes no other man has seen when we say our vows."

"Hmph. It's wasteful, that's what. What are you going to do with the first set?"

"They're in my cedar chest, and they'll stay there. Whoever buries me can choose whichever ones they like; I'll be in no position to argue about it."

Ruth sniffed and attacked her macaroni casserole with vigor. There was nothing she could say; everyone knew that the bridal couple's clothes were all new when they were married—even, Emma supposed, the second time around. Only Ruth Lehman would pinch a penny so thin that it would break tradition.

She cleaned her plate with relish. "That was wonderful *gut*, Amelia. Thank you for saving me some."

"Only the best for *meine Freind*." Amelia's smile flashed. "We took a little of everything before we sent the plates out. And look what I have for dessert. Orange poppyseed cake with orange cream cheese frosting. Your favorite."

Emma groaned. "Now I wish I hadn't eaten that macaroni and cheese. You're going to make me fat."

"You've worked hard enough today to wear off any calories in advance," Carrie told her. "Come and have some, quick, and then we can take the plates out. I've started the coffee so it should be ready in a minute."

On the stove, the big coffeepot gurgled as if it agreed. Amelia's orange poppyseed cake was enough to make you wish you could take things with you to heaven. Emma savored every bite, and then laid three trays of squares, cookies, and sliced cake across her arms, going out the door sideways as Carrie held it for her.

After everyone had finished dessert, she took a moment to breathe outside and visit a little before she went back in to help with the dishes. When someone came up on her left, she turned, expecting to find one of the other helpers.

Instead, Joshua Steiner smiled at her. "No hard feelings about my little joke, I hope?"

"I think the joke was on you in the end."

"I should be used to that." A hummingbird hovered over them, as if trying to figure out if there was any sweetness there, and they watched its zooming path into the trees. "I was hoping to run into you."

"You know where I live, Joshua. You could just come for a visit."

"I think Calvin might get a little upset if I did that. I missed the boat, didn't I?"

"There is no boat. We're just friends, the same as you and me."

"But friends want to be together. I haven't seen you and Calvin within ten feet of each other all day. I almost wonder if the rumors are wrong."

"Rumors usually are. But you and I are together now, visiting as friends will."

"No doubt causing more rumors."

"Which is worse—gossiping, or behaving in a way that provokes it?"

He grinned, and she realized he hadn't taken her seriously. "I had no idea talking to you was so dangerous to the spirits of my brothers and sisters. But I guess someone has to keep them exercised."

"Joshua, will you be sensible? I'm beginning to think that's all you want me for—to get people talking so they don't realize what you're really up to."

The humor drained from his face. "What do you think I'm up to?"

"I hope you're up to the standard God expects from all His children."

Across the lawn, little Katie and Sarah Weaver carried Zachary between them like a hammock slung between two trees. The little boy shrieked, half fearful and half laughing, as he tried to see where they were going.

"If I'm up to anything, it's trying to get your attention for more than the space of a lecture. Would you like to go for a ride this evening?"

His bluntness surprised an equally blunt reply out of her. "*Nei.*"

It took him a second to recover. "Why not? Do you have another date?"

"Joshua, I can't just drop everything when you crook your finger. I have dinner to get for Mamm and work to do."

He gazed at her for a long moment. "This isn't going to happen, is it?"

She didn't toy with him by pretending not to understand. "No, I don't think so. We don't seem to knit together as well as we did when we were children, do we?" Like trees, they had grown up and out, their branches pushing each other away instead of intertwining.

"I had hoped we'd be able to...and I'm still willing to try."

"I don't think there's any point, Joshua." Her heart would never unmake its choice, and she had learned that sometimes it was better to be content with nothing than to settle for second best. "I think we make better friends than...anything else."

"We still have that, at least." He shoved his hands in his

pockets. Katie had dropped Zachary's feet and was tickling his ribs, much to his delight.

"And I hope we always do."

Someone had better rescue little Zachary before the tickling got too rough and brought on tears. She flashed a smile at Joshua and ran over to the children, picking Zachary up and cuddling him. Katie giggled and ran to her sister, who was swinging on the gate into Moses Yoder's pasture.

Zachary subsided against her chest, and Emma soaked in the unexpected luxury of an armful of little boy. Grant Weaver joined her when she reached Amelia's flower border, and she handed him over. "I'm sorry you had to rescue him from his wild sisters."

Emma nodded. *Do not blush. Do not overreact and get all silly. He is speaking to you as any friend would do.* "Tickling is all in fun, but it's one of those things that can become not so fun all too quickly."

Zachary put his arms around his father's neck and closed his eyes. The girls had worn him out. Grant nodded toward the border. "Amelia, she likes flowers, I see."

"She likes the tall ones. I think these are delphiniums here, along the walk. And the hydrangeas against the house look like they're ready to burst into bloom at any moment."

"It would be nice if they did by Tuesday."

She smiled. "Maybe they will."

"What flowers have you planted at the *Daadi Haus*?"

"Some anemones, and the bank of poppies will come up by itself. I also have bleeding heart, fuchsia, and peonies, all blooming like mad."

"They will show nicely against the white house."

"They do, thanks to you." She dared a smile directly at him.

"Showy flowers, for a woman who does not make a show of herself."

What did he mean? Was that a bad thing? "God made them as they are," she said a little uncertainly. "As He makes all of us."

"I had heard things lately that seemed...out of the usual way for you. And now I see that Calvin King has not spoken with you today, except to say *denkes* for his coffee." Grant gazed across the lawn in the direction of the expanse where Eli planned the workshop. "This seems odd for two people who are...friends."

Oh. Oh, my. This seems odd. And personal. And wonderful.

Emma took a deep breath to try to stop her heart from taking off at a gallop. "Calvin was...thinking thoughts that were perhaps...mistaken."

"Was he?" Grant's thoughtful gaze met hers. She could fall into those calm eyes and never come out. "So the talk was not true?"

"I—I don't know. It seems he wanted to come courting, but...now he doesn't."

"Why would that be? Calvin is a fine man, and certainly in need of a capable, loving mother for his *Kinner*." The way he said it was almost like a compliment. Her very soul warmed with it.

"He is, and he does, but...I am not that woman." He gazed at her, and somehow the words fell out of her mouth into the air between them. "He would not let me write."

"Ah," was all he said. Then, "He did not know who the E.S. is who writes to the papers?"

She shook her head. "He asked me to give it up, but I could not. I would give up writing for the papers if I was married and didn't need the income, but I could not give up writing for myself. He would want even that, you see. A whole sacrifice, not a partial one, tied to the altar and given willingly."

Like the noon sun, Grant's long gaze seemed to pierce every curtain inside her that she would have pulled shut against the light. What was she doing, babbling her deepest secrets to this man? Now he would tell her that Calvin had been absolutely right to require that sacrifice—that a wife and mother should be focused on her responsibilities in the home and not fill her head with nonsense that brought no lasting profit.

Except that it did. For her.

Emma braced herself.

"Emma…a woman like you, handy in the kitchen, steady, kind, loyal…how is it you've never married? It cannot be because of the writing."

The words struck her like a hammer on a bell, her whole body echoing with them. "I…I had Mamm and Pap to look after. And now someone needs to keep an eye on Mamm."

"But she has a big family, and many children to care for her."

Drat him. Drat him for asking when he was the last one who should ever want the answer. "I guess I never found anyone to suit me."

"I think you would suit plenty of men hereabouts. I just saw Joshua Steiner a minute ago, for instance."

"We are just friends. And I'm not so sure you're right." The words fell out of her mouth, and she would have given anything to grab them back and swallow them. How self-pitying they sounded! She tried to put a patch on a bad job. "I'm taller than many."

"And smarter than some."

"I'm not much on conversation."

"Words don't mean as much as actions do. I think you speak in that way all day long."

"I'm not—" She stopped. *Pretty, like Lavina was. Pretty and sparkling and always saying just the right thing.* Yet for Lavina, it had all turned out to be vanity and vexation of spirit.

"Not what?"

She pulled herself together. "Not going to talk about me anymore. It's time I got back to work before they finish the dishes without—"

Gravel crunched on the lane, and everyone standing outside on the lawn turned as an *Englisch* car crept out from under the trees and rolled to a stop in front of Amelia's flowerbeds. A low-slung car that looked as sleek as a cat fed cream every day.

Who could this be? A lost salesman? A guest for the wedding?

The door opened and a man unfolded himself from behind the wheel—a man wearing cream-colored pants and a plaid shirt in stripes of pink and pale blue.

Emma's blood froze in horror. She knew only one person who wore clothes like that.

"Afternoon. Um, *Guder Obed*, I guess I should say. They told me at the big farm up the road that Emma Stolzfus was over here." Tyler West pushed his sunglasses up into his hair and raised his eyebrows at the stunned, uncomprehending faces turned toward him. "Anybody know where I can find her?"

The blood rushed out of her head and Emma swayed, certain that for the first time in her life, she was about to faint.

But she couldn't do that. Not when every person outside had turned to gawk at her, and more were clustering inside at the windows. And just as the bending wheat indicates which way the wind is blowing, Tyler West had followed the collective gazes of her friends and neighbors and was coming toward her.

"Do you know this man?" Grant said quietly.

Emma dragged in a breath and forced her head to clear. "Yes. He is a...a friend from New York City."

Tyler's long stride brought him into hearing distance in just a few seconds. "Hullo, Emma. It's good to see you." He shook her hand. "Cold hands. I hope I'm not interrupting anything?"

It was obvious to a blind man that he had, but as she gathered her wits, long years of Lena's training kicked in. "We are having a work party for my friend Amelia Beiler. You remember I spoke of her?"

Amelia came out the front door and ran down the steps as if she'd been waiting all day for Tyler to show up. Tyler held out his hand and Amelia took it with a smile. "Tyler West," he said. "I've heard so much about you."

"And we have heard a lot about you, too. You are very welcome."

"Amelia is getting married on Tuesday," Emma explained. She would find Amelia later and fall on her neck in thanks for her easy greeting. "We're helping her get the house and yard ready."

"Tell me what I can do," he said instantly.

She looked him over. "I think your clothes would not survive it. Maybe you'd better—"

"I have other stuff in the car. Jeans."

To Emma's surprise, Grant leaned in, his hand outstretched. "We can always use another pair of hands. I am Grant Weaver."

Tyler hung on to his hand for a second longer than necessary—and that second told Emma that he had not forgotten a single thing she'd so unwisely babbled during their hours together in New York. "It's a pleasure to meet you, sir."

"Please. We do not use honorifics. Call me Grant."

"That'd be great, as long as you call me Tyler. What can I help you with?"

Tyler didn't look as though he'd be good for much except maybe drying dishes—or signing contracts. But if he thought the same, Grant didn't let a trace of it show on his face. "Can you swing a paintbrush?"

Tyler nodded. "I painted my apartment when I lived in Long Island. And I helped my dad paint our house when I was a teenager. I think I can I remember how to do it."

"I can show you. We're getting ready to start on the barn. Maybe you could change inside and then join us."

"Emma will show you," Amelia said. Clever Amelia, giving her a chance to find out what on earth he was doing here. And wonderful Grant, treating him as he would any other person, and assuming the best of him.

Tyler pulled a gym bag out of the trunk of his car and followed her into the house, where the women turned away and got busy with the dishes as if they had no interest whatsoever in the young *Englisch* man who had driven all the way from New York to find the Stolzfus spinster. This would totally eclipse any desire to wonder why she had been talking alone with the black sheep of the district—or its newest widower.

Emma supposed she should be thankful for small mercies.

"I guess you're wondering why I'm here," Tyler said in the hall.

Emma showed him into the bathroom. "I am, but we won't talk of it now. When we walk over to the barn we might have a minute."

He put a hand on her wrist while he held the bathroom door with the other. "Was that—?"

"Yes, it was, and not a single word from you, do you hear?"

"Yes, ma'am." He was grinning as if he'd just gotten the world's biggest joke as he closed the door.

Carrie met her in the kitchen doorway, her eyes huge. "Was that—?"

"Yes," she said in as low a tone as she could. "I'll tell you all about it later."

"I just guess you will. You sure know how to cause a sensation, Emma Stolzfus."

"It's not me. I didn't ask him to come."

"I'd like to know why he's here."

"So would I, believe me. But since he is here, Grant has claimed him for the painting crew. He'll be wanting to hightail it back to New York by the end of the day, just you watch."

"Grant? That's interesting."

"You have no idea."

Emma had never minded housework; in fact, she rather liked restoring order to chaos. But she had never been more thankful for a dozen extra people's dishes, or for an unending number of windows to wash, because it kept her mind off exactly what might be happening down at the barn.

Why, oh, why had she been such a *Plappermaul* and told Tyler West the secrets of her heart? With one sentence he could ruin even her nonexistent chances with Grant and make her the laughingstock of the entire district. Just by driving in, he'd interrupted what could have been a real conversation—one that might have given her a little insight into Grant's thoughts—and had given everyone something to talk about over their supper.

By five o'clock, people had begun packing their rags and brushes into their buggies, and Amelia and Eli stood hand in hand, waving and calling their thanks as people rolled down the lane. Emma planned to walk home over the fields, so she gave Amelia a hug and waved at Carrie as she and Melvin drove out of the yard. "I guess I'd better find out what's happened to Tyler West. Maybe Grant really did work him to death."

"I'll leave you to it. I need to put some supper together for my menfolk. If you see the boys, tell them to come in and wash up." With a smile at Eli that brought an answering smile of such love that it made Emma's heart hurt, the two of them climbed the steps and went into the house. Only four more days and it would be his home. In the meantime, he stayed with Martin King, as he had been doing all the months of his courtship.

Emma did her best not to run out to the barn, but it was a close thing.

As she approached the doors, she heard voices—two of which were the piping trebles of Matthew and Elam. Around the back, then. She rounded the corner to find Tyler and Grant up on ladders, painting the last of the boards up by the roofline. The two boys straddled the bases of the ladders, holding on to the sides as though their sheer strength alone were keeping them upright.

"*Aendi* Emma, look," Matthew said. "We're holding the ladders so Grant and Tyler don't fall down."

"And it's working," she said, speaking English so as not to be rude. "They're almost done, aren't they?" She gazed upward. "Did everyone go home and leave you to finish?"

"There's only this left," Tyler said. "Grant can't come back tomorrow, so I offered to stick around and help him."

The jeans that had started out crisp and clean were now spattered with white paint, and the pink and blue shirt looked as if it had put in a hard couple of hours. She'd expected him to be miserable; instead, he looked elated.

"Bet you didn't think I could do it, huh, Emma?"

"I can't say; I wouldn't want to hurt your feelings."

"He's a good painter," Grant put in without missing a stroke. "I offered him a job, but he said he already had one." Emma's breath hitched in her throat. Had he told? "Some fancy office job in a big skyscraper."

Relax. Stop this, or you will make yourself crazy. She turned to the boys. "Your mother says to come in now and wash up for supper."

"But we can't. We have to hold the ladders."

This was a male decision. Emma held her tongue and Grant said, "It will be all right, boys. Emma is here to steady the ladder if we need her. You must do as your *Mamm* asks."

Cautiously, they released their grips on the wood, as if both Tyler and Grant would slide sideways and fall fifteen feet without them. When nothing happened, Elam told Emma, "You must hold it firmly, so it doesn't slip."

"I'll do that," she said solemnly. "Off you go, now."

Both boys ran off, and she looked up again to find Tyler climbing down. "Want me to hold it?"

"Nope. I'm down." He jumped the last rung and landed next to her. "Those are nice kids."

"Amelia's a great mother. Even when she was working at the pallet shop and running her home, she always put the boys first." Another glance upward. "Grant, you must come down. We can finish this tomorrow."

"We who?" he asked, and with a flourish, finished the last coat of the last board. "My assistant?"

"Hey, you know I could." Tyler reached up and took the brush and pan from him, and they waited until Grant climbed down. "But I'm just as glad I don't have to. Did I tell you I'm afraid of heights?"

"How could you be?" Emma remembered the size of the building that housed his office. You could put this whole barn in the lobby and still have room for a herd of cows. "You work on the eighteenth floor."

"There's a big difference. No windows that open, for one thing. Nope, that ladder tested the limits of my endurance. But the good thing is, now I know I could do it again if I had to."

Grant just shook his head. "You should have said something. One of the other men could have gone up with me."

"And lose face in front of those boys? I'm sure they thought I was some namby-pamby *Englischer* who couldn't lift a hand to some honest work. My Y chromosome was at stake."

"*Englischer*?" Grant's eyes twinkled. "How do you know our words?"

He didn't even look at Emma. "Oh, it was in something I read. Come on, let me help you get all this stuff in the truck. Er, I mean, the wagon. The buggy."

"We call it a spring wagon, and I'd appreciate the help."

After they cleaned up, each of the men carried a plastic bucket full of brushes and a can of paint, while Emma folded the drop cloths and stacked the trays on top. When the men went back to get the ladders, Emma fetched Grant's horse from the field and began to hitch him up.

Tyler slid the ladder into the back and came around to stroke the horse's nose. "Did you do this?"

"Do you see anyone else around here?"

He leaned in, as if to tell her a secret. "I thought hitching up horses was men's work."

Smiling, she buckled the last strap and patted the horse's flank. "If we waited for our men to do it, we would never get to go shopping, or visiting, or to church either. My sister and I could hitch up our pony cart by the time we were eight."

"Wow. And here I thought I was hot stuff when I could tie my own shoes."

Her smile became an outright laugh. "We had to go through that stage, too. You have to start small and work up."

"If you want to know how to do it, I can show you sometime," Grant said as he slid his ladder into the back of the wagon. "How long are you staying?"

"Just the weekend, I think." Tyler glanced at Emma. "Or not. I haven't actually talked about it with Emma. I suppose what I need to do is work the Expedia app on my phone and find a place to stay."

"You'll stay with us, of course," Emma blurted. "You didn't mean you were going to find a motel?"

"Emma, I can't turn up unannounced and expect you to put me up."

"Why not?"

"Because—well, because it's rude."

"It's rude for friends to visit?"

"It is if they don't call first."

"Oh. Call first. Yes, I'm sure you did that. And the phone out there in the shanty on the highway probably rang a long time, too."

"Well, I didn't actually—"

"Never mind. The point is, you can't stay with Mamm and me because it wouldn't be fitting, but Karen's boys can double up for one night and leave the other room for you. You can take your meals with us."

"Emma, I meant it. I'm not going to just land on you and expect you and your family to—"

"I know you expect nothing. That's why you get something. Now, come on. It's getting late and Mamm will be watching for me."

Helplessly, Tyler looked at Grant and spread his hands. "I guess she told me."

Grant gazed at Emma and nodded slowly. "Then you had better listen."

CHAPTER 16

The car's seat was covered in leather so soft it was almost like fabric. Emma settled into it and felt it cup her body like a hand around a baby bird. Tyler backed it around and then set off up the lane so slowly that by the time they got to the highway, Grant's wagon was already out of sight over the crest of the hill.

But it wasn't her place to criticize. Maybe her driver was afraid of falling into a ditch.

"So what brings you all the way out to Lancaster County, Tyler West?"

"I'll give you one guess."

"I've been racking my brain and I can't think of a single thing. It can't be my book, because we settled that before I got on the train."

"And we also settled that I was an optimist."

"Then your optimism is wasted. If you plan to hound me for the next two days, you'd better drop me off at home and take yourself back to New York."

"Man alive, Emma, do you talk this way to every guy who comes to see you? I think I have the solution to your single-ton problem, if that's the case."

His face still held humor, but his mouth had set. In her panic, she had hurt his feelings.

Dismay and regret stabbed her like a needle through three layers of fabric. "I'm sorry. Forgive me. Mamm is always telling me I'm too blunt—that I speak before I think about the person receiving the words."

"I'm looking forward to meeting your mom."

"You'll like her."

"So in answer to your blunt question, part of the reason I came is to see if it would do any good to ask you again. People do change their minds. And the other part was just to see where you live. Google Earth is great up to a point, but it has its limits."

"Turn left here onto the county highway," she said, her gaze averted from the place where Pap had . . . where the *gut Gott* had seen fit to take him. "I'm not going to change my mind."

"I can see why." He drove with easy confidence now that they were on solid asphalt. His car must be very delicate underneath. "All those people, staring from me to you like they'd never seen either of us before. I suppose every one of them would have an opinion about you being published, wouldn't they?"

"Some of them already do. A man was—well, he thought he might court me, and then he found out about my writing. That was that."

"Court you? Wow, that was totally out of left field."

"The field on the left belongs to Moses Yoder. And that has nothing to do with Calvin King. The man."

"Sorry. Cultural references. I keep forgetting. What I meant was that I'm surprised. I thought the thing that bugged you most was that you were single. Where did this guy come from?"

"If I tell you all this, you must swear to keep it to yourself and not say anything. Particularly not to—" She stopped herself. "To anyone."

"You really know how to crank up the suspense. Turn here?"

She blinked and dragged her gaze to the stop sign. "Yes. Did you remember this from Google Earth?"

He shook his head and pointed to the little screen set into the dashboard. "GPS. I've already been to the house once, remember?"

"It's only half a mile. There isn't time to tell you, so we'll go for a walk after dinner."

"Isn't that what couples do? Won't that make people talk?"

"I don't think so. If we were in a closed buggy, now, and you were driving me...well, that just wouldn't happen."

"I guess not. I can't drive a buggy."

His face was deadpan, but his eyes danced, and she chuckled in spite of herself. "You are a brat, Tyler West."

"So my sisters used to tell me." He wheeled the car into the lane, and every one of Karen's children popped out from among the trees to stare.

When they saw their aunt, who normally lived a quiet and retiring life that did not involve being driven around in low-slung cars, their little eyes practically fell out. "Would you like to meet the children?"

"Sure."

Nathaniel was the first to run over. "*Aendi* Emma, what are you doing in this car?" he squeaked in *Deitch*. "I thought you went to Matthew and Elam's. This man came before. What does he want? Why is he driving you?"

She could barely get a word in edgewise. "*Englisch*, Nathaniel. It's rude to speak *Deitch* in front of our guest. This is Tyler West, a friend from New York City." She opened the door, and he stepped back.

Maryann followed more cautiously, but Emma could see she was full of as many questions as her brother. "Is he courting you, *Aendi*?" she asked in *Deitch*. "That's what Mamm says. You should have seen her when he came before. It's not very often Mamm forgets her words, but she sure forgot them when he got out and asked for you."

Emma could just imagine. Karen was going to have a field day with this, drat Tyler's paint-spattered hide.

"*Aendi*, Maryann is supposed to speak English."

"From now on. No need to translate what you just said, *Schatzi*. Tyler, these are Karen's children, Nathaniel, Maryann, and Victor over there by the garden."

"He's shy," Maryann confided. "He thinks the car will hit him like *Grossdaadi*."

Emma stifled another pang of distress, and went to six-year-old Victor. She knelt and took him in a hug. "The car won't hurt you, *Schatzi*. The man who hit *Grossdaadi* was speeding on the highway. Tyler's car is turned off, you see? No one will speed in our yard. Your *Mamm* wouldn't have it, would she?"

Victor shook his head, then turned to look at Tyler. "That man is your friend?"

"He is. So you must come and say hello, and he will be your friend, too."

Tyler shook hands with them all as solemnly as if they were the ministers lined up at the head of the congregation. Then Emma shooed the boys off to play. "Maryann, can you ask your mother if she can put Tyler up for the night?"

"He can have Nathaniel's room."

"That's very kind of you, *Schatzi*. But please ask all the same." She touched Maryann on the cheek and the girl ran around the corner of the house. "Come and meet my mother."

They found Lena at the kitchen table, snapping green beans. "I heard the car come back. You had no trouble finding Amelia's?"

"None at all. I'm sorry we didn't get a chance to speak before. I'm Tyler West."

Lena dried a hand on her apron and offered it to him. "Ah. The Tyler West who was sending my daughter letters this spring?"

"The same."

"I hope you like chicken and dumplings. It's one of our favorites."

"What she means is, you're invited to supper," Emma translated. "But you already knew that." She removed the kitchen apron that still smelled faintly of vinegar and put it in the basket in the washroom, then pulled a fresh one from the peg on the back of the kitchen door. "Just let me get this going."

"Can I help?"

Lena gazed at him over the tops of her glasses. "Did your mother teach you how to cook?"

"No, but I can read a recipe as well as the next guy."

"We don't use recipes, but if you haven't had enough work for the day, you could give me a hand with these beans."

Emma kept half an eye on him as she cut up the chicken

and browned it, then made cream gravy and dumplings and set the whole pot to simmering. She couldn't tell if he'd ever snapped a bean in his life, but after watching Lena closely, he mimicked her until the whole bowl was cleaned and ready for Emma to cook. A salad rounded out their meal, with a plate of her famous beet pickles for color, and before she knew it, Tyler was leaning back in his chair, weakly waving off the plate of gingerbread pear cake.

"I haven't eaten this much since I don't know when," he groaned. "No food for me tomorrow. At all."

"You'll be hungry by breakfast time," Lena said serenely. "You don't want to miss Emma's biscuits. They're so light they practically float away."

"Mamm." If she didn't stop, Emma's cheeks would be as red as those beets. She collected the plates and ran water into the sink. "I'll take Tyler over to the big house and put his things away, and then I think he might appreciate a walk."

"Please," he begged. "Otherwise I'm going to have to run circles around the house."

Lena smiled as she settled into her chair and picked up the soft shawl she was knitting. Emma could practically read her mind. *That young man appreciates Emma's skill in the kitchen. I don't know what he's here for, and I don't know if she'll tell me, but I can appreciate anyone who appreciates my girl.*

Since they'd come back so late, and dinner had taken a while to prepare, twilight had already fallen by the time they stepped outside. Emma led the way down to the creek at the side of the property. A path next to it went under the bridge, which on the other side met a gravel cutoff to the highway. You could walk along it for a good two miles without running into anyone except the farmers who worked the fields on both sides, and once in a while a courting couple who had pulled off to get a little privacy.

She'd already forgotten how long a stride he had. At this rate, they'd cover the two miles before she'd managed to tell her story.

As if her thoughts had prompted him, he said, "So, Emma. There isn't a soul for acres. How about you tell me about this new guy and then maybe I'll tell you a thing or two about the old guy."

"What old guy?"

"Old as in information previously conveyed. Grant Weaver."

Her heart jumped at the mention of his name. "Tell me what? What do you know?" Oh, she just knew they'd been talking out there behind the barn. Wasn't that just like a man! They were as bad as women—they only did it where you couldn't hear.

"Uh-uh. You first. You promised."

Fine, if he wanted to be like that. She gave him a considerably abbreviated version of what she had told Amelia and Carrie about Calvin King at their last quilting frolic, including the part about the writing.

"He told you that he wouldn't consider marrying you if you didn't give up writing?" Tyler sounded aghast, as if she'd just said the condition to being Calvin King's wife was that she must commit murder. "That—that—" He stopped. "Sorry. I'm trying to keep my language clean. I can just picture someone saying something like that to one of my sisters. There'd be blood running under the door."

"No blood," Emma told him quietly. "No bad language, either. I just told him that I could not marry him."

He stopped walking, his high-topped running shoes scraping a little in the gravel. "I'm glad to hear it." She kept going, and this time it was he who was forced to jog a little to catch up. "So that's what Grant meant about being glad you had people around you who were more than fair-weather friends."

"Perhaps he meant you."

"I don't know. I just thought he meant your girlfriends. Amelia and the pretty blond you told me about who invites her chickens to sit at the kitchen table."

"Carrie. You know perfectly well what her name is. You're just stalling so you don't have to tell me what else Grant said."

He jammed his hands in his pockets, evidently aiming for a jaunty look, but that didn't stop his smile from turning a little rueful. "I'm just savoring my brief moment of having something *you* want, for a change."

"But you do not have the *Ordnung* keeping you quiet."

"You got that right." He paused, and Emma fought down the urge to take him by his shoulders and shake words out of him, like seeds out of a dried pod.

Patience. He said he would tell you, so let him keep his word.

"I guess the bottom line is that he really respects you, Emma."

Respect was not going to put wedding invitations in people's mailboxes. "I'm glad."

"I wasn't sure how much he knew about your trip to the city, so I didn't say much about that. I hope he doesn't have the same opinions this King guy does."

"I don't think he does," she said. "He spoke quite openly about it just before you drove up." *And he encouraged me to paint graffiti on my house.* No, best not say anything about that. A woman had to have *some* secrets.

"I told him about our walk in Central Park, and how you refused to take a buggy ride because you'd be too tempted to tell the carriage driver how to take better care of his horse."

A smile curved her mouth at the memory. "Grant takes good care of his animals. He would have done the same."

"That's pretty much what he said, when he got done laughing."

Laughter was good. Laughter meant the story had pleased him—maybe even surprised him.

"He did say a funny thing, though."

When he didn't go on, Emma choked back a growl of frustration and only poked him in his skinny, underfed ribs. "Stop teasing me."

"He said of all the women in the settlement, he feels most at peace with you." Tyler gave her a sideways glance, as if he were looking for a reaction. But she had been through the hard school of Karen, and had learned that she could choose her moments to react. Or not. When she said nothing, he went on. "Seemed like a backhanded kind of a compliment, if you ask me. Most women want to hear that they get a man going. Charge him up. Turn him on. Not put him at peace. Makes you sound like you're putting him to sleep. Or getting ready for a trip out to the cemetery or something."

The merry words flowed over her like the wind, and she paid it just as little mind.

She made Grant feel at peace.

She could think of no higher compliment, and her soul expanded outward in sheer joy, rising through the night sky.

"...wondered if things were going to change now that he's been widowed?"

Emma came back to earth, a little disconcerted. Her feet were firmly on the ground, and Tyler was still talking about Grant. She needed to pay attention. "What did you say?"

"I said, I was just wondering if you were going to make a play for the guy, now that he's single."

Emma nearly fell over. As it was, she missed a step and had to catch up with a sidestep and a skip. "I will do no such thing. And please don't talk like that about a man who only buried his wife's remains last week."

"He buried the remains of someone who died a long time ago."

"Yes, but he didn't know that. It wouldn't be seemly for him to look around so soon. Or for anyone else to look at him."

"You look at him plenty."

"Not like that."

"Yes, you do. And you ask me, he doesn't mind a bit."

She had never met a man who just said what he thought, with no sieve between his brain and his mouth that would catch the unseemly bits. "What do you mean?"

"Haven't you noticed he's different with you than with the other women? He's...softer. No, that's not it. It's like this bubble forms that has only the two of you in it when he talks to you."

"You're making this up. It's like a game with you. You're talking nonsense."

The scraping of his feet on the dirt track stopped, and she stopped with him. "Emma, get over yourself. You're so determined that he shouldn't like you, you're totally going to miss it when he shows you he does. If you haven't already."

"And you're such an expert on him and me, then? With one whole afternoon's experience?"

"I've got eyes, woman. And a whole afternoon is enough, if you spend it talking about the right things. Which I made sure we did."

"You talked about me." On purpose. With an end in mind. Emma didn't know whether to cry or scream or run away. How was she ever going to face Grant after this?

"Sure. That's why I'm telling you all this. I've done my bit. Now it's your turn."

God may have been free with His gifts, but Karen made no bones about the price Emma would be expected to pay for hers. At six the next morning, she and John walked into the kitchen together, their newest baby wrapped up tight in a blanket against her chest, as Emma was putting the coffee on.

Emma looked from one to the other as her stomach plunged in consternation. "Is everything all right? Is the baby well? Did Tyler take sick?"

John waved off her questions and took Pap's chair at the head of the table. "Little Jeremy is fine, as you can see. Tyler is still asleep, though he told me last night he plans to help out over at Amelia's again today."

It wasn't as though Karen and John never came over here. But at such an hour? And as a couple?

She dropped a kiss on the sleeping baby's cheek. He smelled like baby powder and contentment. "Mamm should be up soon," she said. "Do you want me to wake her?"

"We wanted to talk to you." Karen rubbed the baby's back, rocking gently. "Before this goes any further."

Emma's brain felt as slack as her face must look. "Before what goes any further? *Was sagst du?*"

Karen looked at her husband and real worry stabbed Emma's heart. The number of times her sister had let someone else speak for her could be counted on one hand, with fingers left over. "Is it Mamm?" she whispered. "Do you know something I don't?"

"No." John's voice was as slow and deliberate as the gait of one of his own plow horses. "It's not your *Mamm*. It's you. Your... Emma, I'm speaking as the head of the family, and I want to caution you about your conduct. People are talking."

Emma slumped, her chest caving in sheer relief. "Is that all? Let me assure you, Tyler West will be gone tomorrow or the next day, and it will all blow over."

Karen's face had colored with the effort to be silent and let her husband speak, but with this she lost control of her tongue. "It isn't just Tyler West, though I have to say he's the worst of it. Emma, do you know how it looks to watch you running from one man to the next like the very worst kind of flirt? First Joshua, then Calvin, now this *Englisch* man. I don't understand how you can live for ten years in modesty, and then break out in wild behavior as if you were an irresponsible sixteen-year-old on *Rumspringe*."

Emma's mouth fell open while a dozen different replies zinged through her brain—and not one of them came out.

"I've actually had people ask me if your trip to New York City turned your head—if you learned rebellion there and were going to leave your family and your church. Do you know how that made me feel?"

"They would have got a better answer if they'd asked me," she said, which didn't improve Karen's expression any.

"I'm asking you. *We're* asking you. What is wrong with you, and when are you going to come to your senses?"

Maybe it was the early hour. Maybe it was the fact that she hadn't had any coffee yet. But the skin of her sense of discretion seemed to be very thin this morning, and Karen's exasperated tone, low and discreet as it was so Mamm wouldn't hear and the baby wouldn't be upset, seemed to scratch it raw.

"You started it." She got up. Surely the coffee must be done by now. "You invited Joshua Steiner and—" Karen had not mentioned Grant's name, and Emma must not bring it up. "—and me to lunch and practically pushed me into his arms. Just because someone else sat up and took notice doesn't make me fast and fancy."

"It does when you come to a potluck with one man and are out having ice cream with another, both in the same week!"

Emma got down three coffee mugs and tried to rein in her temper before it bolted and hurt someone.

"We understand that you want a home of your own, Emma," John said. "But you must go about it in a more circumspect way. No man in the community is going to want a woman who flits from one man to another and can't make up her mind. How could he trust that she's really settled when he marries her?"

The unfairness of this would have made her laugh if it weren't so maddening. She poured and served the coffee in silence while she grappled with the angry words that wanted to fly out and attack, then set out the creamer and sugar bowl in front of her visitors and sat in her usual place. They did not know she had made up her mind ten years ago and never wavered in her faithfulness to that choice, foolish and sinful as such behavior might have been. And she was certainly not about to tell them now.

"I can't believe you blame me for this," Karen hissed, trying to keep her voice down. "I thought better of you, Emma."

Emma took as big a sip of coffee as the heat of it would allow. "Do you begrudge me the opportunity to spend time with someone? To be courted?" Ah, now her brain was beginning to clear. She drank some more while Karen left her cup untouched and bristled like an angry dog.

"Of course not! I am not the one being spoken to here. All we're saying is you need to be more discreet. You're inviting too much talk."

"This running around with all these men—and I won't even go into what this *Englischer* is doing here, because I don't want to know—must stop," John said. "This isn't our way. Our women wait for God to show them His choice of man, go with that one, save their kisses for that one, and then marry him." His face darkened with embarrassment at having to have this talk with a spinster on the far side of thirty.

Hmph. It would be good practice for him. Maryann would need it in another eight or nine years.

"If it makes you feel any better, Calvin King spoke to me of marriage." Oh, she should not have said that. The relief that filled Karen's face only made her feel guilty at having to say what must come next. "But I refused him."

"Why?" John asked, bewildered.

"Emma, have you taken leave of your senses? He is a good, kind man and you may not get another chance."

"I realize that—on all counts. But he wouldn't let me

write, and that's one thing I won't give up when I marry. If I ever do."

John was already shaking his head. "Foolish. I never heard of anything so foolish. All this could have been brought to an end and you could have had a home of your own ... and you threw it all away because of your articles in the paper?"

Put like that, it did sound foolish. Reckless and selfish and senseless. And then she remembered Tyler's face in the fading light, and how outraged he had been on her behalf. Some people saw the value in the gift God had given her. And some just did not.

But that didn't change the fact that it had come from God, and with it the responsibility to cultivate and water it wisely, even if it did grow in a desert, all by itself.

"What's done is done," she said, "and there's no undoing it now. I am not going to marry Joshua Steiner, either, so you can set your minds at rest about that."

"And this *Englischer*?" John said. "Are you going to marry him?"

She bit back a shriek of laughter just in time. The last thing she wanted was to wake the baby—or offend her brother-in-law. "He is a friend and nothing more. As he told you, we're going over to Amelia's to join the work party again today, and then I imagine tomorrow he will go back to New York." She couldn't imagine Tyler wanting to stay for Sunday, not with the hours of driving he would have ahead of him. "And then everything will be back to the way it was."

And you'll have put yourselves through this little talk for nothing.

Ach, well. They loved her and wanted what was best for her. It was like the tincture Ruth Lehman had once brewed up for her when she was covered in measles. It had done more to make her mother feel better than it had to actually cure the condition.

Karen followed John out the door without much more protest, and Emma emptied her sister's cold coffee into the sink. A sound in the hall made her turn, and there stood Lena, her oxygen tank next to her foot. "Mamm, you're up early."

"No more than usual."

"We didn't want to wake you."

"Not much hope of that. I wake at five whether I want to or not. I heard every word." Lena crossed the kitchen slowly and took Emma in her arms. It was like being held by a bird, her bones were so fragile, her skin papery and soft.

"Don't you let it harm your spirit," she whispered with all the authority with which she had once run a big household. "If people talk, it's because they haven't got anything interesting happening in their own lives. My girl has every right to wait for the one God has chosen for her, and no one has the right to criticize."

Emma's eyes filled with tears as she rested her chin on her mother's shoulder, and before she knew it, she was weeping in earnest. God's blessings came at odd moments, when you least expected them.

Which, she supposed as she fished in her sleeve for her hankie, was why they were called gifts.

CHAPTER 17

Much to Emma's astonishment, Tyler West did not go home on Sunday morning. Instead, he asked very humbly if he might come with her and Lena to church. "I'd like to give you a ride there, if you think it would be more comfortable for your mother."

Emma turned toward Lena. "Mamm?"

"There's no reason for me to arrive at Isaac Lehman's in a fancy car, as if I were some *Englisch* lady and not his neighbor of sixty years. You can take yourself to church in that thing if you like, but Emma and I will drive the buggy and not get above ourselves."

Which meant, of course, that Tyler folded himself onto the back bench where the children usually rode, and consequently made people's eyes bug out when he unfolded himself again in the Lehmans' yard.

All Amelia's family was here already, and most of Eli's, so the crowd was bigger than usual. Tyler still stood out; in his khakis and blue button-down and tie he looked like a bluebird on a fence filled with crows. Not that it bothered him. He sat through the three-hour service on the backless bench next to Grant Weaver with only a few twitches and the odd twist of his spine. And while the main sermon on bringing in the hay was in *Deitch*, the preachers gave the readings and their testimony in English, out of courtesy to their guest. When everyone visited before lunch, Grant took him under his wing, introducing him to some of the men and talking about whatever men talked about while they waited for lunch.

When Emma went to get her horse later in the afternoon, Amelia hurried after her and they crossed the lawn to the pasture together. "It's nice to see Mark and his family again," Emma said. "And Emily's new husband seems a nice boy."

"He is. They're going to stay for a month for *die Flitterwoch*."

"And when do you get to make *your* honeymoon visits?" Emma teased.

Amelia blushed. "We'll take the boys up to Lebanon County when school is out. In the meantime, we'll do our honeymooning right here."

"I promise Carrie and I won't interrupt."

"You'll do no such thing." Amelia caught the horse's halter and led him over to Emma. "I expect to see you next Tuesday as usual. Nothing will change."

"Oh, I think everything has changed." Emma gazed at her fondly over the horse's back. "In a good way."

Together they led the horse over to Emma's buggy, where they found Tyler gazing at the slats in bemusement. "I'm going to watch you do this and see if I can learn something." She and Amelia backed the horse between them and got to work. "But mostly I'll probably just learn how inept I am and how useless my skillset is here."

"I don't know," Emma said. "I hear you're a pretty good

painter." Even if he didn't know a thing about men and women and how things should be between them.

"And Grant is a pretty good teacher. I thought I knew a lot more than I do."

"How are you going to get back to New York, Tyler?" Amelia asked. "If you plan to work tomorrow, you'll be mighty tired when you get in."

"About that…" His gaze moved from the harness to Emma's busy hands to her face. "I wondered if I could stick around another day? Grant mentioned I might tag along on his work crew if I wanted. They didn't get finished in the barn yesterday."

"Really?" That was awfully good of him, in Emma's mind. Of course, any good thing Grant did wouldn't surprise her. What did surprise her was this urbane young man's unexpected taste for manual labor. Evidently the novelty of it hadn't worn off. And if the entire crew was there, maybe there wouldn't be so many opportunities for man-to-man talks about people who didn't need talking about.

"I guess one of his boys went to something called a band hop over on the other side of Bird-in-Hand and shows no signs of coming back. So he's short a man."

Amelia glanced at Emma, then at Tyler. "Eli and I would be very pleased if you could come to our wedding, then, Tyler, if you're going to be in town and you're doing all this work for us. The service will start at eight o'clock in the morning."

The dawn breaking over the hills couldn't have been brighter than the elation in Tyler's face. "Serious?"

"Serious." Amelia laughed and slid the passenger door back for him. "It would make us very happy."

"I'm—I'm honored, Amelia. I know you don't—that is, not a lot of *Englisch* folks get to—"

"You've been very kind to my best friend, and I'm only returning the kindness. Of course, if you join the cleanup crew, you won't think I'm very kind."

"It can't be worse than the hurricane cleanup in South Carolina," he said. "My grandparents' house will never be the same. *Denki*, Amelia. I would like to come, very much."

Smiling at his gallant attempt at pronunciation, Emma walked the horse and buggy over to where Lena waited on the porch. She had no idea why he was staying on—not that she didn't enjoy his company—but she would have a little talk about what topics of conversation were off-limits. Hopefully before the rumors about him courting her gained so much momentum she wouldn't be able to stop them.

By the time the work party finished on Monday, all Emma could think about was falling into bed. While the men had mowed lawns, trimmed gardens, got the barn cleaned out, and the bench wagon arrived with the benches from the Lehmans' place, the women made the preparations for the wedding feast. For the two hundred people Amelia expected, this would include forty pans of the chicken and stuffing dish called *roast*; mashed potatoes and gravy; forty quarts of applesauce; mountains of coleslaw; bowls of garden vegetables; and of course, jars of celery. Since the wedding was in the summer instead of the fall, Ruth Lehman had gone around to all the supermarkets and cleaned them out of celery because a wedding just wouldn't be right without it. Emma's hands were so clean from washing stalks that they squeaked.

When she went to get the horse to hitch him up, she found Grant out in the pasture doing the same. When he saw her, he caught Ajax's halter and brought him over. "This is your animal, *ja?*"

She patted the horse's neck. "*Ja*, this is Ajax. Have you got all your painting done?"

"Painting and sweeping and carrying and more painting. If Amelia finds a speck of dirt in her barn tomorrow, I'll build Eli's workshop for nothing."

Emma laughed, and was rewarded when Grant's brown eyes twinkled in return. Another gift from God's hand—the ability to bring joy to each other, even for something so silly. The things Tyler had said zoomed through her memory like a hummingbird aiming at the sweetness of a flower, but she shook them away. "And when do you get started on it?"

"Soon, I think. Within a couple of weeks. It will be nice to be working every day on this side of the settlement." He gazed over the pasture to Moses Yoder's gate. "You're just on the other side of the hill."

Had he connected those two observations on purpose? "*Ja*," she said. "It's not very far—maybe five minutes. I only brought the buggy today because of all the cleaning supplies."

"You make a fine cup of coffee. It would be a great temptation to stop in of a morning, before work."

You're so determined that he shouldn't like you, Tyler's voice whispered in her memory, *you're totally going to miss it when he shows you he does. If you haven't already.*

But it was difficult to miss this. What should she say? "*Denki,*" she managed at last.

No, that wasn't enough. He would give up and walk away. She would miss her chance.

Emma, speak up!

"You—you would be very welcome," she blurted, as if the

words had come out under pressure, like steam from under the lid of a boiling pot. "If you think it would be...proper."

He gazed at her over the back of the horse. "Proper? You mean, because of Lavina." When she blushed at her own forwardness, he went on. "The *Kinner* and I, we did our mourning when we lost her, two years ago. To show ourselves to be mourning now, well, I don't think it would be healthy. My girls have learned to smile again, and I would not take that away from them, even after they stood at the graveside. It did not seem like their *Mamm*, then. It was more a farewell to someone they knew once, who would never come again."

Her heart twisted for them—and for him. "And you?" she whispered.

"I want to smile again, Emma," he said. "I never thought I would say this, but it hurts to look back."

"You must have some good memories," she protested softly.

"I do, but they're like memories of childhood, golden and far away. I have been an adult in body for all my married life, but I have not been an adult in mind until just recently. I need to learn how to live again, now. Live differently." He paused, then stepped back and patted the horse's shoulder. "Learn how to appreciate God's little gifts again, like a good cup of coffee and a woman's laughter."

And with a smile, he walked across the pasture to his own horse.

Ajax moved and she went with him to the gate and through it to her buggy. Otherwise, she might have stood in the pasture for the rest of the day, wondering. Had he meant to be personal? Because these were things he could say to anyone.

When Tyler joined her in the buggy, he looked as droopy

as her body felt. "We'll go to bed early," she told him as they drove home, "because we'll be expected back by six in the morning."

Tyler groaned and dropped out of the buggy like a sack of onions to open the barn door for her. Emma drove Ajax in and unhitched him, brushing him down and making sure he had his feed. Then she hung the harness from its pegs next to the sets that John used for the family buggies and the plow horses.

Thank goodness she'd made enough chicken and dumplings yesterday that she could just warm up the leftovers for supper. A few cut vegetables and some potatoes, and that would be that.

Tyler must have worked up quite the appetite, because he took another helping and cleaned up the potatoes, too. But all during supper he seemed distracted, as though he had something on his mind as well. Finally, after Lena had gone to bed, Emma pulled on her shawl to walk him over to Karen's house.

She had no intention of going in. Not after yesterday's early-morning visit. She had no idea how Tyler had broken it to them that he was staying over for the wedding...wait a minute. Maybe that was what was disturbing him.

As they went down the front steps, the scent of Karen's flowering jasmine blew toward them on the evening breeze. She breathed in deeply. "I love that smell."

"It's nice," Tyler said. His shoes scraped on the stones in the walk. "Emma, when we were talking over supper I kinda left some things out, since your mom was there."

"Left some things out? There isn't much about wedding preparations that Mamm doesn't already know."

"It was nothing to do with wedding preparations. Not directly. See, I spent most of the day helping Grant clean out the barn."

"No wonder you're so tired. I am, too."

"And we sort of...talked."

Something in his tone made a spritz of unease shoot through her stomach. "Again? And what assumptions are you going to make this time?" She slowed her steps in the lane under the darkness of the overhanging trees.

"This wasn't like the other day. But I was so tired and your name came up and I..."

Oh, dear. "And you what?"

"I kinda let it slip. It was an accident, Emma. It just popped out and then it was too late to take it back."

She stopped walking altogether, and he stopped beside her. The outline of his tall body in the dark looked like Alvin Esch's might have if his father had discovered his correspondence-school packets. "Tyler West, what did you say?" she asked quietly.

"Well, we were talking about how everyone pitches in, and how you and Carrie were Amelia's best friends and were going to stand up with her tomorrow, and that led to whether a man could be friends with a woman the way two women are, and he asked me if you and I were friends."

Well, that didn't sound so bad. "And what did you tell him?"

"I told him we were...and that we were also business associates. I told him about your book."

Emma let out a long breath. Compared to what he might have blabbed, this was nothing. "Did you?"

"Emma, I'm sorry. It's my business, you know? And I'm

used to talking about my business, but I'm not used to talking about yours. Anyway, he feels the same as that Calvin
guy. Articles you can get away with, but a book is no go."

"I know that, Tyler. I've said so from the beginning. Regardless of what an individual person's opinion might be,
the *Ordnung* is pretty firm on the matter." She didn't think
there was a specific stricture against an Amish church member having a book published, but that wasn't the point.
There were plenty of strictures against women speaking outside the home, or appearing in public offices and such.
They were lucky they got to sell their quilts in their front
yards.

"There's more."

She had relaxed and resumed her leisurely walk toward
the big house. She could just see the lights in the front windows through the trees. "What? Better be quick, we're almost
there."

"So then he asked me just how good a friend you were to
me. He takes a while to get to the point, but when he gets
there, he really lets you have it."

Just like some people she could mention. Emma's heart
began to pick up its pace even as her feet slowed. "So you told
him the truth, of course."

"Of course. I said I valued your friendship very much, but
that's all it was. Friendship. And then I—" He gulped. "And
then I did it again. I swear it was exhaustion talking, Emma.
It was like my mouth said words while my brain was in a
coma. I told him it wouldn't matter even if I was crazy in
love with you, because the only man that mattered to you was
standing right beside me."

Emma's heart gave a great thump and for the space of five

seconds she felt as if her lungs couldn't get breath, as if the world had ground to a halt on its axis.

He hadn't said that. Surely he hadn't. Ach, mein Gott, *please back everything up to before I heard this and maybe I can stop it before I find out it's true.*

"I'm sorry, Emma. I didn't mean to blab your secret, and especially not to him. It just happened. But maybe it's not such a bad thing. I think it's good that he knows. Like I said before, now you can—"

"What did he say?" Her voice didn't even sound like hers. It sounded as if someone had dragged it through the gravel in the lane.

"Well...nothing. We just finished up the horses' stalls and went on to sweeping where the buggies go."

This was even worse.

Grant had nothing to say. Not a "That's interesting" or a "You must be mistaken" or anything else. He'd probably been stricken silent with pity. No wonder he'd made such an effort to be neighborly out there in the pasture. A good friend. Not a man who was interested in courting. And she'd read it completely the wrong way. He might have even thought she'd waited to get her horse just as he was hitching up his. But he was far too kind a man to show it.

So much for Tyler's vain assumptions the other night. But somehow, having him proved wrong felt even worse. "How could you?" she whispered. "How could you do this to me?"

"I'm sorry."

"You of all people. The one I thought I could trust because you're not of my world and have no reason to talk to people."

"But I thought—"

"If this is how you keep someone's confidence, I'm glad I

didn't give you my book. What other kinds of terrible moral behavior are you guilty of?"

"Emma, it's not like that."

"What is it like, then? Do you realize what you've done? Now I have to go through Amelia's wedding knowing he'll be there, feeling sorry for the poor spinster he thought was his friend, with her pathetic little dreams of something more."

"He's not that kind of man and you know it."

So he was telling her what she knew, was he? With his three whole days of experience in her world? Her temper ignited. "Here's what I know. I might have to be there, but you don't. I don't want to see you or hear from you ever again, Tyler West. You just march into that house, get your things, and take yourself back to New York. You're not welcome here any longer."

"What, now? Tonight? Emma, please, you don't mean—"

"I'll tell my sister you've had a change of plans." She pushed past him, and ran up the front stairs, her fury melting into an enormous lump of tears in her throat. If she spoke one more word, she would start to weep and she would never, ever stop.

For once in her life, Karen kept her mouth shut. She simply went to the boys' room and put his things in his duffel bag until he moved her to one side and finished the job himself. Karen nodded stiffly at his mumble of thanks, and stood at Emma's elbow as he tossed the bag into the backseat of his car. The engine fired up, the car wheeled in the yard, and he left the farm at least twice as fast as he had arrived.

As the tires ground at the turn onto the paved road and he accelerated away, Karen asked, "Do I dare ask what just happened?"

"No." Emma started down the farmhouse steps. "It's over and done and I don't want to speak of it."

"I can't say I'm not happy."

Nei? *Well, I can.*

Emma hurried into the lane, where the trees shielded her from view of both houses. Her chest ached, her throat ached, and blast it all, there were the tears, running hot down her cheeks. She gasped for air, and it turned into a sob, and she slid to the grass, weeping her heart out alone in the darkness.

During Pap's decline into dementia, Emma had learned that sleep was one of God's most underestimated gifts. She'd counted every hour like a miser, totaling them up with precision, rolling minutes together like coins. Some nights left her poorer than others.

The night before Amelia's wedding left her impoverished.

It wasn't that she was afraid her swollen eyes and pale cheeks would cause any comment—no one looked at her for pleasure, anyway. But as one of Amelia's attendants, she had duties to perform, and a sleep-deprived brain would not help her do her best for her friend.

At least before the service, and after the *Abroth* where the elders had counseled Amelia and Eli in private, she could sit upstairs with Amelia and Carrie among the wedding presents, which gave her just enough time to whisper to them what had happened. Amelia had a bad case of jitters, so Emma made the sacrifice of her own pride gladly when she saw that indignation on her behalf took Amelia's mind off the singing of "*So will ichs aber heben an, Singen in Gottes Ehr*" downstairs.

Finally it was time. On the third verse of the *Lob Lied* they got up, and Amelia smoothed her new white apron over her blue skirts. In single file, they went down the stairs, and Emma took the hand of Eli's youngest brother, who was barely twenty, and he led her up the aisle to the front. Carrie smiled at Melvin as if she were the one getting married, and they took their places. Eli took Amelia's strong, slender hand as if it held everything important to him on this earth, and led her to her place and then took his seat opposite her.

The *Gmee* picked up where they had left off in the hymn until the elders came in on the eighth verse. When silence fell, Moses Yoder stood and began the opening, the story of Adam and Eve. When he was finished, Emma and everyone else knelt in front of their chairs for a few minutes of silent prayer. After a minister from Eli's congregation read the marriage verses in Matthew 19, Bishop Daniel stepped forward for the main sermon.

Emma put out of her mind all the specters that had haunted the night hours, and concentrated on two people she cared about deeply leaving the loneliness of their separate paths to join their lives in marriage. Grant Weaver and Joshua and Calvin might all have been in the congregation, and Tyler West was no doubt back at home where he belonged, but in front of her she could see love and commitment and the blessing of God. She was their witness, and anything else vying for her attention had no place here.

When Bishop Daniel had made his way through the stories of Isaac and Rebecca, Jacob and Rachel, Ruth and Boaz, and Tobit and Sara, at last it came time for the vows.

"We have here a man and a woman who have agreed to enter the state of matrimony, Eli Fischer and Amelia Lehman Beiler. If any here has an objection to the marriage, he now has opportunity to make it known." Silence fell, hardly more than one tick of the clock. "So, then. No one has any objection, so if you are still minded the same, you may now come forth in the name of the Lord."

Amelia and Eli got up and moved to stand in front of the bishop, and Eli took her hand, gripping it as though he never meant to let her go. Emma reached for Carrie's hand, too, blinking back tears.

"Can you confess, Brother, that you accept this our sister as your wife, and that you will not leave her until death separates you?" the bishop asked Eli quietly. "And do you believe that this is from the Lord and that you have come so far by faith and prayer?"

"*Ja*," Eli said without a moment's hesitation.

When Bishop Daniel asked Amelia the same questions, it took her a moment to get her answer out—not because she didn't want to, Emma saw, but because she was trying not to cry. "*Ja*," she whispered.

Each of them vowed to be loyal to the other, to care for the other in sickness and adversity, in weakness and in moments of lost courage. And then Bishop Daniel took their right hands between both of his, finally allowing the ghost of a smile in the depths of his gray beard. "The God of Abraham, the God of Isaac, and the God of Jacob be with you together and give His rich blessing upon you and be merciful to you," he said. "I wish you the blessings of God for a good beginning and a steadfast middle and a faithful ending, in and through the name of Jesus Christ. Amen." His voice strengthened as he, Eli, and Amelia dipped their knees at the mention of the holy name. "Go forth in the name of the Lord. You are now man and wife."

Ruth Lehman stayed just long enough to see her daughter

safely committed to Eli, and then she and the kitchen crew slipped out to start work. The ceremony ended with a few words of blessing from Isaac Lehman and Eli's father, and after the final hymn, the elders were the first to shake the bridal couple's hands. Amelia and Eli and their attendants nearly disappeared in the crowd of well-wishers, so it was a while before the crowd thinned enough to allow Emma to make her way to the door.

Where the first thing she saw was Tyler West standing on the lawn next to Grant, bold as a day lily in a vegetable garden.

Her uplifted, grateful spirit at seeing her best friend committed to a man who loved her evaporated, letting her down with a bump.

"I thought you said he was gone?" Carrie whispered at her elbow.

The nerve of him! Well, the fact that he was Eli and Amelia Fischer's guest didn't mean she needed to speak to him. "I thought he was. I told him to leave last night and he did. He must have gone to Grant's, who's practically the only other person he knows here." She hurried Carrie across the lawn to the upper floor of the barn. There the men had set up the *Eck* and the two of them had decorated it yesterday.

Calm. You must be calm. Anger has no place on such a happy day, Emma Stolzfus, so you'll just put them both out of your mind.

The embroidered tablecloth where Eli and Amelia would sit looked so pretty with her china, and the blue damask tablecloths Carrie had found for half off at the big-box store in Lancaster were pale as spring rain, and set off the white icing of the wedding cake to perfection.

"I was so afraid something would happen to this on the way over." Carrie moved the second cake a fraction to the right. "I had visions of opening the box and seeing it all splatted to one side."

"It looks beautiful," Emma said sincerely. "How on earth did you get those ribbons to lie so...ah, I see. You edged them with icing." Each of the two layers had a satin ribbon tied around it and a bow, edged top and bottom with a thread of frosting. "How are they going to cut it?"

Carrie dimpled. "The ribbons aren't real. It's candy."

"Oh, my." Carrie was so talented. "When did you find the time to do this? And without Amelia seeing it, no less."

"I did it in the spare room and kept the door closed. I hope she likes it."

Carrie needn't have worried. When the bride and groom and all the crowd climbed the steps to the huge loft, Amelia's eyes shone and it was all they could do to keep her from moving the store-bought wedding cake, with all its curlicues and icing roses, to one side and putting Carrie's cake in its place. The chocolate one with rolled icing that Emma had made paled in comparison, but she didn't mind at all. Chocolate was Amelia's favorite, and what it lacked on the outside would be more than made up in fudge filling on the inside.

In an instance of God's perfect timing, both Tyler and Grant waited for the second sitting, which meant Emma, as a member of the wedding party, could finish her lunch and flee before they came upstairs to eat. The kitchen helpers ate at second sitting, but there was no way she would be allowed in there to help with the dishes. It seemed natural to join in the singing in the afternoon, and in all the crowd, why, it was easy to miss speaking to someone. Besides, she hadn't met

Eli's two brothers and their wives, who were so nice and so interested in the quilt the three of them were making that it was suppertime before they finished their visit.

In fact, it was getting on for evening before the kitchen was cleaned up and set to rights and the first of the guests began rolling home. Cows waited for no man, and milking had to be done on most of the places in the district.

Emma felt rather pleased with herself that her evasion tactics had worked so well. She had no idea where Tyler West was, and only a fair idea of where Grant might be, seeing as his girls and little Zachary had gone back to the farm with their Yoder aunties ten minutes ago. It was time to get home anyway. Mamm had come with Karen and the children, and had gone with them as well, but she would still be wanting to talk over the day in front of a piece of pie and some chamomile tea.

Emma started past the barn, heading for the field behind it and the gate in Moses Yoder's fence.

"Emma." She turned with a start to see Grant Weaver not ten feet behind her, turning his good black hat in his hands.

And then she knew she hadn't been so clever at evasion, and that she'd been avoiding him out of humiliation and nothing more. Now it was time to face the music. "Grant."

"I haven't been able to get close enough to speak to you all day."

"*Ja*, well...standing up for Amelia and all..."

"Are you on your way home?"

She gestured up the hill. "I was just going to walk. You remember...it's only a few minutes through the field."

"Ah. Of course you want to get home, after all your busy day." He took a step back.

What was this? He sounded almost as if he wanted to talk to her. Not avoid her. Not laugh at her.

Talk.

She dragged a breath into lungs that seemed to have been pressed flat as a linen tablecloth. "I'm in no hurry." Nothing like stepping out on a limb with nothing but air beneath you. But this was Grant. Surely he wouldn't deliberately bring up a subject that would hurt her? Surely what Tyler had told him had been firmly put in the past—especially if Tyler had gone running to him and confessed his mistake?

His face brightened. "I thought maybe— Would you— That is . . . could I offer you a ride home?"

If the skies had scrolled back and a choir of angels begun singing, Emma would not have been any more surprised. In a single moment, ten years collapsed away and she was that teenage girl again, too tall and big-boned and awkward, a glad *Yes* ready to burst out like the trumpets of those angels.

Could he still be the boy who would give a girl a ride home and never ask again, choosing instead the prettier face, the livelier eyes? Had he learned, like the adult he said he'd become, which would wear better in the wash? Or was she just fooling herself and making far too much of this?

With a glance up the hill, she said, "It's probably shorter to walk."

"It probably is. But you said you were in no hurry."

Was he trying to convince her? Goodness. "I don't want to put you to any trouble."

A smile flickered at the corners of his lips. If she hadn't been watching him so closely, she might have missed it. "I'm not offering out of the goodness of my heart, to spare your bum knee and your lumbago. I'm asking because I'm a selfish man and I haven't been able to get near you all day for that crowd."

She tried not to laugh and failed utterly. "I do not have lumbago. And my knees are in perfect working order, *denkes*."

"Emma."

"What?"

"Please get in the buggy." He waved a hand in the direction of the fence, where his patient horse stood in the traces, waiting.

She had never been so happy to obey.

CHAPTER 18

This was nothing like the ride he'd given her as a teenager. Then, they'd both been tongue-tied and uncertain, Emma in an agony of self-consciousness and inexperience that had probably done more to chase him away than anything. Now, she was the woman who had fed him and his crew breakfast. Who could take a joke as well as make one. Who had managed to travel to New York City and turn down a literary agent all by herself—something the old Emma would not have been able to imagine, much less do.

The question that plagued her now was, what did he think of the secret Tyler had blabbed? Was he going to let her down easy in the next few minutes, or...?

Emma, there you go again, only thinking of yourself. For heaven's sake, your mind needs a change of scenery.

"It was a nice wedding, *ja?*" she said at last, when she could bear the silence not one more second. "Amelia looked so happy."

"Eli is a good man." Grant's shoulder touched hers with the rocking of the buggy as he turned onto Edgeware Road, and she thrilled at the unexpected gift. "He and I have become acquainted in our talks about what he wants for the new shop. In fact, he doesn't want to waste any time, so he'll start next week. The sooner he gets established, the sooner he'll be able to provide for Amelia and the boys right at home instead of going into Whinburg every day."

"He's taking over the work at the pallet shop until then?"

Grant chuckled. "Oh, yes. The very first thing he'll learn as a married man is how to take instruction from his wife."

"If she gives him a kiss for every one he gets right, they'll have a stack of pallets up to the roof in no time." Then she blushed. She shouldn't have mentioned kissing. He might think that was what she had in mind when she came along on this ride. Maybe he would think she was fast. Or desperate. Or both.

"Maybe," he agreed, smiling at something over the horse's shoulder. "I think there will be a lot of laughter and kissing in that shop. But that's a wonderful *gut* thing. You know his story?"

Emma nodded. If he could speak so calmly about kissing, then her jitters were all for nothing. "Amelia told me. So sad for him. I hope Elam and Matthew can fill the hole that the loss of his little boy left in Eli's heart. Of course no one can replace his family, just as no one can replace Enoch Beiler, but I think with God's help, he and Amelia can heal each other."

"That's true. A person cannot replace one who is gone," he said softly, and her heart sank.

There was her answer, put as gently and considerately as a man could. She could not replace Lavina. Golden memory or not, mourning finished or not, no one could, and she needed to give up hope that he might want her to.

Emma's throat swelled with tears that she must not shed, and she bit the inside of her lip to keep it from trembling. This was why he had asked her to ride with him. He wanted a quiet space of time to tell her, where no one could hear and no one would talk or make guesses or assumptions.

"Do you not think so, Emma?"

"*Ja*. You can't replace a unique person the Lord has made," she whispered. *There will never be another Lavina—at least, the one you married and love still. The fact that she became someone else—someone else's woman, even—doesn't change the golden memory of that girl you hold in your heart, pure and laughing and inviolate.*

"But two people can heal each other," he persisted. Did he not realize he was breaking her heart? "You said so . . . you must believe it."

"I do believe it." She swallowed the lump of tears down so she could speak. "If it's God's will."

"I seek His will every day," Grant said, sounding strangely emphatic, as though she might not believe him. "Every day I ask, and every day it seems as if He is pointing me in one direction. And now I believe He has given me such a shove that I can hardly ignore it."

"Goodness. God shoved you? That never works with horses, but maybe it does with people."

Setting aside her own pain, she was trying to lighten the frown lines between his brows, but it didn't seem to help. The horse slowed, and Grant turned him into a harvesting track that led to the gate of the Lapps' east field.

"Emma, Tyler West told me something as we were work-ing yesterday."

If she could have flung herself out the door and run, she would have done it. But that would just put this conversation off until another day, and there was no way she was going through another night like last night. "He should not have said . . . what he said."

"He came to stay with us, as I'm sure you saw."

"Thank you for opening your home to him."

"He is very unhappy at losing your friendship. I hope you will forgive him."

Amelia and Eli's happiness had soothed her humiliation and distress, and she found she could say truthfully, "I already have. I'm just not going to tell him right away."

"That's good, because you see, he may have broken your confidence, but he opened a door for me."

She turned her gaze from the horse's slow munching of the bishop's grass and dared to lift it to Grant's dear brown eyes. "A door?"

"*Ja*, the kind God shoves you through. Emma, I had no idea that you cared for me in... in that way."

She could not look into those eyes anymore. The horse, at least, would not humiliate her silently with every stricken moment. "I had hoped to keep it to myself," she whispered. "And not burden you with it."

"Burden me? *Burden?*" With one finger, he touched her chin and turned her face toward him. But still she couldn't meet his eyes. "Your love is no burden, Emma Stolzfus. I am not worthy of it."

It's not you, it's me.

"I do not have much to offer you," he said softly. "This heart is broken and dry, like soil that has not been tended. But if you are willing, maybe we can tend each other. And maybe God will make fruit grow there."

For a moment, all she heard was "broken and dry." Then the rest of his words caught up to her, and astonishment gave her the courage to look him full in the face. "What?" she said inanely. "What do you mean?"

His mouth formed a rueful bow. "What I am trying to say,

not very well, is...I would like to court you. And it seems you would like that, too."

He couldn't be saying those words to her. He had brought her out here to let her down easy, hadn't he? Had she misheard? Was this even happening?

When her jaw just hung there with no words coming out of her open mouth, he went on. "You know this is not the first time I've courted a woman, but it's been a long time. I'm more eloquent with my hands than I am with words. Just the opposite of you. But all the same, you are one of God's gifts that I was talking about earlier, and I would treat you with respect and tenderness."

"You...would?" She needed to get something perfectly clear, so there would be no more mistakes, no more wrong information. "*Me?*"

"Yes, you, Emma Stolzfus. Maybe someday you can tell me just why this is so hard to believe."

"Because I thought you still loved Lavina. And there was no room for me."

"I told you last night that it was all in the past, and that my mourning for her was finished. Didn't you believe me?"

She had believed that little voice she had listened to all her life. The one that said *not good enough, not pretty enough, not...enough.* Maybe it was time to take a page from Grant's book and grow up, at the advanced age of thirty.

"Yes," she said. "I believe you. Now."

And when he took her in his arms at last, she was so overwhelmed by the scent and warmth of the skin where her nose was pressed against his neck, and so deafened by the singing of the angels that she didn't even realize he hadn't kissed her.

Not until much later, in the middle of another sleepless night.

* * *

Since Eli and Amelia were not going on their wedding rounds right away, Amelia insisted that their quilting frolic go ahead as usual the next Tuesday. This meant Emma was forced to keep her news to herself for an entire week. She didn't even tell Lena—though sometimes it threatened to burst out of her without warning, and she'd be hard pressed to keep her mouth closed on the building pressure.

Why not tell? she asked herself a dozen times a day. *Mamm needs to make plans. You need to give her and Karen time to decide whether she'll go to live with Katherine as she had suggested, or whether one of our unmarried cousins will come to stay at the* Daadi Haus.

But somehow, the words stayed bottled up inside until she felt like a can of soda that had been shaken by a giant hand. One move and everything would explode.

The wedding cleanup began at 4:00 a.m. and took all of Wednesday, and Emma and Carrie pitched in to help. The women wiped down all the benches, which the men loaded into the bench wagon so that they would be ready for the next church Sunday.

When will they come to Karen's for my wedding? But that was a question she would have to save until Grant someday asked her to be his wife.

The rest of the week saw her busy catching up with everything she'd neglected in favor of Amelia's wedding—laundry, sewing, baking. A letter came on Saturday, with a New York return address.

Dear Emma,

I'm very sorry I didn't get to see you before I left on Wednesday. I'm also sorry about what happened the night before the wedding. Grant says that everything is okay, but he didn't give me any more details and you didn't seem to be around on Wednesday morning when I drove by.

Other than what I caused by my own stupidity, I had a great time in Whinburg, mostly because of you and Grant. I feel privileged to have been part of Amelia and Eli's wedding. I feel I really know the world in your book. I think that's why I came to visit...so I could live what I read in a different way. And can I say, the movie is just as good as the book, ha ha. *Englisch* joke.

Take care of yourself. I hope I hear from you again someday.

Your friend,
Tyler

Emma folded up the letter and slipped it back in its envelope. He would hear from her. Soon. Forgiveness wasn't worth much if you kept it to yourself and did nothing to help the hurt in the other person. Maybe, if she had the joy of planning a wedding, she would even invite him.

The next day, being their off Sunday, Emma and Lena were having a quiet morning while Emma read the story of Ruth aloud. It had always been one of Emma's favorites; Ruth had been so brave. It couldn't have been easy giving up home and family and nation for a man and traveling so far.

Thank goodness it wasn't likely she would ever have to do that. If it were God's will that she and Grant should marry, she would have a new home and a new family right here in her own district. What a marvel. It would be something else to be thankful for.

The sound of a buggy in the lane brought both their heads up, and Emma looked out the window to see Grant in his buggy, the little white *Kapps* of his daughters just visible through the windows. "Mamm, it's Grant. He's brought his children to visit."

"Has he, now. That seems...very friendly of him." Lena eyed her. "Is there something I should know?"

Emma couldn't keep a straight face. The smile just busted out on one side the more she tried to keep the other solemn. "Soon, Mamm."

"Ah." Lena sat back in her chair with the satisfied air of someone who has figured everything out at last. "I'll look forward to that."

"We've come to ask you to take a ride with us," Grant said when she went outside. He climbed down from the buggy and his eyes crinkled in a smile. "Could you leave Lena for an hour or so?"

"I think I could. Go in and say *Guder Mariye* while I say hello to everyone."

Grant pulled his straw hat off as he went, and Emma peeked in to see the girls on the back bench, with Katie, the elder, holding a squirming Zachary. "Hullo, girls. Your *Daed* says we might go for a ride. Is it okay if I come along?"

"I'm hungry," Sarah moaned. "I want to go home."

"I'm hungry, too," Emma confided, though she'd had lunch not an hour past. "How about I put together a picnic basket and we ask Daed to take us somewhere nice to eat it?"

"Like the river?" Katie moved the baby to a more comfortable angle. Small as she was, he filled her whole lap and then some.

The river was the last place Emma would have chosen, considering it was strewn with reminders of that last disastrous conversation with Calvin. But maybe it would be *gut* to go with Grant and his family. They would overlay good memories on bad ones, and make the river their place instead.

"That sounds good," she said. "I'll be back in just a minute."

In the kitchen, she grabbed her carry basket and stuffed it full of everything she could lay her hands on. What a lucky thing she'd got the baking done. Half a dozen doughnuts, a couple of jars of lemonade, some fat slices of cake, and several pieces of fried chicken went into the basket, along with a bunch of apples. Then she tucked a cloth over the top and went to find Grant.

"I can't believe you've kept this from me all week." Lena shook a knitting needle at Emma while Grant smiled quietly, kneeling beside her chair. "Grant just told me we'd be seeing a little more of him—and not for building projects, either."

Emma's shoulders slumped with relief as she knelt on Lena's other side. If he'd told Mamm, then he really meant it. "I didn't want to say anything until—" *I knew it was real.* She risked a glance at him while her soul sang. She should have had more faith. Then she could have told Carrie and Amelia on cleanup day, and they could be celebrating with each other even now.

He stood, and squeezed Lena's hand. "I will have her back in an hour."

"Take your time," Mamm said. "It will take me all of that and more to savor this. And then you'll have to go over to the big house and tell your sister. You don't want her to hear about yet another man over the grapevine."

"She's joking," Emma reassured him as she hurried out ahead of him with the basket. "There aren't any other men, as you know very well."

Down at the river, Emma found a flat spot that wasn't too damp, and not so close to the rush of water that Zachary might stagger over and fall in. It didn't keep the girls away, though. After they'd descended on the food like a plague of locusts, they danced away to play at the river's edge, leaving Emma and Grant alone.

"I feel as though I should be with them, to get acquainted."

Under his father's watchful gaze, Zachary investigated the area immediately around them, particularly fascinated by the gnarled roots of a tree and what he could find in the crevices. "Plenty of time for that." Grant followed her gaze. "If we only have an hour, we should talk while those two are busy getting wet."

"Talk? What about?"

"Before we go much further, I want you to know everything. And then if you feel you must change your mind about us, I would not hold it against you."

The cake rolled uneasily in her stomach. "I won't change my mind." He would be more likely to change his before she would ever give him up.

He was silent a moment, as if arranging his thoughts. "You've been in our home for church, so you know that it isn't as nice as some."

"It needs a woman to care for it." She had hoped this might lighten his expression, but it didn't.

"That is true. But there has been some financial difficulty." He looked up. "The economy has not been kind to many of us. The house is worth less than my mortgage, and while I have enough work, sometimes I live from check to check. The money must go to the bank before other expenses." After another pause, he went on. "And there are...bills from Springfield as well."

Emma had not thought of this. Even though Lavina had not survived, the effort to save her still had to be paid for. "I'm used to economizing. Mamm and I get by on very little." If that happy day ever came, she would rather live with him in a chicken coop than go back to the way things had been, but she wasn't about to say so.

"I must try to get as much work as I can over the summer so I can get ahead a little bit, so we may not see each other as much as I'd like."

Emma took courage. "You will still have lunch hours. I can bring your lunch and we can eat together, at the very least. And supper, too, if you must work into the evening."

"I would like that."

Now he would kiss her.

Surely.

But he did not. Instead, he encouraged little Zachary to come back to the blanket and have a piece of apple. "I think we should prepare ourselves for some talk," he said. "Me because I'm not observing three months of mourning, and you because of all the men you've been running around with." He twinkled at her. "A pair of rebels, we are."

"But people will understand, won't they, about you having done your mourning long ago?"

"Some will. But some will not."

"Are you thinking of the Yoders?"

"*Ja.* They have had the same amount of time to mourn, but I'm sure they will look at it differently." His gaze moved beyond her, checking that the girls were still in view. "I want a home again—a real home. And if the price I must pay is a little disapproval, then I'll pay it."

His eyes met hers again, and she thrilled with the certainty that he was speaking of their future. "I would like a home of my own someday, too," she whispered.

"Already we agree," he said, leaning back on his hands. His smile was even warmer than the sunshine that fell like a blessing on her shoulders.

"What do you mean, he thinks that God is shoving him toward you?" Carrie let their quilt fall to the table, as if she'd forgotten she was holding one end of it. "A man is supposed to run toward you, not wait to be shoved."

"Carrie," Amelia said softly, putting a hand on her arm. "Every man is different. Grant may not say romantic words, but his actions show that he cares for Emma."

"That's true," Carrie conceded, watching Emma carefully. "I heard that young Kelvin wouldn't let Mandy paint every room a different color in their new house. He said they all had to be white, or they'd stay unpainted."

"I wouldn't let her paint them all a different color, either," Emma said. "Every time you made a new quilt, you'd have to repaint the bedroom to match. Either that or make them in the same colors, over and over."

"Now you're just being contrary." Carrie stuck her tongue out. "Oh Emma, it's just so wonderful that the man you've loved all these years is courting you!"

And then the poor quilt got abandoned on the table again as the three of them hugged each other for about the fifteenth time since Emma had broken the news. But honesty ran among them the way the river ran among the rocks in its bed, scouring the truth from between lumps of pride and reluctance and bringing it to the surface. She hadn't wanted to bring her reservations up. It almost felt disloyal to Grant to speak them aloud. But if she couldn't ask Carrie and Amelia, who could she ask? Karen? Not likely.

"Is it...do you think it's strange that he hasn't...kissed me yet?" She could hardly get the words out, but something inside her drove her to it. She had to know.

Amelia smoothed the first section of the quilt on the table-top while Carrie busied herself rolling up the other end. The plan for today was to stencil the rest of the flowers on the fabric, but so far they'd barely managed to get it out of its bag and put it on the table.

"It's not strange," Amelia said slowly. "Many of our men find it hard to even talk about emotional things, never mind demonstrate how they feel. They're more likely to make you a chair or bring home a set of silverware than they are to look deep into your eyes and vow everlasting adoration."

"I don't need adoration or silverware," Emma said shortly. "But I would like my first kiss."

"You've never been kissed?" Carrie blurted. "Ever?"

Emma gave her a look over the metal rims of her glasses. "You need a boyfriend first. And you know perfectly well I've never had one of those."

"Oh. I—well, I thought—I mean, there are all those parlor games and band hops and places where...oh. You didn't go to those, either, did you?"

Emma shook her head. "Now I'm glad that Grant will be my first. First kiss, first real date, first..." Oh dear. No, she couldn't say that. It would mean she was taking the future for granted, and she would never, ever do that.

"First time in the bedroom with the door closed?" Amelia

asked in a completely normal tone, as if she'd said *Shall we start the stenciling here?*

Emma's face felt like it had caught on fire. "*Ja,*" she said in a voice not much more than a whisper.

"She's blushing." You could hear Carrie's teasing whisper across the room. Across the house. Maybe even out in the yard at the end of the lane, where Eli was pacing out the foundation markers for the new shop with Grant and some of the men. "You don't need to be shy about it, Emma. It's a natural part of married life."

"But I am not married, and you're embarrassing me."

"Leave her alone, *Liewi,*" Amelia chided. "You can tease her when she is engaged, not before."

"All right." Carrie gave Emma a squeeze and got out the pencils. "I still can't imagine a man asking a woman if he can court her and not kissing her, though."

Emma's stomach sank. "Does he not want to kiss me?" And then her worst fear sprang out of her mouth like a hen frightened off its nest. "Is he only looking to see if I'll make a good mother for his children, like Calvin?"

Amelia dropped her stencils. "Of course not. The two of you have known each other for years. You're friends. He knows what kind of woman you are, and now he's free to make his feelings public."

Emma released a long, cleansing breath. If she had the sense God gave a goose, she would have realized how he felt when he didn't speak all those days he was working on the *Daadi Haus* and they had talked and laughed with his crew in her kitchen. He had let his eyes speak, which was all he had been free to do, and in her diffidence she hadn't seen it.

"It's only a matter of time before he asks you to marry him," Amelia said. Well, she should know. She had had two men propose. "You're not teenagers. There's no reason to wait."

"He did say he wanted a proper home again," Emma said.

"And so do you, so there you are. As for the kissing," Amelia went on, "some men are more conservative than others."

"Unlike Melvin and me," Carrie put in. "We kissed that first night in his buggy, and I'm not ashamed of it. After him, I didn't want to kiss anybody else."

"I'm glad to hear it." Emma's tone was a little more schoolmarmish than she'd meant, so she softened it. "But you can see why I feel so ... I mean, I have no experience to go on. How do I know what is normal from one man to another?"

"That's why you have us." Carrie handed her a marking pencil, and Emma leaned over a square. "Between us, we've kissed at least four men."

With swift, sure strokes, a rose took shape in white wax. She moved on to the next one. "At least?"

"Well, there was one boy before Melvin, but he didn't count. He was *Englisch*."

Emma looked up in astonishment. All the years she'd known Carrie, and she'd never heard this. "You kissed an *Englisch* boy?"

Carrie shrugged. "It was *Rumspringe*, at a band hop. I think one of his friends dared him to kiss an Amish girl, and there I was at the soda cooler, getting a Coke."

"What was it like?" Amelia looked amused.

"The Coke was fine, *denki*. Just you wait until Matthew wants to run around," Carrie told her. "Then you won't be smiling like that. And for your information, the kiss was nice, too. He was a good kisser, even if he was *Englisch*."

Emma just shook her head. Carrie was so casual about it, as if kissing any boy who asked you was perfectly normal. For Emma, kissing one boy—man—was enough emotional torment for a lifetime.

Maybe she was just thinking about it too much. Another rose formed under her pencil. Amelia was right. Grant was a conservative man by nature as well as by training. She just needed to be patient, that was all. She could make him smile. She could feed his children, that was certain—they'd left nothing but crumbs in the picnic basket. She could tease him with impunity. Even six months ago, she would have thanked God rejoicing at such gifts. The fact that they were courting didn't mean she could cast aside the small gifts and joys because she wanted bigger ones. God had provided in the small ways; He would provide in the larger ones as well.

Besides, maybe she could be the one to kiss him first.

CHAPTER 19

The news broke like a thunderclap over Whinburg Township, and Emma realized just how many people had believed that she had been destined to care for Mamm until the latter was called to be with God, and to care for Karen's children until she herself was.

Her sister Karen being one of them.

Emma and Grant stood outside the home of one of Old Joe Yoder's sons. Together. In public. It was a declaration of Grant's intentions toward her, and a small crowd gathered around them after the service and before lunch. Some of the ladies, like Old Joe's wife, Sarah, had left tact behind them decades ago.

"Well, you've proved me wrong, Emma Stolzfus," she said in a voice that creaked like a rusty gate. "I thought you'd never get a man, and here you are with him and his children, too. I s'pose you'll be announcing a wedding sooner or later. I hope he makes you happier than he made Lavina."

"Happiness is a gift from God," Emma managed. *Oh, please don't let me blush on Grant's behalf. What must he think?*

"Tell me that again when you've been married six months." And with that, Sarah moved the control on her electric wheelchair and trundled off.

"Don't listen to her," said Christina Yoder Hoff, who was

Lavina's sister and the one who had been caring most for the children after Lavina had left. "Some people see life through rose-colored glasses. Great-grandmother Sarah has forgotten where she left hers." She hugged Emma. "I'm glad God has led Grant to you."

Karen hovered on the edges of the crowd, smiling and nodding and generally taking modest credit for orchestrating the whole thing. When she finally got close enough to speak, she kept her voice low. "You certainly know how to make a spectacle, Emma. Why couldn't you have kept things quiet and respectful, and simply let the bishop make an announcement in the fall like everyone else?"

"Can we talk about this at home?" Emma smiled and shook hands with Erica Steiner.

"I can't believe Mamm allowed it. If you'd come to John and me first, we could have talked some sense into you."

"Karen, for once can you just be happy for me?"

"Well, I like that! Where would you be if not for John and me, I'd like to know?"

Emma smiled and acknowledged the introduction of someone whose name she forgot immediately. "Married to Calvin, most likely."

Then, thankfully, Grant led her over to a host of cousins from the Weaver side, and Karen was forced to round up the children and take them into the house for lunch.

Emma tried not to feel guilty. Maybe they should have done as Karen had said, and seen each other discreetly over the summer so that the announcement could be made with all the others in October. That would have been the modest thing to do. But then she would have had no freedom to see and be seen with Grant all summer long. Maybe she didn't deserve that happiness, but she wanted it.

For once, she wanted to enjoy something that Karen hadn't had first. She wanted to bask in the pleasure of standing next to Grant. In the knowledge that he had chosen her and wasn't afraid to say so in front of the whole *Gmee*. Was that so wrong?

By this time Christina Hoff had circled back around and now stood on Grant's other side. "I think maybe it would be *gut* for Emma to take the children in for lunch, don't you, Grant? She may as well get used to having children at the table."

Emma looked from one to the other. "How have you done it before?"

"The children have been sitting with Lavina's family while I eat with the men," Grant said. "Christina and her sisters have been very loving and kind. Without them, I could not have managed."

"I hope we'll see as much of them as ever," Christina said, smiling. "We're their family, after all."

"They'll be very fortunate *Kinner*, then, with more than one family to love them," Emma told her. It might be interesting at Thanksgiving and Christmas, she could tell right now. But she would not think of that. She would focus on happiness—and every time she moved and felt the steadiness of Grant's shoulder touching hers, happiness wasn't hard to find.

"You're positively glowing," Carrie whispered to her as they went in to lunch. "Courtship is a serious matter, and here you are smiling all over yourself."

Emma bumped her, careful not to lose hold of little Sarah's hand. "I can't help it. Maybe in twenty years I'll have learned some decorum."

Carrie tried to keep her frown in place but her face just

wasn't built for it. "See that you do," she said in her best imitation of Mary Lapp, and they both tried to smother their laughter as Carrie went to sit with her cousins.

"Poor Carrie Miller," Christina said as she settled Zachary on her lap. Katie and Sarah sat between the two of them, and Emma tried not to notice that they minded Christina more than they did her. Oh, they were respectful enough, but it would take time for them all to get used to the idea that someday Emma might be *Mamm* while Christina would still be *Aendi*. "Poor? Why do you say that?" Emma asked.

"I remember when she and Melvin were married. They were so much in love."

"They still are."

"We expected she'd be a mother before their first anniversary, and here..." Christina's voice trailed away. "*Ach*, well, it's God's will."

Emma's first instinct was to leap to Carrie's defense. She was not poor. If a hardworking man's love was riches, then Carrie was one of the wealthiest women in Whinburg. And as for God's will...well, it was not for lack of prayer that their little family had not grown beyond two. It was just too bad that some people had to dwell on what God had not provided instead of on what He had.

Thankfully, the bishop stood to indicate they would say grace, and silence fell. When prayer was over, Emma helped Sarah spread peanut butter filling on her bread. Half of her wished the stuff hadn't had the marshmallow topping added that all the *Kinner* loved. With her mouth glued shut from peanut butter, Emma wouldn't be able to speak, no matter what the temptation. But for now, she would just have to rely on self-control.

After lunch and visiting, Grant suggested that she and Lena come by his house for a game of Scrabble.

"You go, Emma," her mother said. "If you could drop me off at home, I think I would like to rest this afternoon."

"Are you feeling well, Mamm?"

"As well as ever. But playing chaperone is for folks like your sister. I don't think you need me watching over you. The children will do well enough for that."

"A chaperone? At my age?"

"Sixteen or sixty, a single woman in a man's house who isn't paid to clean it will cause talk. There will be one or two who think I should mind your business for you, but I'm too tired. Take me home."

After she saw Lena settled in her chair with *Family Life*, she flapped the reins over her horse's back and sipped the pleasure out of the ride over to Grant's house.

I am going to his home because he has invited me. I have every right to be there. And it seems he even wants me to be the mistress of it.

Dear Lord, thank you for such gifts.

The board was already set up on the kitchen table when she arrived, and while Grant led her horse to the field, she found the kettle and put it on for tea.

"Where do you keep the teabags?" she asked Katie.

"I don't know. Daed drinks coffee."

"Then I'll make coffee."

"Only in the morning, though. He says it's too expensive to drink the rest of the time."

"Ah. Then should we have milk?"

"We finished it all at breakfast. *Aendi* Christina will bring it when she comes tomorrow."

It was clear she was going to need to be very economical

indeed. "There's nothing like a refreshing glass of water, anyway, is there?"

She and Sarah played Grant and Katie...and won the game. "We didn't have a chance, taking on a writer," he told Katie as she scooped up the tiles.

"I know my vocabulary words," she protested. "There were just all kinds I didn't know this time."

"Next time it will be words I don't know," Emma said. "Vocabulary is one thing that can always grow, no matter how old you are."

"*Aendi* Christina says you're very old to be courting," Sarah informed her.

Grant pulled the little girl against him. "*Aendi* Christina is mistaken. Emma is the perfect age for me to court, because I am so old." His voice cracked as he mimicked an old man's voice and tickled her ribs. She giggled and wriggled away. "It's time for Zachary to say good night. Take him upstairs and then find something to do while Emma and I talk. We'll all have prayers together before you go to bed."

"Can I read my new library book?"

"I hope so, otherwise why am I sending you to school?"

"Daaaaaaed."

Smiling, Emma watched the two girls lead Zachary upstairs between them, his chubby legs managing one riser at a time. When she turned back to the table, she found Grant gazing at her.

"I apologize for my sister-in-law saying things like that, especially in front of the children."

"It's nothing I haven't heard before—or will again. I'm not ashamed of having waited for you. I'd have waited ten years more if that was what it took." She felt a little brazen saying it, but if a woman couldn't be honest with her own man, then something was out of place.

"Still, she should not have said it, particularly in front of Katie. That little *Maedsche* never misses a thing."

"Never mind what others say. It's what we say between us that's important."

"There has not been so much laughter at our table in a long time. Thank you for that, Emma." He paused a moment. "You have really been waiting so long for me?"

Only the warmth in his eyes gave her the courage to say, "Since I was eighteen. I tried to stop—when you and Lavina were married and so happy, I almost did stop. But when she left and I saw you trying to make a life on your own, trying to be both father and mother to your children... *ach*, it was hard. I wanted so much to offer a shoulder to share that burden, but... of course I could not."

"My dearest wish was to find a faithful woman. And here you were, all this time. I thank the *gut Gott* for Tyler West and his big mouth."

Emma found laughter bubbling up behind her tears—tears for the years they had not had together, and laughter for the years that they would. "He gave me a talking-to as well. He said I was too busy looking at all the reasons why you and I couldn't be, and not the reasons why we could."

"It seems we have each been blind where the other is concerned."

"But no more." She smiled into his eyes.

"No more," he echoed.

She couldn't take her eyes from his. The air in the kitchen seemed to thicken, and her face felt hot. Possibility—hope—anticipation—all of it seemed to flicker across the few feet separating them.

"I am very tired of being alone in my home," he said softly. "But you deserve to be courted."

What was he trying to say? "With Mamm, I am not alone, but all the same, it's good to be together with nothing standing between us." She looked down at the scattered Scrabble tiles, then back up. "And I like being able to say what I want to you, with no fear of misunderstanding or of making a fool of myself."

"I would like to say something, but I'm not sure if the time is right. Then I would be the one making a fool of myself, but that's nothing new."

She held his gaze. "You can say anything to me. I would never think you were foolish."

"You say I am the man you have been waiting for. And you are the faithful woman I have been waiting for. Emma, what are we waiting for?"

His eyebrows rose in a way that was so comical that she giggled. "I don't know."

"You deserve your summer of courtship, but I want something more."

Her breath seemed to back up in her throat, and she whispered, "So do I."

"Then you will not think I am rushing you if I ask you to be my wife?"

"Will you think I am hopelessly forward if I say yes?"

Now her eyebrows rose, and they both laughed. And then he was pushing back his chair and she knocked hers over and finally, finally, she found the refuge she had been looking for half her life—in his arms.

From the top of the hill, Emma could see the skeleton of Eli's new workshop going up at the foot of his and Amelia's property, close enough to the road so that a man could pull in and tie up his horse, yet far enough back so they didn't seem too anxious for business. In the good weather, the foundation had set up quickly, and Grant's crew had made short work of studs and beams. Various men from the community, including, to Emma's surprise, Joshua Steiner, had augmented the core crew so that the building was going up with gratifying speed. Amelia had thought they would be able to finish the sheathing and maybe even begin the roof today, and as Emma walked down the hill, she saw that they'd already finished insulating the walls. Many hands made light work, indeed.

She hoped she had enough lemon cake and chocolate peppermint whoopie pies to feed them all when they broke for refreshments. With men coming and going all the time, it was hard to make a good estimate.

Amelia waved from her garden as Emma let herself in through the gate. "Have you come to see your man?" she called gaily.

He was her man, all right. Emma hugged the knowledge to herself. She would tell Amelia and Carrie soon—probably later today—but for now it was hers alone to marvel over. "I have, and I brought some baking for when they break."

"Oh, good. I made plenty of cookies and a big pan of matrimonial cake, but I'm afraid it's not going to be enough. Alvin Esch and a bunch of his friends arrived to help just after lunch." She paused. "Are you still..."

Emma knew immediately what she referred to. "Not so much anymore. His packets stopped coming, you know, when he finished his course. I don't know if he'll start up again in the fall. It won't be with my help, in any case." *I won't be living here then, so I won't be able to sneak his packets out of the mailbox and into the cupboard.*

Amelia slashed at the soil with her hoe, separating weeds from their roots with cheerful efficiency. "I can't say I'm sorry. It was a risky business. I'm very surprised you were never found out."

"I am, too," Emma confessed.

"Have you told Grant what you were up to?"

"Do you think I should?"

Amelia paused to gaze at her. "You shouldn't keep secrets from your man."

"And I won't—when they're mine. But this one is Alvin's."

Thoughtfully, Amelia swiped the hoe through the soil, swinging it more than using it for its intended purpose. "I suppose."

Time to change the subject. She shaded her eyes with her hand and stepped closer to the corner of the house, where she had a long view down the lawn to the construction site. "It looks like the men are coming down."

Amelia dropped the hoe. "Already? Goodness. I filled the cooler with jars of water. We just need to get the pitchers of lemonade out of the refrigerator and turn the gas on under the coffeepot. It's ready to go."

While Amelia washed her hands, Emma took everything out of her carry basket and set it out on the table on the porch. Then she hustled into the kitchen to turn on the flame under the coffeepot. Amelia took the drinks outside just in time for Alvin and his friends to swarm the table like so many tall, gangly locusts.

When Emma brought the coffee out, the boys were lounging on the lawn with their suspenders slipped off their shoulders, and Grant was standing on the top step looking hot and thirsty.

She put the coffee down and poured him a jar of lemon-ade. He smiled at her as he took it. "You read my mind."

For no reason at all, she blushed, as if this were an in-timacy that belonged behind closed doors. "You seemed to prefer lemonade to water when you were at our place working on the porches."

"Not every woman would notice."

"I noticed everything you did." And then, drat it all, she blushed again.

But he only smiled, not releasing her gaze—which meant she nearly dropped the pitcher. Only when Amelia gently took it from her did she realize she'd dribbled lemonade on the porch floor and it would have to be wiped up quickly be-fore the sticky stuff got tracked everywhere.

Goodness. How was it he could shake her up and make her mind go blank simply by looking at her? And he was so confident about it—already some of the men were teasing him, but he only laughed it off. She felt ready to crawl into the nearest linen closet and hide there the rest of the after-noon.

"Emma, I think we might need more lemonade." Amelia was trying not to smile and failing. "The lemons are in the refrigerator, and you know where the sugar is."

It wasn't a linen closet, but it would do.

When she came out with the fresh pitcher, the men were straggling back to the shed. Alvin Esch grabbed half a dozen whoopie pies in one hand. "We could use that down there," he told her with a jerk of his head. "Want me to carry it?"

If she took it, she might catch another glimpse of Grant—and maybe he would smile that way at her again. "*Nei, denki.* I'll do it. You might carry the cookie tray, though. Amelia wants it emptied."

It wasn't often she got a chance to see Grant managing his crew. The ease with which he gave instructions, and his patience with teenage boys whose enthusiasm outweighed their common sense, was a beautiful thing. Even little Matthew and Elam, who were out of school, hopped to it when he told them to do something. Her man was as humble as any in the *Gmee*, yet he was a born leader—one who wouldn't ask someone to do something he wasn't willing to do himself, even if it was only picking up the lumber scraps and fallen nails at the end of the day, a job usually reserved for the small boys.

Alvin dropped the tray on a plank set on two sawhorses, so Emma set the pitcher and a clean pint jar next to it. Then she walked around the side of the building, keeping so far away from the activity that she was practically in the cornfield. Where was Grant?

Ah, up there on the peak of the partially completed roof. He straddled a couple of planks on the far end as he pulled up the stovepipe from whoever was feeding it to him on the inside. After setting it in place and securing it, he straightened and saw her. She hadn't meant to distract him from his work, but when he waved, she couldn't help the smile that broke out. Who cared if half the crew saw her grinning her fool head off? The man up there on the roof made her happy simply by existing—and it seemed she could make him smile with just as little effort.

Alvin scrambled up the ladder like a monkey, a couple of studs under his arm. It was very high on the roof. The crew were skilled, experienced men. They knew what they were doing. It was the teenaged boys who shouldn't be allowed up there. Alvin carried too many studs. His load was off center, and no one stood at the bottom of the ladder to steady it.

"Alvin!" she shouted. "Drop them!"

Grant shouted something at the same time, and slid down the beams toward him. Alvin wavered, dropped the lumber, and jumped for the roof just as Grant reached the exact same place.

Steel-toed boot met ungloved hand.

Alvin screamed as Grant lost control of his slide, flailed fruitlessly for something to grab on to, and man and boy tumbled over the edge and fell fifteen feet to the ground.

CHAPTER 20

Emma's shriek could have been heard all the way over in Whinburg. She yanked herself into motion and ran as she had never run in her life, arms and legs pumping, skirts flapping against her thighs, heart pounding with fear.

She skidded to a stop just behind Joshua, who knelt beside Grant with a face as bleached as a sheet. "Is he—is he—?" She didn't even know how to finish the sentence.

He lay unmoving, on his back, his left leg twisted up under him at an angle so unnatural Emma was thankful he was already unconscious. Alvin, on the other hand, had landed partially on a pallet of insulation and was already sitting up, looking dazed and horrified at the same time.

Joshua looked up. "Run for the phone. Call nine-one-one."

She was already moving, flying down the lane as if the very hounds of hell were after her. She caught herself on the door of the phone shanty before sheer momentum caused her to barrel right past it, and grabbed the phone off the hook. It took two tries before she got the numbers right.

"Nine-one-one, what is your emergency?"

"*Ein herr hat*—" She caught herself and started again in English. "One of our men has fallen off a roof. We need help."

"Is he conscious?"

"*Nei*. No."

"Broken bones?"

"*Ja*, I think so. His leg did not look so good."

"Where are you located?"

"I'm at the phone shanty. But Grant—the man who has fallen—he is at the Fischer place on Edgeware Road."

"The address, ma'am? The ambulance will need an address."

What was Amelia's address? Why couldn't she think of the numbers? *Dear* Gott, *please tell me the address.*

And then her brain cleared, as if someone had drawn a curtain back from a window. "Eighteen-fifty-three Edgeware Road. Please hurry."

"I'm dispatching the ambulance right now. Please stand at the end of the driveway to flag them, all right?"

"*Ja*. Yes, I will do that. Thank you."

"Will you be all right, ma'am?"

Tears welled up in Emma's eyes. Until she knew Grant was out of danger, nothing in the wide world would be all right. But she couldn't say that to the kind woman on the phone. "I'm fine. Just please tell them to hurry."

She hung up and began to run the quarter mile back to Amelia's place. She had to see him before the ambulance came. Maybe he was awake. He would certainly be in pain. Had someone put something under his head?

Eli Fischer was waiting at the end of the lane, watching for her. "They're coming. Is he conscious?" She was so out of breath she could hardly gasp the words out.

Eli shook his head. "I felt the back of his head and he's got an awful knot back there. But with the leg... I'm thinking it's *gut* he is not awake to feel it."

"Will he be all right?" She couldn't keep the fear out of her voice. A bump on the head was one thing, but hitting it when you fell off a roof was serious. More serious than the leg, maybe.

Ach, mein Gott, mein Gott, *please protect him. Please be with him and keep him. Let him be well. Show me how to help him.*

Eli gripped her arm, and through the gabbling in her mind, she focused on him. "He needs you. Go to him. We will let the Yoders know to keep the little ones while he goes to the hospital."

In the distance, they both heard the wail of the siren. "You'll flag them down?" she asked, already half into a run.

"*Ja.* This is my place. You go take yours."

She beat the EMTs to Grant's supine body by a matter of seconds—long enough to see that his eyelids had begun to flutter. When they worked on his leg and she heard his moan of pain, it was all she could do to beat off the buzzing of the black dots in her vision and stay on her feet. They strapped him down and loaded him into the back with the efficiency of long practice, and one of them looked around at the silent crowd. Emma knew the same prayers were going up to God as were in her mind.

"Are any of you members of this man's family?" he asked.

The men shifted and someone—Joshua—gave her a push in the small of her back, and Emma found herself not hovering anxiously on the periphery, but standing in front of the EMT, twisting her hands in her apron. He lifted his eyebrows and she realized she had to say something before they slammed the doors shut and drove off without her.

"I—I will be," she managed past her fear. "We are engaged to be married."

Somewhere in the back, she heard Amelia gasp, but there was no time to explain.

"Close enough," he said. "Hop in."

Emma didn't remember much about the ride to the hospital. Normally her writer's eye took in details in unfamiliar situations, just in case she could ever use them in a story or an article. Now such things were furthest from her mind. It was all she could do to remember to brace herself for the turns in the road. Every cell in her body was fixed on Grant, as if her watchfulness alone would keep him safe and out of pain until they got to the doctor.

They pulled into the loading bay and she climbed out, trying to stay out of the way while they yanked the wheels of the gurney into position and ran it up the ramp. Doors seemed to open magically as they ran through, and she would have run right into the triage room with him if someone hadn't grabbed her arm.

"Ma'am? Ma'am, you can't go in there. Please wait outside."

"But we are engaged. I am his family." Or close enough.

"Yes, ma'am, I understand. Please, let me take you to the waiting room, and someone will come and talk to you as soon as they know his condition."

"He fell off a roof," she said inanely, looking over her shoulder at the doors as the woman in the odd blue pajamas led her down a hall and into a little room with orange couches and a low table spread with magazines.

"Can I get you something to drink?"

How kind this *Englisch* woman—girl—was. "A glass of water would be *gut*."

A water bottle gurgled as she filled a paper cup and brought it to Emma. "It's nice and cold."

"*Denki*," she whispered, gripping the cup. "Will they know to find me here?"

The girl nodded. "This is the only waiting room in Emergency. They'll come here first. When you've finished your water, you can come with me and we'll get the paperwork started."

And so Emma waited. Two hours and a pile of forms and several paper cups full of water went by, so of course she was in the bathroom when the doctor came out to find her. She found him talking with Amelia and Eli, as well as Daniel Hoff, Christina's man, who must have arrived at the same time. Even traveling much more slowly in the buggy, they had made good time.

"Please," she said breathlessly. "I'm sorry. I was in the bathroom. How is he?"

"We have just been telling the doctor you couldn't be far away," Amelia told her. "We just got here ourselves."

"I'm Kirk Duncan. Are you Mrs. Weaver?" The doctor had gray hair that sprang back from his forehead in a widow's peak. His blue eyes looked particularly piercing under the lights.

"I am Emma Stolzfus. I am engaged to him," she repeated for what felt like the dozenth time. "Please, will he be all right?"

"Your fiancé suffered some trauma to the head, but as best we can see, there's no fracturing of the skull. We're going to keep him here overnight to make sure he isn't concussed. He's got a broken tibia and a twisted kneecap, so he'll be in a cast for a couple of months. We'll put that on tomorrow, once we know he's stable."

Trauma to the head. Broken leg. Twisted knee.

Ach, he must be in so much pain!

"He should be able to go home tomorrow or the next day," the doctor went on. "From what your friends have been telling me, he's a pretty lucky man. Apparently there was a lumber pile quite close to where he landed. A clip from the corner of a beam would have made my job a lot harder."

Thanks be to the good *Gott* that it hadn't.

"Could I see him?" she asked.

"He's a little groggy from the painkiller, but I don't see why not. A nurse will take you into the recovery room." He glanced at Amelia, hovering anxiously at Emma's elbow. "Just you, though. A crowd will only confuse and agitate him."

Reluctantly, but obeying the authority in his tone, they fell back as the little nurse in the blue pajamas reappeared. "He'll be fine," she confided to Emma as they walked swiftly down the corridor. "I've seen patients with a lot worse trauma come out of it with no problems at all."

Without that hope, Emma might have fainted at the sight of Grant, so tanned and strong and capable, lying between the rails of the bed with a needle poking out of the back of his hand, and a lot of tubes and things going who knew where.

"*Ach, mein Lieb,*" she whispered as the curtains shivered closed, shutting the rest of the world away.

Grant's eyelids flickered, and then opened. "Emma."

"How do you feel?" She couldn't imagine. Who could?

"Strange. Am I floating?"

"No, you're lying in a hospital bed. You have to stay here overnight to make sure you haven't got a concussion. The doctor says you're lucky."

"Don't feel…lucky."

"The bone will mend. In a couple of months you'll be good as new."

"A couple…" The word faded into silence, and Emma

thought he had fallen asleep. Then his eyes opened again. "*Kinner?*"

"Safe with *Aendi* Christina. Daniel is here, though. Do you want to see him?"

"*Nei . . .* just you."

His hand—the one without the needle in it—fumbled for hers. She gripped it like a lifeline as he drifted off into the soft cloud of whatever drugs they had given him.

Just her. He wanted just her.

The magnitude of God's goodness—for giving her such a gift in the midst of all this fear and pain—overwhelmed her. Tears of gratitude welled in her eyes. When the little nurse came back for her fifteen minutes later, she found Emma with her forehead resting on both hands, still gripping Grant's hand as she gave her thanks up to God.

As was the case with many active, healthy men, the sickbed didn't suit Grant one bit. Emma came in five days later with an unbaked chicken noodle casserole in her carry basket, plus potatoes, carrots, and a cake for dessert, to find him sitting at the kitchen table with his leg stuck straight out in front of him, attempting to slide a knitting needle in between skin and cast.

"It itches and I can't reach it," he said by way of greeting.

Where had he found a knitting needle? "That's a big one, for afghans." It must have been one of Lavina's. "You need a number nine needle."

With a growl of frustration, he threw it across the kitchen, where it clattered against the stove and landed on the floor. Emma tried not to smile as she stooped to pick it up. "Feeling better, are you?"

"If you're going to tell me what I need, you'd better bring it."

"I will, next time. Meanwhile, supper will have to do."

His face softened and he caught her hand as she passed. "I am sorry, Emma. I'm a bear and I don't deserve company."

She squeezed his hand in return and began to unpack the basket. "The girls will be home from swimming at the pond soon. I need to get this in the oven. It will take an hour to bake."

When she'd slid the pan in, she fished a box of teabags out of the basket and put the kettle on. "I know you like coffee, but if I drink it this late in the day, I'll be up all night."

"I could have bought some tea for you."

"That's all right. We have lots at home." And with her tea in the house, it felt as if the moving-in process had begun, in the very smallest of ways. She wasn't sure if she was being presumptuous, but when the kettle boiled and he accepted a cup of hot, fragrant tea, she figured if he was going to say something about that, he would have.

"I'm glad we have a few minutes before the *Kinner* come back," he said. "I want to talk some things over."

She waited, watching him over the rim of her cup. When he didn't speak again, a tiny *frisson* of concern darted through her stomach. "Is something wrong?"

He set the cup down a little harder than he had to. "You see me like this and you have to ask that?"

She tried not to feel hurt at his tone. Of course he was frustrated. She hid behind the cup once more. "I mean...other than your leg."

"What else is there, other than my leg?"

"The *Kinner* are well, the whole *Gmee* is traipsing in and out of here with food and household supplies, and you weren't killed in that fall. All in all, I don't see very much wrong...other than your leg."

A flush burned into his cheeks, and she was very glad she'd kept her tone gentle instead of matching his frustrated temper with her own.

"Ah, my Emma. You have a way of putting things into perspective."

My Emma. Now a flush crept into her face as she savored the words. In her heart, she had been his Emma since she turned eighteen. Would it have been this sweet if she'd heard those words then? Or would she have taken them for granted and let them fall to the ground, confident there would be more to come?

At nearly thirty-one, Emma had learned that when it came to sweet things, sometimes there weren't more to come.

"What is troubling you, Grant?"

His tea had cooled enough for him to drink it. She pushed a plate of lemon squares toward him, and he took one.

"A whole summer of not being able to work, that's what."

"Are you worried about Eli's shop? Amelia says your crew is keeping up with the job, and the other men pitch in when they can. They got the roof insulated and finished, she says, and they'll be ready to paint next week."

"So the crew will be getting paid, but I won't."

Emma remembered what he'd said about the mortgage. About living from check to check. "Is it—are you—I know I have no business sticking my nose into your finances, but—"

"You're going to be my wife, Emma. It's best you know that if I can't work, you may not have a home to come to in November."

"You have no savings?"

He shook his head. "Everything I have goes into this house, and feeding the children, and buying them shoes and clothes, and equipment for my work. And hospital bills. It's only because of Eli paying me for the shed that I can even make this month's mortgage payment." His throat worked, and finally the words came out. "Do not think I'm asking you to help. I won't think of it. I'll find a way, even if I have to move to do it."

The offer of her meager savings evaporated in her mouth. "But you cannot lose the house. The children need their home."

"Others have walked away and let the bank have the house. My grandparents live here, but my folks live east of Paradise, and my father would be glad to have me. Have us."

The thought of moving away from Whinburg—from her family, from Amelia and Carrie—made Emma's blood run cold. "Can you ask him for a loan, just until you're back on your feet?"

He licked a finger and pressed it into the crumbs on the plate, but didn't eat them. "They are not wealthy people. They have rooms filled with nothing but love, but I could not ask my father for money. He would give what little he had instantly, but I couldn't do it. And even if he did make me take it, the bank cannot make up a shortfall with love."

Thoughts ran this way and that in her head like a flock of chickens frightened by a hawk. What could she do to help? It was too early in the season to harvest vegetables and sell them at a roadside stand. They had the quilt, but the auctions were finished … and anyway, she could not ask Amelia and Carrie to abandon their households to finish it in several frantic days of stitching. Even if they did, who would buy it? If she took it to the quilt store in Intercourse, it might be months before a tourist chose it.

They didn't have months. They had to do something in a matter of weeks.

Unless...

Could she?

You can't. A woman can't have a public voice.

But this is the only way. I can't let Grant's home—the children's home, my home—go to the bank.

He can ask the Gmee *for a loan. Others have.*

For medical expenses, yes. Not for something like this.

The elders will never allow it. Grant will never allow it. His wife-to-be? Putting herself out there like an actress or a person on the television?

The world will never see me. They will only hear me.

They will only hear you. But first, Grant must hear you.

"Grant," she said slowly, "remember when Tyler West told you why he came to visit Whinburg Township?"

CHAPTER 21

By the time she finished telling him the whole story of why she had gone to New York, and why Tyler had really come to Whinburg, Grant's whole body had gone slack with astonishment. "This was your book? You wrote a book about life among us, and Tyler West thinks he can sell it for *Englischers* to read?"

Emma nodded. Put like that, it did sound ridiculous. But at the same time... "It placed among the top seven in a national contest. Tyler seemed to think it would do as well if it were a real book out there being read by real people."

He gazed into the distance, as if he were seeing not the stove but a crowd of people, all reading. "I suppose it's better than one person seeing a word painted on the side of a house." His gaze flicked to her and focused. "I remember what word it was."

L-I-S-T-E-N.

"Is that what you want, Emma? It's not enough for me to hear you, or for the *Kinner* to hear you and do as you say? You must have this, too?"

She hitched her chair over to the corner of the table and took his hand. "It's not that. I put the book on the altar of sacrifice long ago, and Tyler West went away with a no for an answer. But Grant, as things stand now, with what you are facing—what *we* are facing—what if he could sell it?"

He remained silent, but his hand gripped hers as it had in the hospital. Firm. Warm. His fingers rubbed the back of hers in the only evidence of his agitation.

Emma wound her courage around her like a warm shawl. "He told me that payment is usually made in three parts. One comes on signing of the contract, one when the book is turned in to the publisher, and one when it comes out. Even one of those payments would be enough to keep the bank happy for a month. Maybe two or three. Long enough for you to get back to work again. It's worth a try, don't you think?"

"How fast do you think he can sell it?"

This was not a no. He was actually giving the plan some thought. Emma tamped down her excitement and tried to speak calmly. "I don't know. But he seemed pretty confident in it."

His gaze trapped hers and didn't let it go. "A woman cannot speak publicly, my Emma. This would be very public indeed."

"We could go to the bishop. We could at least try. Surely Daniel Lapp and Moses and the other elders would see that I'm not trying to put myself out in the world for praise. If our *Gott* has given me a talent that would keep a good carpenter in the district and keep him from losing his home, then shouldn't I use it, not bury it in the ground?"

His face softened while his grip on her hand became even more firm. "If you had been born into an *Englisch* family, you would have made a fine lawyer."

"If I had been born into an *Englisch* family, I would not have known you."

"Then it's my good fortune you were not."

And before she could react or get up to pour another cup of tea or even take another breath, he leaned across the corner of the table and kissed her.

The world stopped turning on its axis as Emma's mouth parted under his, and she marveled that a man's lips could look so hard and determined and yet feel so soft and persuasive. An hour could have passed…or a moment…or maybe it was just the space of the breath backed up in her lungs. She drew back and raised her gaze to his, feeling the blood race into her cheeks as fast as it was racing through her veins.

"Is it all right, my Emma?" His voice was gruff, as if he had been affected as much as she.

"Oh, yes," she whispered. "I never knew…" He raised a brow in silent question, still holding her hand. "I never—you—this is the first—" She stumbled to a halt, words deserting her like a box of pins knocked all over the floor.

"The first time you have been kissed?" She could barely manage a nod. "Then I am glad. Glad," he said fiercely. "You have far more to give me than I have to give you. Your talent, your kisses, your generous, practical self…these are gifts I may open for the first time. I wish I had them to give to you, my Emma."

"You have gifts, never doubt that," she said softly, daring to look up into his face. "Your children. Your home. Your love. I have waited for you for twelve years, Grant Weaver. Do you think I would do that for a prettily wrapped box with nothing in it?"

His expression turned bleak. "People fall for prettily wrapped boxes every day. And they find out too late what is inside."

"But you and I," she said softly, "we know what is inside. We have known each other all our lives. I have seen you managing your crew, seen how you are with men and with your children."

"And I have seen how good you are to your *Mamm*. I have even seen your patience under your sister's..." He paused.

"Thumb?" she suggested with a twinkle.

"I was going to say *authority*, but that didn't sound quite right."

With a laugh, she squeezed his hand and got up to get the teapot. "Karen means well. She's a good manager. She just forgets that some people can be managed better than others."

"There's that independent spirit that's about to get us in trouble with the elders," he teased.

"I hope not." She settled in her place once more, the teapot warm under her hands. "I hope they will listen."

If Grant had heard her, maybe there was hope that Moses and Daniel and the others would, too.

If not, then the only One left to listen would be God.

Amelia took off her away bonnet and hung it on a peg next to the door. "Sorry I'm late. Matthew is home with a cold and when he's sick, all his bravery deserts him. Even knowing Eli is at the bottom of the lane painting the shed, he didn't want me to leave him alone." She hugged Emma and bent down to hug Lena. "Carrie's with me—she saw Karen on the porch and got distracted by the new baby. She'll be over in a minute."

Emma already had the quilt top laid out on the table. "We'll be able to start marking the feathers today. I'm anxious to see how it will look."

Amelia surveyed the borders, almost as if she were dividing them over and over into feather widths. "Should we start in the corners or in the centers?"

"Better wait for Carrie. I vote for corners, but she may think differently."

Amelia looked her over with the eye of long friendship. "What's happened to you?"

"Noth—"

"I'm here, I'm here." Carrie came through the door like a whirlwind, swinging off her shawl and hanging it up, all in the same motion. "What did I miss?"

"Emma was about to tell me a fib," Amelia told her over her shoulder. "Don't you think she looks different?"

Carrie gave them both a hug and greeted Lena, who smiled into her knitting and didn't say a word. Then Carrie focused her clear gaze on Emma, who gestured at the quilt. "Should we start the feathers in the corners, or not?"

"You do look different." Carrie ignored this poor attempt at distraction. "I mean, you've been looking happy since we all found out so dramatically that you were engaged, but this is more. This is…" And then understanding dawned. "Emma Stolzfus. He's kissed you, hasn't he? Or something pretty close to it."

Oh, drat this blush that seemed to rise in her face whenever anyone mentioned Grant or anything to do with him. She was thirty years old, not thirteen!

She mumbled something and Amelia pounced like a kitten on a piece of yarn. "I knew it! When did it happen? What made him finally break through and do it? Or—" She made big eyes at Carrie. "Did you kiss him first?"

"I did not!" Emma said at last, goaded beyond endurance. "And it's private, anyway." Some moments were too sacred to share, even with your very best friends. "He kissed me, and I'm happy, and that's that. Now can we talk about this quilt, please?"

Laughing, they settled down to work and soon decided that quilting the roses first would be the best plan. "We're going to work from the inside out, anyway, and stitch the plain diamonds in the ditch, so it makes sense to do the feather borders last," Carrie said. "My fingers are itching to do some stitching, anyway. We've been working on this quilt so long that it's time it was done."

And then she shot Amelia a look. Hm. What was that for?

Amelia pretended not to notice as she threaded a quilting needle. "We have until November. This quilt is more an excuse to get together, not an actual project. If it were, we'd have had it done by last Christmas."

Wait a minute. "November?" Emma said. "Why November? The auction is in September, isn't it?"

Amelia straightened. With another glance at Carrie, she said, "Sunrise Over Green Fields isn't going to the auction. It's going to you. It's your wedding gift from Carrie and me."

Emma looked from one to the other. "No, it's not. If anyone should have it, it's you and Eli. Besides, I need—" She stopped.

I need the money it will bring...though by November, if the elders don't agree to my plan, I could be living in Paradise. Or, as Grant had joked about the distance his folks lived from town, cast out of it.

Carrie turned up her nose. "Amelia and I decided back when we were piecing it that it would go to you. Though at the time we wondered if it would sit in a cupboard until God got around to leading a good man to you."

"But—"

"There's no point in arguing," Amelia told her in a tone the boys must know well. "It's two against one, so there."

Tears welling up and blurring her vision, Emma gazed at the white markings in the squares and imagined how the borders would look—feathers twining around a central column, just as she had imagined months ago. Carrie's clever sketches would be a reality by the autumn, if they took their time. And then the beauty of their work—their shared labor, their friendship—would go with her into her marriage, to wrap around her and Grant when the nights got cold.

She had been crazy to think for a moment she could sell this quilt. How could she when it had come to mean so much?

"Emma, what's wrong?" Amelia, used to ferreting out the reasons for tears, slipped an arm around her shoulders. "I don't think these are tears of happiness. Are you upset about the quilt? Did we do wrong?"

"No, how could I be?" she choked out. "But the money it would have brought at auction..." Her throat closed.

At a loss, Carrie and Amelia turned to Lena, who merely shook her head. "Emma, tell us," Amelia said.

And so she did. About Grant being one payment away from losing the house, about Paradise, about the impossibility of the elders' agreeing to let her publish, everything. "I love him so much," she concluded, still half in tears, "but I'm so afraid that loving him will mean losing everything else I love. That's why this meeting with Bishop Daniel tomorrow is so important. If the elders don't let me publish the book, I don't know what we're going to do."

"You can't leave Whinburg." Carrie's tone brooked no argument. "It's unthinkable."

"I would go where Grant goes," Emma said, controlling the wobble in her voice, but only just. "It would break the piece of my heart that the two of you live in, and Mamm, and the *Kinner* here. Now I know how Ruth felt," she whispered.

"It won't come to that." Amelia hugged her. "I think your plan is a good one. Tyler West must know his business. If he thinks the *Englisch* would buy your book, then they will."

"And maybe we should encourage the men to hire Grant for lots of building projects once he's on his feet," Carrie said. "I bet Melvin would bring it up with all the people he talks to, once they're done talking about pallets."

"I would appreciate that," Emma told her. "And now that I've finished unburdening myself, why don't we get to work on these borders? At this rate we'll only have one feather to show for our afternoon together."

As Emma got out the marking pencils and tape measure, she reflected that she had much more than that to show for an hour spent in her friends' company.

She had a basketful of encouragement, and a room full of loyalty. Whatever the bank thought of their ledger book, at least she knew one thing. She and Grant were rich in everything that really counted.

"It's been a long time since I rode in the back of a spring wagon," Grant called through the rolled-up rear window. "I feel like a sack of potatoes."

"Your eyes are much nicer, though." Emma flapped the reins over Ajax's back and started him up the lane. The sound of Grant's laughter brought a welcome lift to her worried spirits.

She was trying not to borrow trouble—worrying about the future meant you didn't have enough faith in God's keeping—but the more she tried not to think about what awaited them at the bishop's home, the more the doubts and secondary plans and fears buzzed in her mind, like flies that would not be shooed away.

Luckily for Grant's patience, the Lapp farm was only a mile or so down Edgeware Road, and Ajax set a brisk pace. She had worried about Grant's leg, stuck straight out in the back of the wagon with no support, but he had wedged it securely between a crate full of coffee cans filled with nails and a rolled-up canvas tarpaulin. Short of her overturning the wagon, his leg was immovable until she came to help him.

She pulled to a gentle stop in Daniel's yard and looped the reins over the rail. "You stay here," she told the horse as she patted his ribs. "We won't be long."

She slid the tarp out from between Grant's legs and helped him slide out the back onto one foot, then handed him his crutches. "I hope you didn't get any slivers."

"I wouldn't tell you if I did." His eyes crinkled with humor and she took her place beside him, walking slowly to match his hitch and swing.

Mary Lapp met them at the door. "*Guder Mariye*, Grant. It's nice to see you, Emma. Come in." She stood aside as Grant negotiated the porch steps sideways, using his crutch to hop up one at a time. The Lapps held church in the machine shed, which had a nice big wheelchair ramp, but that didn't help their guests now.

"The men are in the front room," Mary told them. "I've got coffee on. It will just be a few minutes."

Emma wasn't sure she could swallow anything, but she thanked her anyway. And then she was in the front room, where Daniel Lapp located a hassock and slid it under Grant's leg. She sank into the chair next to him and folded her hands in her lap, each gripping the other as she tried to relax.

She'd known these men all her life. They were all friends of her father's—especially Moses Yoder, who had grown up with him and had even been *Newesitzer* at her parents' wedding. They would understand. Surely they would allow her to help.

Daniel Lapp cleared his throat. "*Guder Mariye*, Grant, Emma. How is the leg?"

Grant shifted so that he sat a little straighter in his chair. "It's as well as can be expected. The doctor tells me I have another eight weeks in this cast, and then he'll put me in a walking cast. I hope that allows me to work."

Moses nodded sympathetically. "It is difficult to be forced to rest. Not everyone enjoys it."

"I cannot enjoy it," Grant said bluntly. "Every day I'm in this cast is a day I cannot work. And my financial situation is such that eight weeks without work means I will miss at least two mortgage payments. I may not be able to catch up quickly enough to prevent the bank from foreclosing."

"Is it as bad as that?" A frown gathered between Daniel's eyes. "You have no savings?"

Grant shook his head, and explained to them what he had explained to Emma. When he stopped and drew a long breath, Moses spoke. As the deacon, he was responsible for the finances of the *Gmee*. Fortunately for them all, he had a gift for management—of his farm, of his family, and of the tithes that came in monthly.

"Are you asking this congregation for a bridge loan, then, Grant?" His tone was cautious, his eyes concerned. "Because if you are, I am very sorry to have to tell you that we cannot use the gifts of the family of God for such things."

Before he finished speaking, Grant was shaking his head. "*Nei*. That is not it at all. I would not ask the congregation for anything more. They have paid the hospital bill for me, and that is enough."

"Then what?" Abram Steiner, father of Brian and his brothers, was preacher. Confusion fought with calm in his expression. "What would you ask of us, if not money?"

"Permission," Grant said. "And a little patience."

"Go on." Daniel glanced at the others and sat back. Emma could see him wondering if at last they were going to get to the reason she was here. It wasn't normal for a man to consult with the elders about finances with a woman who wasn't yet his wife.

"As you know, Emma and I plan to be married in November. I have told her everything, even the possibility that she may not have a home to come to if I cannot see a way out of these troubles. And yet, she tells me she is still going to go through with it." He smiled at her, and even stern Abram Steiner's mouth softened. "But Emma has a talent—something that could bring in enough money to tide us over until I am fully able to work again."

"A talent?" Moses Yoder, who had known her in her cradle, gazed at her, puzzled. "Sewing? Cooking? Many of our women have something of this nature on the side, but I do not see it satisfying the bank if the situation is as grave as you say."

Grant glanced at her, and Emma gathered her courage. "Neither of those. My talent—what God has given me—is writing."

Silence. Perplexed, the elders gazed at her.

Oh, Lord, please, if ever there was a time for You to give me words, it is now.

"I have written a novel," she said slowly. "Earlier this year I sent it away to a contest, just to see how it would do. It placed in the top seven, and a literary agent from New York wrote to me to offer to represent it. Sell it. To a publisher."

"Tyler West," said Moses in the manner of one who has figured out the answer to a riddle at last. "And did you accept this offer?"

Emma decided to leave out the details about going to New York. Best to stick with the essentials. She shook her head. "At the time of Eli and Amelia's wedding, he came to Whinburg to try one more time to convince me, but I had already put the book on the altar of sacrifice. It was enough to know it *could* be published. I didn't need to have it actually *be* published."

Abram shifted in his seat. "I do not see what this has to do with Grant's money troubles."

"It is this," Grant said. "Tyler West was confident he could sell her book. Apparently the *Englisch* are very interested in how we live, and her book is about Amish people. If he does this, then the money would be enough to get us over the hump, with maybe a little left over to begin housekeeping."

Abram's brows had begun to climb at *sell her book.* "Am I hearing this correctly? You would have this book published, with your name on the front for all to see? How does this fit in with *Gelassenheit*, Emma Stolzfus?"

"It would not be my full name," Emma said weakly. She had been wrong to hope. Abram was even more conservative than Daniel, and he would sway them against the plan. "It would only have E. Stolzfus on the cover. That could be a man or a woman."

"Regardless, our people do not publish books and put them out for sale in shops."

"We would not be doing it. The publisher does it."

Daniel held up a hand. "I must confess this concerns me— a woman of my district speaking out by means of a book. And you say it's about Amish people? Are any of us in this book?"

Abram's cheeks reddened and before he had a chance to say whatever burned on the tip of his tongue, Emma blurted, "No one from Whinburg is in the book. I made it all up. The town, the people, the—the horses. A person might recognize a turn of phrase or a description of a house, but there is nothing offensive in it. Nothing recognizable."

"Lies," Abram muttered. "She puts lies on paper and expects us to give her permission to sell them."

"It's not lies," Grant put in gently. "It's fiction. Like what I read to the *Kinner* of an evening, from the library. Like the stories Jesus told His disciples. And it seems to be the only path open to us—other than letting the bank have the house and going to live in Paradise with my people."

Moses, who Emma knew had hired Grant to reroof his hay barn as soon as the leg healed, straightened. "We do not want to lose a good carpenter, Daniel," he said to the bishop in a low tone. "Grant's work is known well outside Whinburg Township, and many churches would be glad to get him. But that doesn't mean I want them to have him."

"His place in one district or another is God's will," Daniel said, but Emma could see he was thinking hard. His gaze flicked up and met hers. "And how is this becoming to a modest woman, to offer her money to a man to whom she is not married?"

"It is Emma's choice," Grant said before Emma could gather a soft answer. "But if you wanted to marry us next Tuesday, that would solve that question."

Moses Yoder gave a bark of laughter, and Abram glared at him. "It was a serious question. It should have a serious answer."

Grant sobered. *He was just trying to lighten the mood. Oh, I hope that wasn't a mistake. Abram is becoming stricter the older he gets.*

But it was her answer to give.

"If the *Gmee* permits me to do this thing," Emma said, "I choose to give Grant the money. With it, we will be able to make a home together in November, and won't have to move away from family and friends we have known all our lives. Without it, I..." Her throat closed, and she swallowed desperately. "Without it, well, we will put our trust in God." *Say it. You must tell the whole truth.* "I feel that He has given me a talent for a reason. If now is the time that I take that talent out of its napkin and put it to use, then I feel I must at least try." She looked down at her hands, knotted together like snarled yarn. "Tyler West may not be able to sell the book. If not, then that is God's will, too."

Again a silence fell, only this time it was full of thought. At length Daniel looked up. "We must discuss this and pray together, and weigh what you have said. Grant, I will come by the house tomorrow and let you know our decision."

"*Denkes*," Grant said. "We appreciate you taking the time away from your fields to listen."

Oh, if only they would, Emma thought as she drove the spring wagon back the way they had come. If there was ever a time for someone to listen, surely it was now.

CHAPTER 22

Emma could hardly get the baking done fast enough.

She'd got up at five and mixed up the bread, and while that was rising, got a batch of doughnuts going. When they came out of the deep fryer, it was time to put the bread in the oven, at which point Lena came into the kitchen.

"My, you're getting an early start."

"I want to take these doughnuts over to Grant."

"Before he's even had his breakfast?"

Emma glanced at the clock on the shelf over the stove. "He eats with the children, and they're up early."

"Emma, I was teasing."

With a sigh, Emma poured Lena a cup of coffee and settled at the table, where she'd already laid out the ingredients for a cranberry square and one that tasted like pecan pie—both of which were easy to cut and transport.

"Daniel said he would give us the elders' answer this morning. If I don't keep myself busy, I'll go crazy waiting until a decent time to drive over there."

Lena put a hand over hers—a hand that was worn practically transparent from hard work for her family. "Whatever happens, it is God's will. You and I must both be willing to accept it."

"I am." Emma turned her hand over until it was palm to palm with her mother's. "But if they don't let me do this, I don't know if I can bear to move away and leave you."

"You will be moving away anyway."

"The other side of the settlement is not Paradise, Pennsylvania."

"But in both cases, I will be well looked after. Katherine and Joel are fitting out the *Daadi Haus* at their place even now. It's cozy and all I have to do is open a door to join them for meals, or for the *Kinner* to come and visit. There is no need for you to feel you cannot leave."

"Yes, there is." Emma smiled at her, even if it was a wobbly excuse for one. "I will miss being with you. We've had good times here."

"And we will have good times in your home with Grant when I come to visit, and at Katherine's when you come to visit us." Lena squeezed her hand and released it. "Now, finish your coffee and I'll help you mix up these squares. Grant must be partial to pecans if you plan to use that whole sack."

By ten o'clock, when the carpentry crew that started at seven had been in the habit of breaking for coffee, Emma's bread was cooling on the counter, the doughnuts had been dipped in powdered sugar, and the squares had cooled enough to be cut and stacked in an airtight container.

Ajax couldn't trot fast enough for her. But it would be foolish to make him break into a gallop—racing buggies was for teenage boys who still believed they were unbreakable, not for women of a certain age who had the life they dreamed of just up ahead. She tied him in Grant's yard and let herself into the kitchen, her carry basket filled with bread and goodies over her arm.

Christina Hoff, with Zachary in her lap, looked up when

Grant did. "Oh, hello, Emma. Grant was just telling me he was expecting you any minute."

She managed a smile, but her whole being was focused on Grant's face. Was it relaxed because Daniel had set his mind at rest? Or was it tense because he didn't know how to break the news to her?

"I'm expecting the bishop at any moment, too," he said. "Whatever you've got in that basket will be just the thing to offer if he's hungry."

He had not come yet. There was no news.

She tried not to feel let down. If he had not come, then there was still hope. Even though their decision was already made, for good or ill, she could still have hope as long as she didn't know what it was.

"Are you sure you'll be all right with Zachary all day?" Christina went on as if there had been no interruption. "I'm so sorry, but I have to take my three to the dentist, and it's all I can do to manage them."

"Of course." Grant blew bubbles in the angle between Zachary's neck and his shoulder, making him giggle with delight. "We'll have a good time together, the five of us." He set the little boy down, and Zachary trundled off to the box under the window where the children kept their carved wooden toys, blocks, and puzzles.

When Christina finally let herself out with a cheery wave and set off across the field that separated the two places, Emma felt as if she could breathe again. With a glance at the clock, she said, "I will be offering him lunch if he doesn't come soon."

"Patience, my Emma. Bishop Daniel is a busy man. Come and sit here by me, and tell me what you have in that basket."

She sat in the kitchen chair next to his, and he slid an arm around her shoulders. Leaning into him, she buried her nose in his shirt and breathed deeply. Then again, maybe it would be better if the bishop could take his time.

"Bread," she mumbled into his shirt front. "And doughnuts and pecan squares."

"Food fit for a king." He had taken a breath to say something more, when they both heard the crunch of wheels in the lane and the jingle of harness.

Emma sat up ramrod straight and leaped to her feet, narrowly missing a pile of blocks that Zachary was stacking next to her chair.

"Emma, breathe. Whatever happens, it is God's will. We must rest in that."

She showed Daniel into the kitchen and he bent to shake hands with Grant. "Don't get up. I will not take long—the vet is coming to look at one of the horses and I must get back."

Emma stood next to the stove, wishing there were somewhere useful to put her hands.

"We have prayed about this, Abram and Moses and me, and we have come to the conclusion it would be a greater sin to uproot your family and lose you to the good folk of Paradise than it would be for your wife-to-be to have her name on an *Englisch* book."

Emma's breath went out of her in a rush, and tears of gratitude sprang into her eyes.

"We feel that as long as the name on this book is E. Stolzfus and no one can identify our community by it, there is no harm in allowing her to help financially now as opposed to when she is your wife. But Grant—" He held up a hand. "The church's portion must be given first. This money, whatever it amounts to, must be tithed."

"Of course," Emma blurted. It had not occurred to her to

do anything else. "*Denkes*, Daniel. You don't know what this means to us."

He gazed at her, then put his hat on slowly. "I hope it is just a means to an end, Emma. I hope that you will not become filled with pride and attract attention to yourself. You have a place to fill here that no one else can fill. If you get too big for that place, well..."

"I won't," she said. "I'll make sure Tyler West understands that, too."

He nodded. "I must be off to my horse. Good morning."

When the door shut behind him, Emma grabbed little Zachary up off the floor and whirled him around the room. After one astonished look, he decided she had not gone mad and his shrieks of laughter joined hers.

Grant struggled to his feet and when her orbit brought her close to him, slid his arm around her waist and hugged the two of them up against his chest.

"The way is clear, my Emma," he said gruffly as Zachary grabbed at his beard. "It is God's will to take your talent out of its napkin and put it to work. May He cause it to increase."

"Thank you for having faith in Him," she said.

"In Him, *ja*. But mostly, I have faith in you."

And then, for the second time in two days, he kissed her.

July 26, 2012

Dear Tyler,

Thank you for your letter. I'm afraid it is I who must ask your forgiveness for being proud and stubborn. Let us forgive each other and be friends again. What you said to Grant has opened so many doors that my hands cannot hold all the blessings God has given us.

In this envelope I'm enclosing the complete manuscript for <u>Inherit the Earth</u>. Please send it out to see if anyone will publish it—the sooner, the better. In fact, if we had a contract by the end of the month, that would be very good. This enterprise is in God's hands, and I know He will make it successful.

I imagine you are very surprised at my change of mind. I'm surprised, too, and I'll explain it all in another letter. For now, I'll just say that I have the elders' approval to do this, so you should go ahead.

I hope you will come and see us in Whinburg this summer. If you cannot come, I hope you will save November 1 on your calendar and come to our wedding. Grant says that you are responsible for all this fuss, and that you should be here to witness the consequences of talking too much.

I look forward to hearing from you soon.

Your friend,
Emma Stolzfus

Glossary

Spelling and definitions from Eugene S. Stine, *Pennsylvania German Dictionary* (Birdboro, PA: Pennsylvania German Society, 1996).

Aendi: Aunt
Alliebber kumm: Everyone come.
Bann: ban, state of being shunned
Bekanntmachung, die: advertising
Bruder, ein: a brother
Buhnesupp: bean soup
Daadi: Granddad
Daadi Haus: grandfather house
Daed: Dad, Father
Deitch: Pennsylvania Dutch language
Denki; denkes: thank you; thanks
Docher: daughter
Dokterfraa: woman who dispenses home remedies
Eck: corner; tables where the bridal party sits
Eireschpiggel: folk character full of wisdom and pranks
Flitterwoch, die: honeymoon visits to family and friends

Fraa: wife, married woman

Gelassenheit: self-surrender, yielding to God's will

Genunk: enough

Gmee: congregation; community

Gott: God

Grossdaadi: Grandfather

Guder Mariye: Good morning

Guder Owed: Good evening

Gut: good

Haus: house

Hoch Deutsch: high German

Hochmut: haughtiness; pride

Ich wisse nichts: I don't know.

Ischt gut. Aich gut.: It's good. Very good.

Ja: yes

Kaffi: coffee

Kamille; Kamilletee: chamomile; chamomile tea

Kapp: woman's prayer covering

Kinner: children

Leddich: single

Lieber: dear (adj.)

Liewi: dear; darling

Maedsche(r), die: the girl, girls

Mamm: Mom, Mother

Mammi: Grandma

Maud: maid

Meinding, die: shunning, the

Meine Freind: my friends

Nei, nix: no

Newesitzer(n): attendant(s)

Ordnung: discipline; order

Pickder, es: a picture
Plappermaul: blabbermouth
Rumspringe: running around
Schtobbe Dich.: Stop it.
Uns: us
Verhuddelt: confused
Was sagst du?: What are you saying?
Wie geht's?: How's it going?
Willkumm: Welcome.
Wunderbaar: wonderful
Youngie: young people

CROSSES AND LOSSES QUILT INSTRUCTIONS

(Part 2 of 3)

In the Amish Quilt trilogy, the characters make a quilt they call "Sunrise Over Green Fields," signifying the hope of the Cross rising over our lives and work. I hope you'll join me in making it as well, so I've divided the instructions into three parts to go with the three books in the series. In *The Wounded Heart*, we began by piecing the quilt blocks. (You can find those instructions on my website, www.adinasenft.com, and also on the FaithWords website, www.FaithWords.com.) In Emma's book, *The Hidden Life*, we'll assemble the blocks together with background blocks and triangles, then sew the borders. Then, in Carrie's book, *The Tempted Soul*, coming in spring 2013, we'll choose quilting patterns, mark them on the fabric, and quilt. Lastly we'll bind the edges, and our quilts will be finished!

Design

Number of pieced blocks: 15
Number of solid blocks: 8
Number of side triangles: 12
Number of corner triangles: 4

Lay out your pressed 15 blocks on a clean surface, 3 across and 5 down. You can lay them on their points for one look. For another design, you can lay them horizontally on the flat side, alternating pieced and solid blocks and forgoing the triangles, so the design goes in a diagonal. Move the blocks around until the colors look good to you. For my quilt, I laid the blocks on point, so the design runs up, drawing the eye to the top. The colors in the piecing went from dark blue at the bottom to light peach at the top, like a sunrise. These instructions reflect the way I did it. Use your creativity and lay yours out in a way that pleases you.

On point, then, the blocks have empty spaces between them that we'll fill with solid blocks and triangles of the background fabric. Cut the following:

Corners: 2 blocks, 6¾ inches square, cut to yield 4 triangles measuring 6¾ x 6¾ x 9½

Sides: 6 blocks, 9½ inches square, cut to yield 12 triangles measuring 9½ x 9½ x 13½

Interior: 8 blocks, 9½ inches square

Assembly

To keep things simple, I always try to assemble pieces and blocks using as many straight seams as possible (which is probably why I've never attempted a Double Wedding Ring quilt). If your blocks are on point and you look at them sideways, you'll see the greatest number of straight lines is actually formed on the diagonal. So we're going to assemble this quilt top in diagonal rows.

If you've laid your blocks on the straight side, your assembly is even easier, and you won't need to use corner or side triangles at all. Just alternate pieced and solid blocks.

Row 1

Starting in any corner (I started at bottom right), with right sides together in a ¼-inch seam, sew a corner triangle to the bottom of the pieced block. Sew the short side of a side triangle to each of two sides of the pieced block, as shown. Press toward the background fabric.

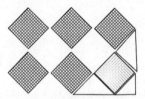

Row 2

Assemble the next row. From the bottom, stitching order would be: side triangle + pieced block + plain block + pieced block + side triangle. Press toward the background fabric. Then, stitch the short side of this row to the long side of your corner row, as shown, matching the seams of the blocks together. Press toward the bottom.

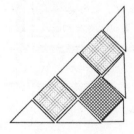

Rows 3 through 5

Continue assembling your diagonal rows as you did Row 2, alternating solid and pieced blocks, with side triangles on the outer edges. Complete the corners as you did in Row 1. Press each row toward the bottom as you finish it.

Row 6

Sew side and corner triangles to the last corner block as you did in Row 1, and press toward the background fabric. Then stitch to Row 5, pressing toward the bottom.

Borders

Many quilters like to add borders to their quilts to add balance and visual appeal. Your borders can be simple strips of fabric from the yardage you used in the pieced blocks, or you can piece them in triangles or squares. My borders are simple strips of fabric, as seen in the diagram below.

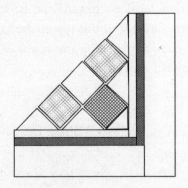

First border

> **Step 1:** From your background fabric, cut two 2½-inch-wide strips equal to the width of the pieced top.
>
> **Step 2:** With right sides together, stitch one strip to the top, and one to the bottom. Press.
>
> **Step 3:** From your background fabric, cut two 2½-inch-wide strips equal to the length of the pieced top, plus the length of the strips you just stitched on. You may have to cut four strips and stitch two of them together first to make up the length.
>
> **Step 4:** With right sides together, stitch a strip to each side of your pieced top. Press.

Second border

In the story, the Amish women use blue for the second border, to symbolize the sky surrounding the fields. Choose whatever color appeals to you and looks good with your piecing.

> **Step 1:** From a contrast fabric, cut two 2½-inch-wide strips equal to the width of the pieced top.
>
> **Step 2:** With right sides together, stitch one strip to the first border on the top, and one on the bottom. Press.
>
> **Step 3:** From the contrast fabric, cut two 2½-inch-wide strips equal to the length of the pieced top. You may have to cut four strips and stitch two of them together first to make up the length.

Step 4: With right sides together, stitch a strip to the first border on each side of your pieced top. Press.

Final border

Step 1: From your background fabric, cut two 9½-inch-wide strips equal to the width of the pieced top and its two borders.

Step 2: With right sides together, stitch one strip to the top, and one to the bottom. Press.

Step 3: From the background fabric, cut two 9½-inch-wide strips equal to the length of the pieced top and its borders. You may have to cut several strips and stitch them together to make up the length. Or, simply cut them with the grain in one long strip.

Step 4: With right sides together, stitch a strip to each side of your pieced top. Press.

Now that your quilt top is pieced, you're ready to mark the patterns, add the batting and backing, and begin quilting. Instructions for the next steps will be in Carrie's book, *The Tempted Soul*.

READING GROUP GUIDE

a. Emma is the youngest daughter, unmarried, and expected to stay home and look after her aged parents. How does Emma feel about her place? Is she conflicted?

b. The Amish do not believe in divorce (Matthew 19:6). How do you feel about the fact that Grant could not marry again, even though his wife left him for another man?

c. Do you think Emma was committing a sin (Matthew 5:28) because she loved a man who was married, even though he was alone?

d. Emma, Amelia, and Carrie tell each other everything. What kinds of things do you talk about with your best friends?

e. Emma's biggest struggle is that aside from Amelia and Carrie and her mother, no one really listens to her. Do you ever feel the same way?

f. What word would you have painted on the side of the house, if you knew it would be painted over and covered up the next day?

g. Do you think it was wrong of Emma to enter the contest when she had no intention of allowing her book to be published?

h. In the Bible, a "talent" is a weight measure of precious metal such as gold or silver. But Emma chooses to use the meaning of *skill* or *ability* when she tells the bishop she believes God wants her to use her talent, not hide it in a napkin (Luke 19:20). Do you think this is appropriate in this context?

i. What are the talents God has given you? How do you use them?

j. The character of Emma was inspired by real-life Old Order Amish author Linda Byler, whose novels of Amish life are very popular. Have you read any of her books?

WATCH FOR CARRIE'S STORY,

THE TEMPTED SOUL,

COMING IN 2013 FROM
FAITHWORDS.

TURN THE PAGE FOR AN EXCERPT!

There hath no temptation taken you but such as is common to man: but God [is] faithful, who will not suffer you to be tempted above that ye are able; but will with the temptation also make a way to escape, that ye may be able to bear [it].

—I Cor. 10:13, KJV

Chickens and babies had a number of things in common. They needed food and protection. They made their needs known with a variety of sounds. And they loved to be loved.

Carrie Miller sat on the top step of the porch, and within a few moments Dinah, one of her six Buff Orpington hens, had climbed into her lap and settled there with a contented sigh. If ever a woman were rich in love, Carrie was that woman. She had a husband who loved her and wasn't afraid to show it. She had a home to care for, and friends she adored. And now, three quarters of her flock had seen her sitting, hopped up the wooden steps, and clustered around her. Some lay on their sides in the warm September sun, some preened their feathers, and some circled, waiting for Dinah to leave so they could have their turn in her lap.

Her best friends, Amelia Fischer and Emma Stolzfus, would laugh and ask if the chickens also sat at the table with her and Melvin every night. Or worse, make pointed comments about the intended use of barnyard animals, which God had said were for food. But Carrie would just smile and let them have their fun.

Most days, she enjoyed the chickens as comforting, affectionate companions who would never see the inside of a soup pot if Carrie had anything to say about it.

But on some days ...

Days like today, when her monthly had made its scheduled appearance. On days like these, she teetered on the edge of grief and despair, knowing she must not fall in, and yet finding it impossible not to. On days like today, even the chickens couldn't help. Her left arm tightened around Dinah's fluffy golden body, making the shape of a cradle that, in almost eleven years of marriage, had never been filled with what she wanted most—a child of her own.

In their district in Whinburg Township, Pennsylvania—in every district, every Amish community, no matter where you were in the country—the *Kinner* were celebrated as a blessing from God. Some women had families of eight or ten, a miracle Carrie could hardly comprehend. In Whinburg, five or six was the average number, and if you weren't expecting by the end of your first year of marriage, why, the married women would start asking gentle questions.

Some were more sensitive than others, when it became obvious their humor and concern caused her pain. Some, like her mother-in-law, Aleta Miller, saw it as their duty to act as a kind of coach, blissfully unaware that their remarks and hints and general helpfulness on the subject were enough to make a person run for the chicken coop, where she could find acceptance and blessed, blessed silence.

And some, like Amelia and Emma, had stopped asking altogether.

This was only one of the reasons why Tuesday afternoons meant so much to her. The three of them met every week, in the two hours before Amelia's two boys got home from school, ostensibly to work on a quilt, but really to refresh themselves at the wells of each other's friendship. There were some weeks, when Melvin's work on the farm had not produced as well as it might have, that their time together literally saved Carrie from physical hunger. Certainly it saved her from a kind of hunger of the heart—the kind that a husband, no matter how beloved and caring—might not even know existed.

And today was Tuesday.

Emma had an eye for the little gifts that the *gut Gott* sprinkled upon His children from the largesse of His hands. For Carrie, Tuesdays were among those gifts.

"All right, you," she said to Dinah, sliding her hand under the bird's feet and gently setting her on the warm planks of the porch, "it is time for both of us to give up our idle ways. I'll be back in time to make Melvin his supper."

Dinah stalked away to inspect the flowerbeds, the rest of the flock scrambling to their feet to follow her, just in case they missed out on something.

The quilting frolic was to be at the *Daadi Haus* where Emma lived with her elderly mother, Lena. The Stolzfus place being way over on the other side of the highway, it meant that either Carrie planned forty-five minutes' walk or simply hitched up and drove. But today, as on most days, Melvin had the buggy to go to Strasburg to talk to one of the businesses there about building shipping pallets. She could take the spring wagon, which was their only other vehicle, but decided against it. Walking was good for you, and she often observed more on foot than she might when she was watching traffic and keeping an eye out for hazards that might spook Jimsy, their old gelding.

Besides, she knew a shortcut or two that Jimsy couldn't manage, and that included a walk along the creek that ran through the settlement. It was a good place to watch birds and see the occasional fox or raccoon, and an equally good place to pick flowers and leaves to make things with.

By the time she let herself in through the back gate of the Stolzfus place, she had spotted out a loop of Virginia creeper and some wild grape that would make the perfect base for an autumn harvest wreath. Her sister Susan's birthday was coming up, and she knew just the place in the hallway of her house where it would fit perfectly.

Emma waved from the back porch of the *Daadi Haus.* "You're early! Amelia isn't even here yet, and she's only ten minutes over the field."

"I didn't want to rush the walk on such a pretty day, so I left a little sooner." Carrie hugged Emma, then held her at arms' length. "You look so happy, *Liewi.* Wedding plans must agree with you."

If you wanted to transform a plain, workaday woman into a beautiful one, just apply happiness. It worked so much better than face paint.

Emma's smile flashed and her green eyes sparkled. "They do indeed. Every job I finish, every jar of tomatoes I can, every quart of beans I put up brings me closer to November first. I'm canning my way through the calendar, vegetable by vegetable. By the time I get to potatoes, I'll be married."

Carrie laughed. "That's a good way to look at all this work." In the kitchen, she could see that Emma had only just stopped for the day. Rows of tomatoes in glass jars sat cooling on towels laid out on the counter, and empty ones filled the drain rack for tomorrow. "I don't know about you, but my garden has been huge this year. I suppose it was because we had such a wet spring."

"God has been very good." Emma put the kettle on the

stove, but didn't light the gas burner. It was better to have tea and a snack after you got your work done, not before. Otherwise, you might never get to it. "Lots of vegetables means we can begin married life with a full pantry, and leave plenty for *Mamm* to take with her when she goes to Katherine's to live. And with your big garden, you will have enough to feed Melvin until April at least."

"Longer, if he travels to the auctions to talk to people about buying pallets. I'll be on my own for those weeks."

Emma's gaze settled on her, and Carrie resisted the urge to look away. A gaze like that commanded honesty—and of course they were honest with each other. You couldn't very well offer counsel to a friend if she hid her true feelings and thoughts from you. But some things lay so close to the heart that it was all too easy for words to bruise them.

"Does he have to go?" Emma asked quietly.

"It...it's what he's good at." Melvin had worked so hard at being a farmer, which he was not good at. He'd sunk money they didn't have into the soil, where seed seemed to rot and plows churned up more rocks than crops. In a good year, when something actually grew, the market would be down and the price of corn or tobacco would be poor, and they would look at an oncoming winter with a feeling akin to panic.

God had always provided, but in those moments before He did, Carrie had gazed into her empty cupboards and resigned herself to another supper of eggs on toast instead of the creamed potatoes, pork chops and gravy, and buttered beans she knew other women in the settlement were preparing for their families.

Thank heaven for the chickens. They had sustained her through some thin times. And not once had Melvin suggested she put one of them on the table.

He was a good man. Things were looking up for them, now that he had leased his fields out, bought into the pallet shop, and found his calling as one who could bring in business simply by talking to people. Carrie had even put on a little weight, and was now pinning her belt apron closer to the back. She needed to eat good things and get her strength up, and then maybe a tiny seed would sprout in a more fertile environment.

She must take a page from Emma's book and look at all the gifts God was providing, taking her mind off those that He was not.

Not yet, anyway.